UNDER
the
COVER
of
MERCY

also by

REBECCA CONNOLLY

A Brilliant Night of Stars and Ice

UNDER
the
COVER
of
MERCY

a novel

REBECCA CONNOLLY

SHADOW
MOUNTAIN
PUBLISHING

Image Credits:
Chapter openings and dingbat: Max Filitov/Shutterstock.com
pp. 284, 287, 288, 289: Photographs of Edith Cavell and Elizabeth Wilkins, public domain

Visit us at shadowmountain.com

This is a work of fiction. Characters and events in this book are products of the author's imagination or are represented fictitiously.

Library of Congress Cataloging-in-Publication Data
CIP on file
ISBN 978-1-63993-105-7

Printed in the United States of America
Publishers Printing

10 9 8 7 6 5 4 3 2 1

To Rachel, Alicia, Heath, Jill, Valerie,

and all of my other family members and friends

who work in nursing or medical-related fields.

Your dedication to your work,

your skills in treatment of injuries and illnesses,

and your devotion to your patients are truly inspirational.

You are the future Edith Cavell dreamed of,

and it is an honor to have you in my life.

And to Kleenex—

thanks for getting me through this book.

CHAPTER 1

August 20, 1914

Brussels, Belgium

The serenity of working the earth on a summer's day was not to be taken for granted. There was such a peaceful feeling in the gift of using one's hands to overturn good dirt, in removing weeds from the vicinity of blooming flowers, in creating places for new flowers to grow.

One could almost imagine in some small way how the Good Lord might have felt as He showered beauty upon His glorious creation of Earth itself.

Surely this sort of pride was no sin.

Edith Cavell wiped her perspiring brow with the back of her wrist, keeping her dirt-splattered glove from touching her skin. This simple act of gardening was not something she would have much opportunity to enjoy again for some time.

The German army was marching into Brussels now. At this very moment.

It was unthinkable.

The Belgian government had fled almost from the moment the fortresses along the border had fallen, leaving the country open and exposed for German taking. Villages had been pillaged and ransacked, citizens massacred, homes burned to the ground. The barest resistance had earned the entire country a wrath too reprehensible for words.

As matron of the Berkendael Medical Institute, Edith was, perhaps, wasting her time with gardening in front of the hospital when war was upon them. But since all of their private patients had left— either having the means to escape Brussels entirely or having been deemed well enough to be conscripted into the army—and none of the military patients had yet been delivered to them, there was only so much to take up her time. If she sat still for too long, her hands would begin to tremble, her chest would tighten, and her thoughts would turn to the unimaginable suffering taking place scant miles from her hospital. So, for now, she was gardening, forcing her mind to simpler tasks.

Dr. Antoine Depage, her associate and founder of the school, had been called away to establish a military hospital closer to the conflict, just as he and Edith had suspected he would be. It was a wrench for him to be gone, but Edith was especially disheartened by the absence of her steadfast friend, Marie Depage.

Marie was a staunch supporter of nursing in Belgium, and she had softened disagreements between Edith and Dr. Depage on several occasions, allowing both to see the view of the other with less irritation. The Institute was quite a different place without either Depage around, which seemed as much a casualty of the war as anything else.

The Belgian Red Cross sisters had begged Edith to provide more of her highly trained nurses, and she had done so with pride. She knew her nurses were exceptional in both their training and their professionalism, and to have them so highly sought-after proved to her that her work mattered.

New sounds met Edith's ears—the call of an officer, the shuffling of many feet, the creaking of heavy wagon wheels—and she sat back on her heels. Several of her nurses had asked permission to go out into the city to watch the spectacle of the Germans marching in, and she had given it. Curiosity over such a sight was natural, she supposed.

Edith had not personally felt an interest in seeing such a thing, but now . . .

She rose from her garden and removed her gloves as she entered the row houses that made up their clinic, moving to her rooms to wash her hands and tidy herself. She would see no soldiers here, not so far from the city center, but she had seen quite a bit of the war in recent days. Each evening, as battle raged closer, the sky would flame red with rockets and exploding shells, the sounds of cannons and conflict rising in volume with each passing day. Only the evening before, the war had raised such a din that she had felt the concussions in the ground beneath her feet, and panes of glass had shattered.

More than one nurse had been in tears with fear, and Edith had done her best to comfort each one, offering words of consolation: Do not give way to fear but welcome the chance to help. It was the advice she continually gave herself, after all, when the world around them now seemed so foreign and fearsome.

Even in her rooms, she could hear the pounding of many steps marching into her beloved city, and she paused a moment to catch her breath. German superior officers had already set themselves up in the government buildings, but the army, thus far, had remained out of Brussels itself.

Today that would change.

"Offer sacrifices of righteousness," Edith recited to herself, taking up her cloak, "and put your trust in the Lord." She examined her reflection in the mirror to ensure her Sister Dora cap was straight and still in place. Her hair seemed grayer of late, but at least her complexion showed little wear. She had no vanity about her looks, being close to fifty years of age, but she did desire a clean, professional appearance.

With a nod of satisfaction, Edith turned away from the mirror and left her rooms, her steps sure and proud as she started down the stairs and out of the building.

The German invasion was a precarious situation for Brussels, and for Belgium as a whole, but it need not be so for the Institute. Though not as large as St. Gilles hospital, her Institute was still an official Red Cross facility, which meant she could do a great deal of good here, if given the opportunity. And that opportunity needed to be addressed before the Germans became too comfortable or settled into a routine.

She could continue to teach her students and probationers whether the Institute had patients or not, but without the practical experience to corroborate such instruction, her nurses would only receive half of their education.

She would not settle for half, nor would she let the wounded suffer while she and her nurses could offer aid.

Brussels had become a quiet place of late, and walking through it only reminded her of that sad fact. The waving flags and proud music were gone, replaced by silence and bare windows and walls. Businesses had been destroyed, the windows smashed in, though the buildings themselves remained in place. Homes, at least for now, had been left alone. The whole world seemed a trifle grayer. The few citizens who were out and about were likely with her nurses watching the transition of power, witnessing a surrender of their home into the hands of those who had already set parts of Belgium aflame.

It would not be long now before the occupation would be complete and the Belgians would return to their homes, having so much of their lives altered, and it was in this sliver of time that Edith wished to approach the German authorities.

Sure enough, the closer she got to the city center, the more she began to see local citizens walking in the opposite direction, their expressions hollow.

A surge of tenderness and pity rose within Edith as she watched face after face pass her by—poor, proud people relegated to a cage of someone else's making. They would continue on with courage and dignity, she knew that well enough, but she felt the sympathy now of a friend within the gates, watching such souls endure the desecration of their homeland and the eradication of their way of life. The city of Brussels itself had been spared from bombing, but would the people emerge equally unscarred?

Edith approached a newly installed German guard at the stately, whitewashed military offices and smiled kindly.

"Good day," she greeted in French, her German being too poor for conversation. "I am Matron Edith Cavell of the Berkendael Medical Institute. Might I speak with the governor general?"

The young guard looked at her impassively. "He is very busy," came the unconcerned reply in neat French. "Call another time."

Well, that would not do.

Edith nodded once, keeping a polite expression. "I am certain he is very occupied today. Is there, perhaps, someone on his staff with whom I might meet? I shall be brief."

He did not look convinced, but he glanced over his shoulder, then indicated she wait while he disappeared into the building.

Edith laced her fingers before her, inhaling a small, careful breath while she kept her mind focused on the task before her.

The soldier reappeared and waved her in, his expression blank.

Edith followed him into the building, passing several uniformed men speaking in rapid German. A few glanced toward her with curious looks as she moved by.

She was led into a tidy, threadbare office where a man sat behind a desk. His thick mustache twitched with a sniff, and his perfectly parted and slicked hair reflected a sheen of daylight. He gestured for her to speak, using no words himself.

"My name is Edith Cavell," Edith told him in fluent French. "I am matron at the Berkendael Medical Institute in Ixelles. Rue de la Culture. We are a Red Cross facility, and I have come to let you know that we are at the services of the wounded, under whatever flag they are found."

The man lowered his chin, giving her a direct, rather frank gaze. He cleared his throat and rose from his seat, standing tall and proud in his uniform. "Governor von Lüttwitz, Miss Cavell. Military governor of Brussels."

Edith barely avoided widening her eyes. So she had been permitted a word with the governor after all. Or was there more than one governor? The military government hierarchy was not entirely clear to her, but it was obvious he was a man in a position of power.

"I will accept the offer of your Institute's service," Governor von Lüttwitz said in French. "There will, of course, be certain expectations."

There was something cold in that final word, and Edith's brow furrowed at the change in his tone. "Such as?"

His smile was very slight. "When treating the wounded French, British, or Belgian soldiers, the nurses should be given formal undertakings to be their guards. We cannot have our enemies slipping away, and we will rely on your nurses to keep them in their place."

Edith could not restrain her surprise. "Guard them? While they are our patients?"

"Of course," Governor von Lüttwitz replied, his smile as cold as his words. "In your service to us—the military government—that would be your duty."

Righteous indignation filled Edith's heart. Did he truly believe that she and her fellow nurses would be complicit in the German occupation of this country? That they would go so far as to imprison the patients they tended?

With the vows they had taken and the Christian duty they undertook, that was impossible.

Edith clamped her lips together, her tongue pressing against her teeth as she collected herself. "We are prepared to do all that we can to help wounded soldiers to recover," she told him, keeping her words even and controlled. "But to be their jailers?" She shook her head firmly. "Never!"

Von Lüttwitz's smile disappeared, his brows narrowed, and he leaned against the desk. His eyes held an almost predatory light in them. "Never, you say?"

"Never," Edith repeated, the word clipped.

He banged his clenched fist against his desk, the sound as explosive as a cannon shot, sending shocks of surprise along her frame.

"I say you will!" he demanded. "We are in control now. We are the government, and we will not abide any resistance or disobedience to our laws. Do you understand?"

"I understand," Edith answered as a wave of blessed calm fell upon her, warmth spreading from shoulder to shoulder and from head to toe. "As I said, we will treat each patient with the same unbiased care and see them recovered. But we will not be jailers, sir."

Rage distorted his dignified demeanor into a murderous mask, and Edith knew he would have been only too pleased to shoot her where she stood.

"Get out," von Lüttwitz snarled, jutting his head hard toward the door. "Now. *Aussteigen!*"

Edith nodded and turned from the room, striding out of the building with the same calm she had felt when she refused his demands, though her heart positively quivered within her chest.

It was, perhaps, ill-advised to make a personal enemy out of the newly installed German officials, but there was no help for it now. She had her personal convictions—extend compassion and humanity to all, be of service and do good, give life back to those on the brink of death—but she also held patriotic convictions, remaining wholly devoted to King and Country and staying firmly planted on the side of what was right rather than what was powerful.

And those convictions were made of iron.

CHAPTER 2

Some people considered folding linens menial work, but Elizabeth Wilkins was not one of them. She found satisfaction in the neat, orderly task, and it took her back to Wales, making beds at home with her sisters, though they were far less efficient in the work then than she had to be now.

A devoted career in nursing would do that to a task, no matter how nostalgic it could be at times.

She did not get to fold the linens often, not with the younger nurses and trainees about, but today, she had managed. And it made her smile.

She hadn't smiled nearly enough since the Germans had marched into Brussels.

"Sister Wilkins, have you seen the matron?"

Lizzie turned from her linens and offered a fond smile to Jacqueline Van Til, one of their Dutch nurses. "She has gone to the hospital at St. Gilles with Jack."

Jaqueline's expression turned into a wry smirk. She shook her head. "Jack went with her? That explains why the morning has been so pleasant."

Lizzie restrained a sigh and avoided giving the young woman a scolding look. The matron's mangy but beloved dog was utterly devoted to her, and he took great pains to protect her, even from those with whom she resided. The nurses and probationers did not care for the mongrel or his attitude.

Poor Jack.

Lizzie cleared her throat. "After the hospital visit, I believe the matron will be visiting the site of the new training school."

The nurse nodded, her expression clearing. "Good. We will need the additional space once this war is finished, certainly. Right now, however . . ."

"I know," Lizzie agreed with a sigh. "The matron told me this morning that the German Red Cross nurses have arrived and are replacing all Belgian nurses at the hospital base, so even what few patients we do have will likely go there first. And we will take in all of the displaced nurses."

"Again?" she asked, biting down on her lip the moment the word had been said. "Apologies, Sister. I should not complain."

Lizzie give her a sympathetic smile. "I understand. A hospital full of nurses but no patients makes our tasks hardly fulfilling."

"Yes," the nurse admitted in a rush. "And Matron still wants the beds and rooms prepared, but there is no one to put in them! Only a handful of Germans, and, after we heal them, they go back out and murder our fathers, brothers, and friends."

Now Lizzie did give her a patiently scolding look. "Sister Van Til, your feelings are valid and understandable, but do take care."

She nodded and fell silent but did not apologize.

It was a rather obvious omission.

"Was there something you needed the matron for, Sister Van Til?" Lizzie inquired, forcing a note of authority into the question.

Jacqueline twisted her lips in thought, her fingers seeming to match the action by entwining with each other. "One of the new girls heard about the proclamation at Namur—about delivering up any hiding French and Belgian soldiers to the Germans—and she was frightened by it."

"That was weeks ago," Lizzie murmured, more to herself than to Jacqueline. "How did she only hear about it now?"

"I didn't ask, but she was in tears. Her brother is fighting, and she said she could not bear to imagine him being dragged from a place of safety and shot in the street." Jacqueline rubbed at her brow, shaking her head. "We've all told her that such a declaration has not been made in Brussels, nor are we hiding soldiers within our walls, but . . ."

Lizzie exhaled slowly, absently drumming her fingers against the pile of folded linen. "I will let the matron know. Perhaps she can address such fears in this evening's chat."

She nodded again. "I think that would help, Sister. I truly do. The matron is so good at setting us all at ease. Even those of us who have seen some of the uglier parts of this war."

The unanticipated boom of a distant cannon broke their conversation, and Lizzie jumped with fright. Her heart still jolted at the sound, even though the explosions had started weeks ago. The timing of the concussions was never regular, and she hated the feeling of the ground beneath her feet quivering at sporadic intervals and the ringing in her ears that beat like a pulse.

Lizzie closed her eyes as she forced her breathing to calm even as Jacqueline said something rather harsh-sounding in Dutch.

"And I daresay having *that* every so often does not help matters either," Lizzie said.

"No," came the agreement, now returning to French. "It does not." She exhaled roughly. "Thank you for listening, Sister. I will return to my work now and anticipate Matron's evening chat." She smiled tightly and turned from the room, striding back toward the empty patient ward.

Lizzie watched her go, wishing there was more she could have said, more comfort she could have offered, more words of advice for such concerns.

But there was nothing.

Even now, a full six weeks after the invasion, Lizzie still flinched at the sound of cannons and exploding shells. Still felt her stomach clench when she saw the German notices about Brussels. Still went colder than ice when any German soldier was brought into the clinic, his expression full of hate, his gun fixed on the nurses as they tended him.

There was no comfort here. There was only haunting reality.

Worse than that was what the matron had confided to Lizzie and the other senior staff that had *not* been relayed to the nurses and probationers. What was happening outside of Brussels that did not always find its way to the ears of those within it.

Only the week before, a curate near Valenciennes had been arrested for carrying certain letters relating to the mobilization of Belgian reservists. He had been court-martialed in the railway station and shot for his offenses. The soldiers had buried him at once, and some of the local citizens of Valenciennes claimed they could see his feet protruding from the dirt.

There had also been the story of the thirteen or so Allied soldiers who had been found hiding in a barn. They had been marched out into the barnyard in an orderly fashion, like the soldiers they were, and shot in turn. No questioning, no imprisonment, only death.

There was only death in Belgium, it seemed.

If Lizzie and her fellow nurses had patients to treat, people who they could see recover from wounds and returned to health, perhaps they might not feel so hopeless. Their patients were few and far between, and then they were only those irate young Germans. The matron had assured her staff that she had offered their services to the local authorities as a Red Cross facility, and yet their halls remained empty of those in need.

Yet more and more nurses were coming to them from larger hospitals, their positions having been filled by German nursing staff who would do the bidding of the German authorities to guard the Allied soldiers, treat them, and then return them to the vindictive authority of those who only wished them alive to beat them into submission again.

The matron had refused to follow such demands, which perhaps was why they had no patients now. Why they were not entrusted to do their duties. Why the only work they had was to occupy their time with education and attempt to ignore the booming sounds in the distance.

Yet there was not a nurse within the walls of the Institute that did not stand behind the matron's decision.

Lizzie shook her head and moved toward the matron's office, more to check on her arrival than anything else. In moments of such disquiet, the matron had the ability to envelop a person in the comfort of heaven simply by the calmness of her voice, the gentleness in her eyes. The touch of her hand.

Just as she could tend to patients by merely being near them and offering comfort, she could settle and soothe the most agitated heart.

Before Lizzie reached the office, she heard the *click-clack* of Jack's paws against the floor, and her heart instantly settled into a more natural pace, knowing his mistress would be in there with him.

Miraculous what Edith Cavell was capable of without a single word.

Lizzie knocked on the partially ajar door, fixing a slight smile on her face as she peered within. "Matron?"

Edith turned at the greeting, apparently in the midst of pacing, her expression tight. "Sister Wilkins. Please, do come in."

Lizzie shut the door behind her and gave the matron a concerned look. "Are you all right, Matron? Was all well at St. Gilles?"

"Yes, yes, they are quite busy," Edith replied quickly, almost absently. "The nurses send their regards. Time will tell if the German Red Cross takes over there as well, but for now, they seem content with the Belgians." She paused, drumming her fingers on the desk next to her, her brow creasing and creating pale furrows in her paler face.

Lizzie had worked for Edith Cavell for more than two years now, and she had never seen the woman so unsettled.

Something was wrong.

"Matron?" Lizzie pressed, coming further into the room. "What is it?"

Edith exhaled slowly, shaking her head. "My heart is heavy, Sister Wilkins. Heavy and weary and utterly bewildered by the things I witness as I go about my usual matters. I do not understand."

"None of us do, Matron," Lizzie murmured softly.

Her throat moved on a swallow, and she suddenly slumped into the chair behind her desk, sighing. For a woman with perfect composure, the change was jarring to see.

"I have seen suffering, poverty, and human wretchedness in the slums of London, Lizzie. It was everywhere, and one grows accustomed to such things. But nothing I saw there hurts me the way it does to see these proud, happy people humiliated and deprived of their men, their homes invaded by enemy soldiers that are quartered

in them, their businesses ruined. I can only ask myself why these innocent people should be made to suffer like this . . ." She looked up,
meeting Lizzie's eyes. "And I do not have an answer."

Tears welled in Lizzie's eyes to see her beloved matron in such despair. Of course, they all felt echoes of this agony to see their beloved
city overrun and altered, to see their neighbors abused and demeaned.
Lizzie had heard the quiet tears of the nurses and probationers regard-
ing it and had cried several of those tears herself. But knowing that
the matron felt it as well? Felt it so deeply that it literally weighed her
down?

Lizzie stepped to the desk, her heart aching. "What would you
have us do, Matron?"

"I am not yet certain," Edith told her, creases still perched upon
her brow. "What I would *wish* done and what *can* be done are not
always neatly aligned. But I greatly fear that this rise of such superior attitudes, of such brutality, will not end. And, heaven forbid,
if Prussianism should triumph, it will mean the entire collapse of
Christianity."

Lizzie's eyes widened, glancing behind her at the door, knowing
full well she had closed it yet fearing it might somehow have opened
and such comments would be overheard. "Matron, is it prudent to say
such things?"

Edith's eyes met hers suddenly, a dark, reproachful light in them
that smoothed her brow. "Prudent?" she repeated. "In times like
these, when terror makes might seem right, there is a higher duty
than prudence."

She rose from her chair, clasping her hands before her and appearing almost majestic in her bearing. "Sister Wilkins, would you
ask the nurses to come to my office, please? Not the probationers; I
will speak to them tonight. The nurses only. As soon as possible."

"Of course, Matron," Lizzie said quickly. She turned and hurried out into the Institute, curiosity piqued.

It did not take long to round up the group, especially when there were no patients to occupy any of them. They were all available and eager to see what the matron wanted of them.

"Will we finally be getting patients, do you think?" one of them asked with a bright smile.

"One can only hope," another replied, her tone ringing with a desperate fervency that seemed to speak for them all.

"It will not help any of us to speculate," Sister Beatrice Smith told them all, trying for severity in her expression, though there was no denying her own anticipation.

Another nurse came to Lizzie's side. "Do you know what this is about, Sister Wilkins?"

Lizzie shook her head, sharing a smile. "I do not, I'm afraid. We shall all have to wait and see."

A half-hearted groan rose from the group, making Lizzie chuckle to herself. There was a natural impatience when their desire to serve went unmet by the work at hand, though they would never have shown such impatience to the matron. Lizzie was forever reminding them to maintain their composure and exude serenity in their manner, particularly with their patients. Even now, when there were no patients to be had, she wished for them to practice such restraint so it would become a habit, not an act.

Most of them were still working toward that goal. The matron, however, had perfected exactly what she was asking of them.

How could any of them refuse to do the same?

They filed into the matron's office in their matching nurse uniforms in relative silence.

Edith bore a far calmer countenance than what Lizzie had

witnessed earlier, though she wondered how closely it reflected her inner feelings.

"Thank you for your prompt attendance to my request," Edith began, meeting the eyes of each nurse, as she was inclined to do. "I have some news, and then I have a request of each of you."

Lizzie blinked in surprise. News and a request?

"The German army has reached the French frontier," Edith announced without emotion. "I need not tell you of the destruction that lies in the wake of that pursuit."

A few of the nurses gasped at the revelation, while others simply looked shocked, faces pale and drawn and worried.

It was just one more miserable part of this wretched war that none of them could do anything about.

Edith released an audible exhale. "More than that, however, is this: many Belgian soldiers are without food and shelter. With all there is to contend with in this sad country of theirs, surely that is a cruel compounding of their suffering. So I come to my request." She paused, her lips compressing into a thin line.

All eyes were on her, rapt with attention and energy, if not curiosity.

"I believe it would be a worthy and charitable act," their matron continued, "if we, each of us, were to give up our salaries to those hungry and destitute men."

The silence was complete, without even a breath to interrupt it.

"Our salaries?" Sister Smith repeated. "There's not much to it, Matron. We're already economical with it as it is."

"Yes," the willowy, beautiful Mania Waschausky agreed. "A few five- and ten-franc pieces only. What good would that be?"

Heads bobbed in agreement around the group.

"I have been saving carefully for the future," Helen Wegels told the matron, her reluctance palpable. "How can I now give that away?"

Lizzie held her own opinions silent, though they were fairly aligned with the others. Money was scarce, and their own food was already harshly rationed. Yes, they took great care with the poor where they could, but for all of them to sacrifice what little they had . . .

How would she ever explain that to her family, who already wished her to use her funds to return home to Wales?

"Matron," Sister Smith broke in, her tone the most reasonable of any to speak thus far, "you have not shown any particular interest in this war as yet—only in treating wounds and saving as many lives as we may see here in our clinic. Why is it your intention to intercede like this now?"

Edith nodded, clearly unruffled by the reminder. "I know it is a sacrifice for each of you—each of us. But I, for one, feel the need to do something more, and for now, this is what I can offer. Perhaps we may find an elevation to our thoughts and something noble in our giving."

She smiled at the group, her affection evident and almost motherly toward them. "Surely, we have all seen the sacrifice our neighbors are making in times like these, sending their fathers, brothers, and sons to fight, though the country is torn with indignities and strife. Should we not give something of ourselves to relieve suffering, if we can?"

The air about the nurses seemed to shift with their matron's gently impassioned words, and the nods resumed, this time agreeing not to a complaint but to a course.

They would give up what they could to help those less fortunate in this time of great need, and, in their small way, take a stand against the brutality they saw daily. If their meager contributions could help the poor Belgian soldiers continue to fight against the Germans, be they fighting in France or elsewhere, then there could still be hope in spite of everything.

Not much, perhaps, but some.

Perhaps that was enough.

CHAPTER 3

"Matron, another one of the Germans is threatening the nurses. This one will not lower his weapon, and he shouts at anyone who comes near him, even the German nurses."

Edith forced her groan into a silent sigh. It was not the first time a German soldier had turned belligerent in the weeks since they had begun to receive them at the clinic, and she was certain it would not be the last.

"Thank you, Sister White. I will speak with him."

"You don't speak German, Matron."

She looked at her senior nurse with a flat smile. "Charity transcends language. As Miss Luckes was so fond of saying when I trained with her, 'Patients come first.'" She rose from her office chair, her smile turning a little more genuine, though she took no joy in what she was about to say. "And besides, we are under military rule. We must do as they demand."

Sister White exhaled noisily, shaking her head. "The nurses will not like it, Matron. They *don't* like it. We are facing unprecedented conditions and injuries in all of our patients, regardless of their nationality—but to then be threatened with rifles and bayonets by those patients who take part in brutalizing our communities and soldiers? It is more than one can bear."

Edith gave her friend a careful look, understanding all too well the frustration she expressed, but having no comfort to give her. "We took a vow, Sister. Hard as it is, we must keep to it."

Sister White nodded, the strain of recent days and weeks evident on her features. "The nurses may need encouragement, Matron. They are struggling."

"I know, Sister. I think we all are." She stepped closer to her and put a hand on her arm. "I will talk to them. Once I settle our agitated German."

"Which one?" Sister White muttered as Edith quickly moved toward the patient ward.

That was, unfortunately, a rather good question.

The German military rule of Brussels had only grown more stifling over the past few weeks, with patrols of soldiers occurring more regularly and curfews set for all civilians. Belgians and other foreign nationals were being arrested for no reason, while others were conscripted for munitions factories. Anyone who provided any sort of resistance risked death—a few had already been shot.

More signs had been posted throughout the town that anyone who was found to be hiding an enemy of the German army would be punished to the severest extent of the law.

Military law, of course. Not peacetime law.

The nurses' complaints of no patients had ceased, as they were now treating quite a few, depending on the status of the larger hospitals and the conditions of nearby battlefronts. Each day, more soldiers arrived. Edith had sent a few articles to *Nursing Mirror* magazine, if for no other reason than for other nurses to learn of their experiences in Belgium.

And still they faced patients who would threaten them at gunpoint while demanding priority in their care.

Were they an impartial hospital of the Red Cross, as the Geneva Convention had agreed, or weren't they? Yet, for all the oppressive nature of the Germans ruling the city, there was no enforcement of any code of conduct for those the nurses were expected to treat.

And any perceived indication of fault or error toward any German soldier on her part would be met with harshness from those in authority.

Still, Edith believed in the humanity of people in general, that they were inherently good, and if she could only reach them, show them understanding and consideration, they might do the same in turn.

Walking into the patient ward, Edith forced her expression into a picture of calm serenity, even while moving down the line of beds at a rapid pace. Her nurses tending other patients glanced at her, some pausing to watch her pass, others smiling as though they knew what would happen.

It was not the first time she'd had to settle an unruly German patient.

Nor was it difficult to determine which patient was causing the trouble.

The terrified Belgian nurse currently facing a rifle held by a bloodied and bandage-wrapped soldier made that perfectly clear.

He was no more than seventeen by the looks of him, and yet he was filled with anger and mistrust at being tended for wounds that could easily have ended his life had they been a touch more severe. He was not the youngest soldier they had treated, and he would not be the last who seemed too young for such horrors, but he had been turned into a man by what he had experienced thus far, and now bore the weight of a man's burden upon his back and in his heart.

How long would his young life extend in this war, and what sort of a man would he be when the war eventually ended?

"Sister Wegels, please tell me about this patient," Edith said calmly in French when she reached the bed.

The rifle immediately swung toward her, and the soldier shouted hoarsely in German.

Edith kept steady eyes on him, nothing affecting her smile. "Sister Wegels?"

Sister Wegels came to her side, nearly hiding behind her when she got there. "Matron," she said softly, her voice thickly accented with her natural Belgian tongue, "this soldier has suffered a shrapnel injury to his left arm and thigh. We were able to remove the shrapnel from his leg, but when we started to work on his arm, he became agitated. He picked up his gun and said we could not take his arm, that he would not let us maim him. He said he would return to his regiment and continue to fight, but we were not to make him a cripple. He will not let us touch him, and still he bleeds."

Edith studied the man's thigh, the bandages neatly wrapped and holding nicely. The shredded sleeve of the soldier's shirt and jacket revealed deep cuts and scratches that continued to bleed. The young man would have more of a chance of losing his arm as a result of an infection than from anything her nurses might do to him.

"Do you speak French?" Edith asked the soldier with all the patience she could muster.

He barked something in response.

Edith turned her head toward the nurse behind her, still keeping her eyes on the soldier. "Sister?"

"He said, 'A little, but not enough for conversation,'" Sister Wegels replied softly.

"I am the matron of this hospital," Edith explained, slowing her words to make them clearer. "I am in charge. My rules."

The soldier's eyes narrowed. "Your rules?"

Edith nodded once. "Yes. We must treat your arm. Remove the shrapnel, so that it heals. We will help you. Not hurt. Help."

He rambled something, his tone defensive, and hoisted his rifle more firmly into his shoulder.

"We will not hurt you," she repeated. "You may point your gun at me while the nurses tend your arm. Mend it. Yes?"

Sister Wegels hesitantly moved around the bed toward her supplies, her hands trembling. Another young sister joined her, though Edith could not see who, given her attention remained on the soldier.

He started to move his rifle to them, but Edith shook her head. "On me," she reminded him firmly, gesturing for him to bring the gun back on her. "My rules. They help. Yes?"

He frowned but settled back against the bed, his gun pointing at Edith. "They help. You stay. Gun stays."

Edith nodded, clasping her hands before her. "Thank you. Sisters, be about it."

The nurses worked quickly, cleaning each wound and carefully removing the delicate shrapnel pieces.

Perspiration wreathed the soldier's face, his fair hair clinging to his skin, and he ground his teeth as each piece of shrapnel was removed, then each wound cleaned. But he never cried out. He kept his attention and his rifle steady on Edith.

The nurses carefully bandaged the arm, their actions efficient and smooth, exactly as Edith had trained them. Once fastened, they stepped back, waiting for Edith to be freed from the soldier's aim.

"Done," Edith told him, pointing at his newly bandaged arm. "Good?"

Warily, he broke his eye contact with her and glanced at the dressings, moving his arm this way and that, flexing his fingers together, then each in turn. Only then did he return his attention to Edith.

"Good," he grunted, lowering his rifle at long last. "Water."

"Of course." Edith nodded and turned to the nurses. "Would one of you fetch him a glass, please? And a blanket. I think he needs his rest."

She nodded again, this time to the soldier, who tucked his rifle beside him on the bed, the muzzle pointing toward his feet instead of anyone else.

Edith glanced to a corner of the room, where a German soldier usually stood guard over their work.

Tonight, however, it was Governor von Lüttwitz himself.

She lifted her chin as she stared at him, and he returned her stare, a small curve of a smile accompanying his simple, patronizing nod of approval.

Edith swallowed the burning sensation in her throat, hating that he thought her actions were in obedience to his command. She was simply doing her job to heal the wounded, nothing more. And he needed to witness it for himself, did he? Wait for her to make a mistake? Hope to catch her in some criminal act?

At least he would not have such a pleasure tonight.

Turning on her heel, a thrill of pride racing up her spine, she moved back down the row of beds, nodding at every soldier who met her eyes, regardless of his nationality. They each needed to know that in this hospital, they would be treated well and would be safe.

Insofar as she was able to do so.

The British, French, and Belgian soldiers who were brought in were all prisoners of the Germans, so she could not attest to their treatment once they left her care. It was a miserable feeling, watching these brave boys and men leave in German custody with no hope and a weakened resolve. What was she saving them for?

It was that question that had driven Edith to begin circumventing the law, just a little. It was common knowledge that once Allied soldiers were ready to be discharged, they were informed of the need to report to the military police. What was *not* common knowledge was that they were also given a secret alternative.

If they chose, the soldiers could go to the nearby home of one Madame X. Edith had once tended the defiant local woman for gout, and Madame X would hide the soldier until such time as she could spirit him away from Brussels. The destination was entirely up to the soldier, though he was not to tell Edith or any of the nurses of his choice.

The nursing reports to the authorities stated clearly that all soldiers falling under such requirements had been directed as ordered. If they did not arrive . . . well, the poor soldier must have become lost on his way, for which the nurses could not be blamed in the least.

"C'est la guerre!" had become a frequent utterance about the clinic.

It's the war.

No one could argue that point.

Still, Edith would tend any who came to her, just as she tended those dear local friends whom she visited in the evenings or those sick and injured in the streets of Brussels who were suffering from the war as her patients did, though perhaps in other ways.

She was a nurse, whatever may come, and she would continue to serve as one.

Once in the hall, out of sight of the nurses and the governor, Edith leaned against the wall, closing her eyes and letting the odd trembling of release take over. It was not the first time a gun had been held on her, but there had been something about the fear in the soldier's eyes that made the situation more fraught. She had not thought of anything but keeping her nurses safe, but now that it was done . . .

One slow breath in, one slow breath out, neither of them steady.

How much longer would this go on?

"Matron? Is everything all right?"

Edith opened her eyes and smiled quickly at Lizzie Wilkins. "Yes, thank you. Would you ask a few of the sisters to meet me in the hall for a moment? I don't want to alarm the patients, but I must say something."

Lizzie nodded immediately. "Of course, Matron." She hurried along while Edith allowed herself a few more calming breaths.

In a few moments, nurses began to trickle into the hall to join her, and when most of the ones she had seen in the ward arrived, she looked at them all in turn.

Tired but eager eyes met hers, and a wave of empathy rose within her.

"I know this is not easy," she told them softly. "I know the injuries you have seen are gruesome, the illnesses harsh, and the infections unimaginable. I know the German soldiers are trying your patience and your kindness with their threats of violence and their attitudes toward us."

Nods rippled all around the gathered nurses.

Edith swallowed, her throat dry as her emotion sank deep. "We will continue to treat whomever God places in our path and in our care, regardless of nationality. That is who we are as nurses. That is what we do. Thank you for all you are doing and have done. Please continue to do so."

Again, the group of them nodded.

She waited a moment, seeing her own strain and frustration reflected in the eyes of her nurses. She hoped they might see that she was not unaffected by this situation either, by their circumstances, by what they were enduring together. She held their gazes longer than she might normally have done, wanting her words to take root as much as possible, then nudged her head toward the ward.

The nurses filed back out without a word, last of all being Lizzie, who smiled warmly at Edith and nodded before going to see to her own patients.

"Matron?"

Edith turned to face Sister White, who was approaching from the other side of the building. "Yes?"

"There's a man to see you. He has a letter of introduction from Madame Depage." Sister White frowned slightly, looking worried. "He says it is a matter of some urgency."

Edith nodded and followed Sister White into the parlor where a man stood. He was of average height, with dark hair and a full mustache. "I am Miss Cavell. How can I help you?"

He handed over the letter first, then bowed to her. "Miss Cavell, my name is Herman Capiau. Madame Depage has told me you are a woman of mercy, of loyalty, and worthy of great trust," he said, his voice almost impossibly quiet. "So I have come to inform you that there are two gravely wounded British soldiers presently hiding in a convent not far from here. I must know if you would be willing to hide them and treat them for their injuries until they are well enough for myself and my associates to get them out of Belgium."

Edith stared at the stranger for a long moment, the letter in her hand only partially opened, his words seemingly impossible to comprehend. She blinked and scanned the lines of the letter, recognizing the hand and the signature as indeed belonging to her friend Marie Depage. She asked in her note for Edith to trust Mr. Capiau, and then apologized for the situation she was putting her in. Marie would have helped the soldiers herself, but she had to think of her children.

All of which meant this man must be who he claimed, his words must be true, and the cause must be just, or else Marie would never have sent him to Edith.

But how could she help?

To house and treat British soldiers who were not prisoners of war would mean going against the German authorities and their warnings of harboring enemy soldiers.

Failing to report them would be an act of defiance.

Assisting in their escape would be treason.

Leaving them to their fate would condemn them to death, if not from their wounds, then by execution at the hands of the Germans.

But to do as Mr. Capiau suggested could condemn herself to that same punishment.

She took a moment, lowering her eyes in a semblance of prayer, her heart thudding furiously within her. But she felt no panic. No fear.

No doubt.

Edith exhaled slowly and met the eyes of her new acquaintance. "Yes, Mr. Capiau. Bring them here. We will take them in."

CHAPTER 4

Lizzie stood beside Edith in the darkened corridor of the clinic, forcing herself not to gape at her matron for the outrageous admission she had made scant moments before.

They were going to hide British soldiers. Not prisoners they needed to tend and send on their way, playing their little game with Madame X against the Germans. These were soldiers who were not known to the German authorities, soldiers the nurses could not—and would not—report on.

Treason. They were committing treason in a time of military rule. The governor himself had been watching them only hours before.

Lizzie was committed to the course and Edith's leadership, but that did not lessen the rather paralyzing sensation of fear currently clawing its way through her stomach at sporadic intervals. Only she and Sister White had been made aware of the situation, and as far as was possible, no one else would know, for the safety of all concerned.

What physical state would these men be in when they arrived? What care would they require? How long would it take to see them recovered and on their way to the next secret place?

Would there be more where these two came from?

So many questions flooded her mind, and she did not dare ask any of them aloud.

"Sister Wilkins," Edith murmured without provocation, "it is no small prudence to keep silence in an evil time."

Lizzie forced a difficult swallow. "Is that scripture, Matron?"

"From my morning devotional in *The Imitation of Christ*," Edith told her. "I was reflecting on the twenty-eighth chapter. I believe it to be true."

"Perhaps I should join you for these devotionals. It might bring me the same consolation you seem to find in them." Lizzie exhaled slowly, shaking her head. "I have no doubts, Matron, but that does not remove my fear."

Edith put a hand on her arm, squeezing gently. "To move forward in the face of fear takes the greatest faith of all. Trust that our Lord will guide our steps and renew our strength. Remember what He said: If you have faith as a mustard seed, you can say to this mountain, move, and it will move."

Lizzie could only nod at the suggestion. She had never met anyone who was so filled with faith and devotion as Edith Cavell, so wholly dedicated to her Christianity that it was impossible to separate it from her person. It was not a trait of her character; it was the center of her existence.

What would it be like to be so certain of something, so immersed in belief, that it defined every action and thought? Lizzie came from a good Christian family in Wales, had attended Sunday services regularly, acted with charity, prayed often, but there was something hallowed about the faith that Edith lived with.

Standing beside Edith now, Lizzie felt a touch of that faith reach into her own heart, squeezing warmth into her chest, as tangible as Edith's hand on her arm.

The quivering in her knees began to settle, and she hoped it would do the same with her fingertips.

A man with a dark mustache entered the building, assisting a thinner, limping man with a beard and a black hat. Another painfully thin man followed without assistance, though his shoulders were broad and slightly deformed. The difference between the soldiers and their guide was stark, the health of the mustached man reflecting the dramatic lack of it in the others.

The soldiers were haggard and pale, drawn in ways that spoke of deep suffering. Their clothing was dirty and tattered, hanging on their frames in shocking tribute to the men they had once been. Lizzie wondered if the men had had to "borrow" the clothes at some point on their way here.

Lizzie moved quickly to take the bearded one's arm.

"Thank you," the mustached man said when she offered assistance.

"Come, let's find a place to talk," Edith told them all in a low voice, going to the other soldier. "Quickly now."

The small group awkwardly made their way up the stairs to Edith's private room, their pace more of a hushed shuffling than any sort of hasty retreat. The wounded soldier Lizzie helped was barely able to move of his own power; she and the mustached man had to nearly carry him at times.

They made it to the matron's room, even with their shuffling and carrying, and if any of the nurses or probationers had seen them, they did not ask questions. Edith settled her soldier in a chair before turning to close the door behind them.

"There," she told them on a relieved breath while Lizzie and her companion helped their own soldier into another chair. "Now we may speak more freely. Mr. Capiau, if you would."

The mustached man nodded, wiping his brow. "Matron, this is

Colonel Boger and Sergeant Meachin, both of whom were wounded at the Battle of Mons in August. They were taken to the convent hospital at the village of Wihéries and managed to escape from the German guards. Mademoiselle Louise Thuliez found them and brought them to me. Eventually, we made our way to Brussels by train, but we have been unable to find lodgings secure enough for them to heal and rest until they are well enough to get out of Belgium entirely."

Lizzie listened intently, each moment growing more impressed and more astounded by the risks that had been taken, and successfully at that. It was incredible that these soldiers had not been captured during the weeks since their escape, and, more impossibly, that they had made it to the clinic now.

And judging by the state of them, they had arrived not a moment too soon.

Mr. Capiau offered a consoling smile to the bearded soldier. "I believe Colonel Boger here has a fever. We have done our best with his foot, and yet . . ." His words trailed off, his expression showing his true concern.

Edith nodded and came to the man, pressing her hand to his brow. "Yes, he is feverish. We will see him settled in a room shortly." She looked at the other soldier across the room. "And you, sir?"

He offered a hesitant smile but said nothing.

"He does not speak French, Miss Cavell," Mr. Capiau informed her. "Sergeant Meachin."

"Welcome, Sergeant," Edith said, switching to English. "You are safe here, and we will see you restored to health."

"Thank you," he replied in a voice so weak and raspy that Lizzie wanted to cry at the sound of it.

Edith turned to Lizzie, straightening. "Sister Wilkins, in an effort to maintain normalcy, would you kindly go to the classroom and teach as planned? I will come in shortly and take a nurse to settle our guests." She glanced over the two men. "To protect their identities, Colonel Boger will be known as *Louis*, and Sergeant Meachin as *Pierre*."

Lizzie nodded and looked at the soldiers once more, her heart aching at the dismal picture they presented. Two noble men, far from their homeland, serving King and Country, and reduced to such a state in their attempts to avoid capture and imprisonment.

How could Lizzie and her fellow nurses not help them?

"Sister Wilkins," Edith murmured softly, as though she could sense the rising tears in Lizzie's eyes.

Lizzie sniffed once, averting her eyes from the soldiers, her heart begging to tend them herself. "Yes, Matron." She turned from the room, pausing only when Edith reached out to place a consoling hand on her arm.

She took strength from that brief connection and focused on the task ahead of her: instruction.

It could prove a useful distraction.

Thankfully, her class materials had been prepared ahead of time, so the instruction required little fresh thought from her. The probationers were eager to learn, asked thoughtful questions, and were so intent on her words that she nearly forgot that Edith had said she would come to fetch someone to tend to the soldiers until the matron herself appeared in the doorway.

"Sister Wilkins," Edith said softly in greeting. "I am going to take one of the students now, if that is quite all right with you."

"Of course," Lizzie agreed with a quick nod.

Edith smiled and turned to the class. "I am sorry to interrupt your education, my dears, but I presently have need to borrow Sister Van Til."

Jacqueline looked surprised but rose, glancing quizzically at

Lizzie, who smiled back in encouragement. The two of them left, and Lizzie resumed teaching, though her mind was certainly occupied with Jacqueline's new assignment more than her own.

Still, she was able to make her way through the lesson and keep her students engaged long enough to finish the class. She allowed herself a small breath of relief, hoping her inner turmoil and scattered thoughts had not been noticeable to the students. It was complicated enough to have two English soldiers within their walls, but to hide the truth of their presence from the nurses and the students only added to Lizzie's stress. And if the soldiers' wounds were any indication, the men would not be quickly made whole and sent on their way.

The longer they remained, the more dangerous for them all.

How would they manage?

She was asking herself question after question, trying to process the last several hours as she readied herself for supper in her room, when a soft knock sounded. She opened the door, expecting Edith to have come to take her to the soldiers for treatment. To her surprise, Jacqueline stood there, her brow wreathed in creases of confusion.

"Sister Van Til?" Lizzie cocked her head, curious and concerned. "Can I help you?"

Jacqueline bit her lip, then entered the room. "Sister, I need to speak with you."

Her fingers linked and unlinked with each other in a show of nerves, and Lizzie could only imagine what the poor girl was feeling after having seen the wounded, hidden soldiers. As Lizzie was entirely ignorant as to exactly what Jacqueline had been told, she was not about to offer information first.

"What troubles you?" Lizzie asked as gently as she could. "Are you well?"

Jacqueline shook her head. "No, Sister. I . . . Sister, may I confide in you?"

"Of course," Lizzie encouraged. "You know you may."

Jacqueline nodded once. "The matron had me come to her private room where two injured and ill soldiers waited. She asked me to take the one she called Pierre to room nine, and the other, called Louis, she wanted taken to room twelve where Beatrice Smith would tend to him."

Lizzie pressed her lips together tightly, wondering what answers she could possibly give to the questions she knew were coming.

"I took Pierre to room nine, as instructed, and talked to him, though Matron said he could not speak," Jacqueline went on, her fingers still twisting with each other. "I gave him some supper, and he ate it as though he had not eaten in months. His eyes were so bloodshot, so haunted . . . I prepared a warm bath for him and helped remove his shirt, only to find—"

She shook her head and began to pace. "Sister, an English flag was binding a wound on his chest. An English flag! I asked him if he was English, which you know I do not speak, but he nodded and said 'Yes, yes.' So he *can* speak, but perhaps not French. I stared at him in shock; I could not think what to do. There was no guard with him, so we cannot be treating a prisoner, which means the Germans do not know he is here. He looked so pathetic, so pleading . . . He kissed my hands, Sister."

Jacqueline's account of Sergeant Meachin would have broken Lizzie's heart had she not already set eyes on him and known of the situation. As it was, hearing this account of him was more moving than she would have expected.

Jacqueline suddenly stopped pacing and stared at Lizzie boldly. "Sister, why are there two British soldiers here who are *not* prisoners?

There are signs all over the town warning us against this very situation, yet we are taking them in and treating them?"

Lizzie exhaled slowly through her nose, seeking wisdom and calm before answering. "I suppose we are doing as the matron has always said. Nursing knows no frontiers. Knowing the matron as you do, how do you believe she would have responded to seeing those soldiers?"

"But she knows the risks!" Jacqueline said.

"Even so, I don't believe the matron would refuse." Lizzie gave the capable, concerned nurse what she hoped was an encouraging smile. "And she would not have specifically asked for your help unless she felt she could trust you with this."

Jacqueline nodded slowly and finally unlocked her fingers. "I will not betray that trust, Sister. I will give my report to the matron before supper. Thank you for listening to me. Seeing the soldiers was rather . . . disquieting."

Lizzie took Jacqueline's hands. "I can only imagine, but you were perfectly right to come and express your thoughts and fears to me. Please, continue to feel that you can do so in the future."

That earned her a nod and a wavering smile. Then Jacqueline was gone from the room, her footsteps fading down the hall.

When silence returned to her room, Lizzie sank onto her bed, her legs giving out in relief at not having to lie or hide more than the necessities. She fully believed Jacqueline would keep the secret of the soldiers and could be trusted implicitly with their care, but it was a heavy weight for any of them to bear. And until the soldiers started to improve, the length of their stay would be impossible to determine.

A bigger question rose in Lizzie's mind: Would Mr. Capiau or his associates bring more soldiers to them under cover of secrecy from the German authorities?

How far would Edith have them go after these soldiers left their care?

What else was Edith willing to risk?

What was Lizzie willing to risk?

She did not know the answers to those questions, and perhaps she would not know until she was actually presented with those risks.

Shaking her head to herself, Lizzie pushed up off her bed and made her way out of her room to the patient ward, needing to check in on their new patients before she could be satisfied for the evening.

Jacqueline had given her a fair enough idea of "Pierre's" condition, so she felt comfortable leaving him to his quiet recovery. Colonel Boger, however, had been in a worse state, and Jacqueline would not know anything about him. It would soothe Lizzie's mind to check on him personally, rather than wait for Beatrice's report since the sister likely would also not know the true nature of the patient's stay.

Lizzie quickly made her way to room twelve, where she found Colonel Boger resting in bed, and Edith sitting beside the bed rather than Beatrice.

"Matron?" Lizzie said softly, not wanting to disturb the sleeping soldier.

Edith looked up, a little pale, but smiling. "Lizzie. I sent Sister Smith to prepare for supper and thought I would sit with Louis for a while."

Lizzie nodded, her eyes studying the frail frame of the man while he slept. "How is he?"

"If he were in good health, he might recover from his wounds shortly," Edith murmured as she also turned her attention to their patient. "But as he is so weak, I fear it will take longer. And his foot will require an operation. Would you send a request to Dr. Gyselinck to come here tomorrow and advise us?"

"Of course, Matron." Lizzie hesitated as she came to Edith's side, weighing her next words with care. "Matron, did Mr. Capiau leave you any idea if we might receive more such patients in the future?"

Edith shook her head, turning to face Lizzie, her expression unreadable. "No. I expect I will hear from him in the next few days as these soldiers improve. Someone must have an idea of how to get them out of Brussels safely, after all." She glanced back at Colonel Boger, her brow creasing.

What Edith thought was not at all clear, though Lizzie could see the concern written in her features. What else did her esteemed matron worry about? The colonel's condition? His family in England? The danger for themselves? The danger for him?

All of those questions and more?

Edith rose then, surprising Lizzie and forcing her to stand a little taller in expectation of an assignment. But the matron only turned to her with a gentle smile. "Come, we mustn't be late for supper. I will check on our patients once more before I retire for the evening, but I trust both Beatrice and Jacqueline to take care of them. I don't think we need to inform the rest of the nurses. These men are simply patients, and they will be treated as such."

Lizzie nodded, though she bit her lip in hesitation. People were naturally curious, and under the strict operations of the German military, anything new and different was bound to play upon that curiosity more than usual. There was little possibility they could keep the soldiers' presence a secret, but could they at least keep them safe?

So many questions, and only time and risk would reveal the answers.

Edith nodded as if she had heard Lizzie's unspoken thoughts. But that reassurance had been needed, and she had seen that in Lizzie's eyes. Despite everything Edith had to contend with in her life, and all that presently lay at her feet, she could still give Lizzie that.

How could Lizzie not feel comforted?

CHAPTER 5

The two British soldiers stayed with them for three weeks, leaving just before dawn. The matron went with them to see them safely to their next destination, and Lizzie was positive she had not breathed a full breath until the matron safely returned. Even then, she fully anticipated General von Lüttwitz would appear at the door of the clinic at any moment, carrying scraps of the two men's disguises, and arresting the lot of them for daring to defy orders.

Every sound made her jump, and every knock at the door or ringing of the bell sent her heart racing.

But thus far, the general had not appeared, the soldiers had not returned, and nothing unusual had taken place at all.

Sister White would be returning to England tomorrow to take care of her aging father and would take with her Colonel Boger's dispatches for the War Office. Lizzie had her doubts about how Sister White would manage that when every parcel was subject to search, as was every portion of a traveler's person, but she said she planned to strap Colonel Boger's documents to her thigh, so as to keep everything that much more difficult to detect.

Sister White was both a Red Cross nurse and a British national, and she was traveling by return ticket. It was doubtful anyone would suspect her or look upon her as the enemy. All would be right and correct.

Colonel Boger's sensitive documents should have no trouble being delivered, no matter what might potentially befall the man in his own attempts to return home.

Lizzie could only hope that both would be successful without incident.

She made her way to the matron's rooms, having been asked to meet her there privately after the matron had rested. What Edith could possibly need after the night she had endured, Lizzie could not imagine, but she was not about to object. She knocked softly, her curiosity reaching almost untold heights and, upon hearing the response, entered with as little noise as possible.

If the matron had indeed taken her rest, she gave no sign of it, nor that any rest was needed at all. She sat at her desk, working away at some correspondence, her hair perfectly in place, her complexion smooth, and her eyes just as bright as any other day in their clinic.

"Sister Wilkins," Edith began in her usual low, gentle tones. "Lizzie. I realize that I have asked a great deal of you and the other senior staff in the last few weeks while we had our guests with us."

"It was nothing, Matron," Lizzie replied at once. "We were happy to help and to do all that was necessary."

Edith smiled her true smile then, which always created an impressive aura of youth in her features. But it soon faded, and she folded her hands atop her desk. "I fear I must ask more of you, and them, in the coming days and weeks."

Lizzie's limbs went a little cold at the statement. "Oh?"

There was a slight pause, and then the matron continued, "We will be receiving nine new guests tonight, and beds must be prepared for them."

The difficulty in swallowing had never been so great in her life. "Nine?" Lizzie repeated. "So many?"

Edith nodded. "Mademoiselle Martin will be arriving later to discuss the details with me, but I am told there will indeed be nine. I do not know their names, nationalities, or injuries, but they are to be treated with the same precautions as our previous guests. Do you see?"

Lizzie matched Edith's nod, barely feeling the motion. "Yes, Matron, I quite follow. Erm, am I to also understand that this new arrangement will continue even after these new guests have left us?"

She watched the matron's face carefully, so perfectly composed it revealed nothing. The somber gray eyes seemed to weigh Lizzie's worth and measure, yet the love and trust her matron had always showered upon her were there in abundance.

"Yes, Lizzie. It will continue for the foreseeable future." Edith smiled and tilted her head. "I know I ask more of you than I have a right to. If you would prefer to be kept out of the operation, I will understand."

Lizzie swallowed the sudden doubt and fear that rose within her and simply said, "What can I do to help?"

February, 1915

Had Lizzie known what she had been taking on when offering to help Edith, she might have rephrased her words.

With the arrival of the new year, the Germans had imposed a curfew on the town and its citizens. Brussels was without electricity or gas, and all coal was being shipped off to Germany for their war efforts. The Belgians were using candles and oil lamps for light, some even breaking up pieces of furniture to burn for warmth.

More guests to the Institute had come and gone since the curfew had been imposed, and the numbers in each group—and the numbers of groups themselves—were continuing to grow. There were currently two English soldiers who were also patients on the ward, under strict orders to speak no English whatsoever. During a recent surprise inspection from the Germans, the nurses had cleverly described Lance Corporal Doman as a Belgian peasant with a chronic rheumatic complaint in order to explain his odd posture and bandages as his back healed from his shrapnel wounds.

Corporal Chapman had no shocking wounds, but his weakness when he had arrived made it easy to claim that he was another poor, malnourished Belgian in need of care. The German authorities had asked no questions about him either, and no further inspections had taken place since. The two soldiers would undoubtedly be departing soon, though the details of how they would do so were kept secret, even from Lizzie.

Given the steady influx of guests at the clinic, Edith had begun to assign some of her most trusted nurses as guides to accompany the men, which kept her from having to make most of the ventures herself. How exactly those ventures took place and by what means the soldiers were delivered to their next place of safety, Lizzie did not know, which was perfectly comfortable for her. The fewer details known the better, especially if the nurses wished to remain protected from the German authorities.

Lizzie had been instructing newer nurses on techniques for binding head wounds when she had seen Mademoiselle Martin arrive earlier, which undoubtedly meant more guests would arrive just as the others were departing. It was becoming an odd sort of routine at the clinic, and questioning looks among the nurses and probationers had long since stopped.

Whoever Mademoiselle Martin was, if that was even her true name, she appeared to be heavily involved in finding or transporting these unfortunate soldiers to safety. It seemed strange, given the woman was rather young, slight of build, and altogether unremarkable in bearing and appearance, apart from her strikingly dark eyes. But Lizzie would never have suspected the matron of engaging in such work based on her appearance, so it was a poor judgment of the thing, indeed.

How many wounded would Mademoiselle Martin have for them this time, and when would they come?

Lizzie glanced out the window near Edith's offices while waiting for an opportunity to speak with the matron, and her heart sank into her stomach.

A number of their current guests were sitting out in front of the clinic as though this were a holiday destination and they were simply taking their leisure in the winter sunshine.

Out in the open. Where anyone could see them. Including any passing Germans.

Governor von Lüttwitz himself walked by the clinic at least once a week, occasionally stopping by to ask questions—mostly of an innocent nature—but more often than not, to simply watch the building as though he expected to see something amiss. As though he knew what the matron was attempting. As though there was something of extreme interest in the place that he needed to inspect personally.

He could come by at any moment and ask his questions of the soldiers, which would be disastrous for everyone.

How could the soldiers not sense the danger they were in? How could they not consider what all of the nurses and staff at the clinic were risking by housing them? Did they not consider the danger to

Edith herself? The clinic housed a decent number of French soldiers at the present, but several English soldiers were with them as well. It was not safe for any of them to be out and about so freely. There were rules in place for specifically this thing!

Lizzie nearly started outside to scold them when she heard the door open to the matron's office, and she turned to face her instead. Edith walked out with Mademoiselle Martin, neither of them seeming agitated or concerned at all. Considering the topic of their discussions, Lizzie found that simply remarkable.

"Matron," Lizzie greeted with a slight smile. "Mademoiselle Martin."

Mademoiselle Martin gave her an almost bright smile. "Sister Wilkins, good day. I bring the gratitude of Dr. Détry, whose guests have all arrived in Holland. I trust that news will be of comfort."

Lizzie exhaled a small breath of relief. Dr. Détry had sent them ten or so French soldiers, and arranging for their travel to the frontier had been a feat for the matron. But, after sending them out in small intervals, all had gotten away, and, as per usual, the nurses had not heard anything since. Hearing of the soldiers' safe arrival was a pleasure, to be sure. Would that Lizzie could be so reassured about all whom they cared for.

"That is excellent news, Mademoiselle," Lizzie told her. "Thank you."

The young woman nodded and continued past her. Edith made to follow when Lizzie put a hand on her arm.

"Matron," she murmured, "I fear our guests are becoming too comfortable. Several of them are sitting outside and taking their ease."

Edith's gray eyes darted to the window and narrowed slightly. "Thank you, Sister Wilkins," she replied in a soft, almost gentle way. "I will see to it." She bade Mademoiselle Martin farewell, and then

Lizzie watched as the matron went out in the front of the clinic and spoke with the soldiers lounging there.

One by one, each of them returned indoors, not a single face among them seeming perturbed or disgruntled.

How did the matron manage to do that?

There was no doubt the soldiers hated being cooped up in the clinic, though none of them had ever blatantly expressed their frustration. But anyone would have felt trapped under the circumstances, and hearing the constant sounds of war in the distance, these brave men must have felt even more desperate to get out and do something.

Unfortunately, it was her task to keep the soldiers secret and safe.

After a few minutes, the matron was back and came to Lizzie's side. "There," she said simply. "I've told them we cannot have them appearing so casually before our doors—this is a medical facility, not a hotel—but that we will arrange for any who wish to take short walks, singly or in pairs, about the town in Jose's company."

"Yes, Matron," Lizzie replied, hoping their guests would strive to obey the matron's orders.

Edith looked out the window again, her expression thoughtful. "These are not the first soldiers of late to take such risks. The good people of Brussels continue to live their lives, despite the sanctions of the German authorities, and so it seems natural for the soldiers to go about as well. But an English soldier, especially, has a very characteristic walk and manner of speaking, and if several men are being seen leaving our house . . . Well, it is bound to draw attention, and we cannot have that."

Lizzie shook her head, swallowing. "No, Matron."

"Which is what I intend to tell the Prince of Croÿ when he comes today."

Lizzie had been turning to look out the window when the matron's words fully processed, and she jerked to face her. "The Prince of Croÿ?" she repeated, her tone almost shrill.

Edith gave her a very small smile, betraying her real amusement by the reaction. "Yes, Lizzie, the Prince of Croÿ. He has come before, but I believe you were occupied. He and his sister, Princess Marie, are quite involved in these activities. I do not know if they are the leaders, or even if there are any, but when our guests arrive, they usually provide me with a code word: Yorc."

"The name of Croÿ in reverse," Lizzie breathed in awe, beginning to smile. "I had no idea, Matron."

"That is as it should be," Edith assured her. "I only tell you now because Mademoiselle Martin seems to think our numbers will continue to grow, and I may not be quite able to personally oversee as much. And with the construction of our new clinic in Uccle nearly being completed, I must begin planning for the removal of our equipment and nurses to the new premises. So I shall leave most of the clinic duties to you, of course. For the time being."

"Of course," Lizzie echoed quickly, nodding. "I will take care of everything, just as you would see it done yourself."

Edith's smile grew further, the warmth of it filling Lizzie with a quiet peace, despite their tense circumstances. "I know you will, Lizzie. You always do." She patted her arm, then said, "Oh, and a few of the French guests will be visiting Chez Jules later today for a glass or two of wine. Some of the English guests have asked to attend. They cannot pass for a local Belgian as easily as a French soldier can, but they have assured me they will behave themselves and not betray their identity. I see no harm in it, so I have given them permission to do so."

It was all Lizzie could do to keep from blurting out all manner of objections, and only the steady pressure of her teeth against her tongue kept her in check. The matron saw no harm in it? After she had just been forced to send the soldiers inside for taking their ease in the sun?

"Yes, Matron," she managed to say without too much of an edge to her words.

If Edith heard her unspoken objections, she said nothing about them. The matron released Lizzie's arm as she returned to her office.

When she was gone, and the door safely closed, Lizzie released a sputtering breath. This could be a truly terrible idea, and the matron ought to have known that. The French soldiers were freer to move about, being able to blend in far more easily among the local Belgians, but the English . . .

For all their attempts to imitate French or Belgian allies, the Englishmen almost never succeeded. Their accents would not be quite right, or their mannerisms a trifle off, or their bearing far too superior, or any number of small details that gave away their nationality as blatantly as though they wore the Union Jack about their shoulders.

And they were going to the snug little café to drink with French compatriots?

There was no promise that any carefully constructed disguise of person or manner would remain when under such influence.

Chez Jules was a popular café for local workmen who would stop in at the end of a day for a drink before returning home. While she would never suggest that the locals would report suspicious things to the authorities outright, given the general animosity toward the Germans, there was the danger of rumors reaching the enemies' ears if word spread too far and too freely.

Anticipation and anxiety built within Lizzie for the remainder of the day, and she feared the feelings would likely not subside for several more, given the length of time it could take for word to spread. But perhaps the soldiers truly would behave and keep their identities secret. Perhaps all would be well and she was worrying and fearing for nothing.

But perhaps . . .

Perhaps the matron ought to have worried a little more.

No, Lizzie scolded herself. No, the matron knew more than Lizzie could hope to about this situation and about the soldiers they were housing. Edith knew perfectly the dangers they were facing and the risks the soldiers were taking. She was no fool. In many ways, Edith was the wisest person Lizzie knew.

That would have to be enough. Faith in the matron and faith in her faith. Just a mustard seed.

She could manage that, surely.

CHAPTER 6

Of all the places for Edith to find herself, sitting in an unfamiliar tavern on the other side of Brussels on a crisp evening in March was not one she had ever imagined.

Nor would she have anticipated having a pint of beer on the table before her. She did not drink, after all. But for the sake of appearances, when she entered the tavern with her two Tommy charges, they had all ordered beers as though there was nothing else on their agenda.

There had been no guide to spare to escort the two soldiers to the local priest who would take them to the next step of their journey, so Edith had done the task herself. She and the soldiers had taken a tramcar from the clinic and had now only to sit and wait for their next contact.

Whoever he might be.

The tables around them were as rowdy and raucous as Edith expected a soldiers' café to be. But waiting among them, knowing if a single person reported Edith or the two British soldiers to the authorities . . .

A bout of loud laughter nearby startled Edith, her hand slipping from the handle of her untouched beer. Her fingers splayed for a brief spasm, and she set her hand in her lap to hide her nerves from any onlookers. Her heart pounded furiously against each rib, a miserable rhythm of anxiety unlike anything she had ever known.

What was she doing here? She was not a soldier, she was the host of soldiers in need, a nurse to the wounded. She was not a guide leading men across the frontier. She was not a hardy, impenetrable thistle in the highlands; she was a chrysanthemum in a vase on a shelf.

Or safely tucked in a garden, perhaps. Carefully tended, weeded, watered.

She did not belong here. Why was she doing this? Why had she thought she could?

Edith paused her own spinning thoughts, scolding herself as though she were one of her own students. She was not having a heart attack for pity's sake, nor was she about to begin to fear her surroundings. She had stood before a furious German general without cowing; she could certainly sit calmly in a room full of drunken soldiers and wait for her contact to arrive.

With a sniff of calm resolve, she reached into her pocket and pulled out the torn half of a visiting card, setting it on the table just in front of her, slightly to one side. Just as she had been instructed.

And now they would wait.

She glanced across the table at her two soldiers, both seeming as calm as the dawn. They had been so kind to the nurses who had cared for them, and the soldiers had come so far. No one looking at either of them now would think they had ever been ill or weak or injured. Edith was quite proud of that and reminded herself to commend her nurses when she returned.

Lizzie, really, was who ought to be commended. While Edith became more and more occupied with the hiding, transporting, and organizing situations for the soldiers, Lizzie had shouldered the bulk of the nursing work in the clinic. Instructing the students, watching over them, ensuring that all was in order for their work to continue. It was imperative to the protection of everyone that the nursing standard did not slacken or even appear to falter, and Lizzie was the reason that could be said.

A few years ago, an opportunity had arisen for Lizzie to work elsewhere, but Edith had been able to convince her to stay in Brussels. It had been a blessing then as much as it was now. She would be lost without Lizzie. They all would.

The two soldiers sipped their beers, while Edith continued to stare at hers. How much longer would they have to wait? Or could they wait? When would she know if her contact was not coming and all was lost?

How long had they even been sitting there?

A figure approached them and, with a quick flick of a hand, placed the matching half of her card on the table. He then sat at their table as though he had always intended to join them, slapping Doman on the back, and ordering a beer for himself.

Edith closed her eyes on a slow breath, her heart seeming to fall to her knees. Relief had never been so sweet.

He exchanged pleasantries with Edith, smiling cordially, and she returned them. She had never seen him before. She could have crossed paths with him in the street and never known it. What was better, he was of such an average nature that she would likely not know him again, should their paths again cross.

Perfect.

When enough time had passed, the group left their table and returned to the streets of Brussels, the soldiers and their new guide going one way, and Edith another.

She enjoyed every blessed breath she took as she made her way back to the clinic. Her heart still beat with a hard edge, but soon enough, she felt the fatigue that seemed to follow her everywhere these days return.

The many tasks she had to tend to, none of which dealt specifically with the calling of her profession, weighed heavily upon her. The clinic was now taking in eight or so soldiers nearly every time, and sometimes there was overlap between groups.

The growing numbers put more strain on both her staff and the soldiers. The group she had allowed to visit Chez Jules last month had not entirely contained themselves, and though no one would have accused them of making a scene, rumors were beginning to spread across Brussels. The Rue de la Culture suddenly sported more than the occasional German soldier walking by, apparently without particular intentions.

Edith arrived at the clinic just as another pair of soldiers was heading out with Gilles, one of their guides. She moved to one of them, reaching out her hands. "Had I known you were leaving us now, I would have arranged a better tea for you today."

He grinned in response as he took her hands. "Matron, had you arranged anything better, I would have thought myself on holiday," he replied in perfect French. "Thank you for all you have done."

Edith nodded, squeezing his hands. "It was my pleasure. Might I ask a favor of you?"

"Of course."

She reached into the pocket of her apron and pulled out the small Bible she had placed there that morning. "When you return to Norfolk, will you go to Norwich and give this to my mother? There is a letter inside, and I believe it may be safer transported by you than by the post."

The lance corporal took the Bible and ran his thumbs gently over its cover. "I would be happy to, Matron. And I will give her my own account of the care I received here."

"Thank you," Edith murmured, smiling slightly. "If you would kindly be vague as to the details of your stay here, it would be much appreciated."

He smiled in understanding. "Of course, Matron."

She had no doubt the lance corporal would do as he said, and there was something inherently comforting in that. Her mother would receive the Bible and the letter, and her anxieties would be somewhat soothed. Until the war was over, however, they would likely linger in some form.

There was not much she could do about that. She would not leave Belgium, and the Germans were not going to ease their policing of the post. Messages sent via her guests would be the best option to circumvent the trouble, assuming those guests could get through the difficulties and make the trip to Norwich.

Gilles, a tall, rosy-cheeked man in his thirties, stepped forward. "We must go, Matron, or we will miss our window."

Edith nodded and smiled at the soldier. "God be with you."

"And God bless you, Matron." He saluted, though she was not tied to the military in any way, and turned to follow Gilles out into the streets.

She smiled softly and turned, sensing someone approaching. "Lizzie, how are you?"

"Well, thank you," came the soft reply. "And you? Is all well?"

Edith put a hand on her friend's arm, gratitude for her and all that she did threatening to overflow. "Yes, my friend. All is well. But I am tired, as you can probably imagine."

Lizzie laughed and took her arm. "Yes, I most certainly can." She paused, peering out the door with a slight frown that was quickly replaced with a smile. "Although it does not appear that you will be able to rest just yet. Here comes Mrs. Depage."

"At this hour?" Edith turned and looked, shaking her head.

"Edith!" Marie called, waving at her. "I have news for you! Hello, Lizzie!"

They both waved back, laughing. Marie entered as freely as she had ever done, the clinic having been founded in part by her husband, and the three women walked together toward Edith's personal rooms. Marie chatted about her children, about the doctor's frustrations with certain conditions imposed on him, about her desire to do more to help.

It was not until they were safely ensconced in her rooms that Edith realized Marie had, in fact, been leading up to a certain topic with her conversation.

Edith's chest tightened in anticipation. "Marie, what is your news?"

Marie gave her a soft smile, though her eyes contained several emotions within their depths as they began to well with tears. "I am going to America. I intend to seek help there for wounded soldiers and to speak on behalf of war relief for Belgium."

Edith nearly gasped in amazement but managed to maintain her poise. To get out of Belgium at all was one thing, but to go so far as to America . . .

There would be no certainty Marie would even be able to return! She was a Belgian national, of course, so she had a greater chance than others of crossing back into the country, but nothing was certain. And the voyage was long; so much could change in the country during that time alone, not to mention whatever length of time she stayed in America.

What if the war descended into deeper dangers and Marie was trapped in America for the duration? Had she and her husband considered that? Was the predicament really so dire as to require such a risk?

Words refused to form in Edith's mind, leaving her only able to stare at her friend in a mix of horror, shock, and, she had to admit, a touch of admiration. There was no denying Marie's cause was noble, no matter the dangers stacked against her. And was Edith not engaged in a precarious situation of her own?

"I have many American cities to visit," Marie continued after the heavy pause. "It has all been arranged. I shall even travel as far west as Chicago and Pittsburgh! And I will bring back some new assistance—the able Dr. James Houghton of New York, for one. I shall bring more if I can manage it."

Edith nodded almost absently, still feeling numb at the prospect.

"That will be a great help and comfort," Lizzie added, her voice not quite steady.

Edith cleared her throat and tried to smile, though her emotions, still so near the surface, began once more to rise. "How long will you be gone?"

Marie sniffled, a sign of her own feelings wavering. "I have reservations at the end of April on the *Lapland*. I may change my plans for a faster liner, though—perhaps the *Lusitania*." She shook her head. "It will be a wrench to part from Antoine and the children for so long, but I must do something."

That was something Edith could understand all too well. The longer she was involved in the hiding, healing, and shuttling of soldiers, the more passionate she felt about it. The more risks she was willing to take. Not in an overly confident or arrogant way—she would never allow her pride to exceed her good sense—but in an attempt to devote more time, more energy, more of herself to saving others.

Marie was trying to do the same thing, in her own way.

Edith's heart ached about the departure, though, filled with some deep foreboding she could not understand, and a wild uncertainty that frightened her.

There was no restraining her tears. Marie's eyes were also wet, and Edith shook her head, moving forward to embrace her friend.

"God be with you, my friend," Edith choked out amid her tears. "May He watch over you, protect you, and send your pleas to willing ears."

Marie nodded, holding her tightly. "And may He keep you safe in your endeavors."

Edith closed her eyes on more tears, willing herself to feel comforted by the words. To be parted from Marie at a time like this felt impossible, and suddenly she felt more keenly how her own mother must fret over her in these troubling and uncertain times.

All the more reason for Edith to do her part to bring about the end of this war so that hope and peace might once again prevail.

CHAPTER 7

"Have you seen this?"

Lizzie looked up from folded bandages to see Sister Taylor, Sister White's replacement, coming toward her. "Seen what, Sister?"

Sister Taylor waved a sheet of paper. "This!" She thrust it out for Lizzie to see, her hand almost shaking as she did so.

It took a moment for her to realize what she was looking at. When she did, the notes and stanzas of a familiar tune playing in her mind, her jaw dropped. "Tipperary?"

Sister Taylor nodded once. "Tipperary. Printed and sold on the streets as an anthem for the Belgians to resist the Germans. Do you have any idea how a British song has turned into such a signal in Brussels?"

Lizzie met her eyes in horror. "The other night," she breathed. "Some of the soldiers were playing it and singing."

"Exactly." Sister Taylor lowered her arm, putting a hand to her brow. "And now half of Brussels is singing it. We might as well post a sign on our clinic as a designated point of resistance to German rule. We all felt so delighted to be singing it again, and now this . . ."

"Has the matron seen it?" Lizzie asked, placing her hands on the table and shaking her head. "She has been under such strain since she returned from taking those nurses to Antwerp; this will hardly help."

Sister Taylor nodded. "She has, but she did not seem to care, even though I heard her talking with Mr. Capiau this morning, and he asked if she could keep the soldiers better hidden and quieter."

Lizzie's brows rose. Edith might be a quiet individual, but she was not to be pressed or intimidated. "How did she respond?"

"She said, 'They are not animals to be caged. What can I do about it?' and that was the end of the discussion." Sister Taylor shook her head, shrugging. "It sounded so cavalier for her. Should we be concerned?"

There was no good way to respond to the question, so Lizzie only bit her lip. In truth, Lizzie *was* concerned, but there was no one to whom she could express those concerns. She had tried to talk with the matron, but received only repeated assurances that she was fine and there was nothing to fear.

She wondered if the matron might be forcing herself to continue day after day with her show of unflappable strength, unable to admit her own fatigue and cares even to herself. Who did she unburden herself to? Or did she at all? With all that she had to contend with, all the risks she was taking, all that they were enduring with the occupation and their work and the secrets the clinic now contained, was it possible Edith was becoming more cavalier as a means of coping?

"I don't know what to do, Sister," Lizzie admitted finally. "She shows no sign of slowing or stopping, and if they are taking more risks—"

"They are not the only ones," Sister Taylor interrupted, sitting beside her and lowering her voice. "The cook's daughter has been caught holding hands with soldiers, and two days ago, she kissed one of the French ones."

"Oh, heavens." Lizzie closed her eyes, shaking her head. "Has she no sense? I've heard some of the soldiers have given her their true names as well."

"Yes, and I gave them my thoughts about that quite clearly, and reported it to the matron at once."

Lizzie's eyes snapped to her friend's face. "And?"

Sister Taylor exhaled. "She was irritated, but nothing more. She said she was too occupied with other matters and asked me to speak with her."

"Too occupied . . ." Lizzie repeated, trailing off in disbelief. "She's never been too busy to attend to important things personally."

"Well, all is different now, isn't it?" Sister Taylor sat back in her chair, looking toward the corridor with a slight crease in her brow. "And getting worse."

Lizzie watched her steadily. "How so?"

Sister Taylor glanced at her. "The Germans sank a Dutch ship carrying a cargo of grain near Flushing last week. The *Katwijk*. Holland is livid, close to declaring war on Germany and giving up their neutral status."

"But that would mean it could become even more treacherous for crossings," Lizzie cried, thinking about all the soldiers they were currently housing and the ones due to leave shortly, not to mention the new ones they would get almost immediately afterwards. "If the Dutch place troops at the crossings, they could require papers of anyone they see."

Sister Taylor nodded slowly, her expression somber. "Indeed, they could. And already there are suspicions in that area, and spies are on the watch. Some guides have already been shot. Not ours, but others. Gilles insists he is not afraid, but I don't know how any of them can keep going like this."

Bless Gilles. He was always so confident about his abilities to get soldiers across the border, and he had never failed yet. He was not their only guide, but he was the one they were most familiar with. He had developed a bit of a soft spot for the clinic and the nurses, and he would occasionally drop by just to see that all was well. It was an affectionate sort of relationship between them all, and yet, none of them knew if Gilles was his true name.

It was undoubtedly best that way.

"How many new Tommies did we get in the last bunch?" Sister Taylor asked in a low voice, eyeing the doorway that led to the rest of the clinic.

"At least eight," Lizzie replied just as softly. "I haven't managed the names of all yet, but Private Scott was the one with wounds to his chest and his feet—do you recall?"

Sister Taylor nodded and made a sympathetic click with her tongue. "Poor lad. He seemed so young and so unwell. Each time I have gone to check on him, he has been sleeping. How is he recovering?"

"Well enough. He would recover faster if we could avoid more inspections." Lizzie frowned.

The trouble was that the inspections were happening more frequently and with far more intensity than any of the previous ones. Almost as though the German authorities knew there was something to find, if only they looked hard enough. It caused a sense of panic throughout the clinic each and every time.

And the more soldiers they had staying as secret guests, the worse that panic became.

"Has he recovered from the last one?" Sister Taylor pressed. "He's the only one staying on the ward, right? So the only one who needed to be moved?"

Lizzie nodded. "Yes. The matron hid him in a barrel in the garden and covered him with apples. I was tasked with bringing him back to bed after the inspection was over, and he was in good spirits. Apparently, before he came to us, he had been staying with a family related to Mr. Joly and was living in a boarded-up cellar. The military police were suspicious, and there were several close calls, so he was brought here. Imagine going through all of that, beginning to heal in relative peace, and then still needing to be hidden from the Germans in a barrel with apples."

Sister Taylor was quiet for a long moment, her expression suggesting her thoughts were far away. "I cannot imagine what any of them are going through. What we endure is hard enough, but for them . . ."

As though to emphasize her point, the sounds of shelling could be heard in the distance. It was a sound Lizzie heard every day, but it felt more painful and more harrowing today.

Odd how the sound no longer made Lizzie jump. Until this moment, it had been weeks since it caused even a twinge of discomfort in her heart. What once had terrorized her days and her dreams was now no more remarkable than the chirp of a bird.

And that was terrifying.

Lizzie exhaled a long, slow breath. "I suppose we had better see to our patients, hadn't we?"

Sister Taylor nodded and pushed to her feet. "There's a new crop of German soldiers in as well, though they are not necessarily as pleased to be here as our other soldiers."

"They never are," Lizzie mumbled, standing and moving toward the corridor and the patient ward. "Some of them have been polite, at least, but others . . ."

"I think it's the same for any soldier, isn't it?" Sister Taylor mused as they walked together.

Lizzie nodded to Sister Taylor as they split off in the ward. She noted that each of the patients seemed to be resting well or tended by someone already.

Except for one man resting in a bed without any neighbors, looking far too young to be in uniform at all.

She moved to his bedside, smiling warmly. "Good day, my friend," she greeted in French. She knew only a few words in German, but almost everyone in Europe spoke French, and certainly almost everyone in Belgium did.

The boy looked at her with wide eyes, showing no understanding at all. He appeared closer to twelve than anything legally approaching adulthood. No one should be seeing war so young. No one.

Lizzie looked over the uniform again, noting the insignia, realization slowly dawning.

She bit her lip, swallowing hard amidst the tightening in her throat. "*Sprechen sie English?*"

His eyes lit up. "Yes. Some little."

Lizzie closed her eyes against the wash of anger, disgust, and irritation. She could not think of this *child* as a German soldier. He was her patient and nothing else. As Edith had told them in the beginning, nursing knew no nationality.

She opened her eyes and tried to make her smile more encouraging. "What is your name?"

Tears welled in the young man's eyes. "Why matter? I am German. You hate me. I hate me too. Hate war. Hate . . ." He looked away, a tear rolling down his cheek.

Lizzie felt her heart creak with the deep, resonating echo usually reserved for endless caverns and broken dreams. She instantly took the lad's hand in hers. "Oh, darling. You don't even want to be here, do you?"

He shook his head, sniffling. "I barely turn fifteen when they make me join. I want to stay on farm, but they make me go to war.

I do not know war, do not know why they have this war. Belgium is beautiful. Why we here?" He looked down at his hand in hers, then met her eyes. "I want to go home. Can I go home?"

Oh, how painful to see his sorrow, to hear his plaintive plea. She wished she could give him an answer that would rid him of his tears. But the German soldiers documented their soldiers as carefully as the nurses did their secret soldiers, only the Germans enforced their count with rifles. There was no way this poor boy could go home, not with his injuries healing as well as they were. The authorities would not let him go even if he were at death's door.

How did an innocent child manage to get plucked up for an army when he was so clearly unprepared for it? What use could someone like this be for any military at all? Why did any country do this to its citizens?

She knew full well that Germany was not the only country conscripting soldiers, nor the only one to send young and ill-equipped men to fight their wars. But now, seeing this poor boy alone in a hospital bed and so very far from home and loved ones, she hated each one that did.

"What is your name, soldier?" Lizzie asked again gently, rubbing his hand.

"Lukas," came the soft, childlike reply.

Lizzie nodded. "Lukas. I don't hate you. None of this is your fault. I cannot do anything to keep you from being returned to the army, but while you stay with us and heal, I can keep you company, and you can tell me all about your home and your farm. I can be your friend. Will that help?"

Tears filled the lad's eyes once more, and Lizzie was hard-pressed not to join him in his emotion. "*Ja,*" he whispered. "It will help."

CHAPTER 8

Edith sank onto her small bed, pinching the bridge of her nose as a wave of fatigue swept over her.

The work grew more precarious as it did more ambitious. The resistance newspaper, *La Libre Belgique*, was alive and thriving, which angered the German authorities considerably. They had been unable to find the editors or printing press used to bring it about, though they certainly tried to quell its distribution.

There were even a few copies of the paper here in the clinic, though the nurses were careful to confine those to the private rooms and cellars that housed their hidden guests. Should the Germans decide to inspect the premises again, there would be a great deal of shuffling to do.

Edith knew Philippe Baucq was involved in the printing somehow, and on the rare occasions when they met, he told her such tales. One of the priests in the city, Pere Meeus, was actually an informer for the paper, often entering German officers' clubs in the city to obtain plans of raids.

What Edith wouldn't give to have an advanced knowledge of

inspections of her own clinic. But she was quite certain Governor von Lüttwitz was taking the surveillance of the clinic personally as well as seriously, so it was entirely possible that he ordered inspections on simple whims.

Fortunately, Edith's options were expanding.

There were a number of safe houses in Brussels now, as well as a number of locals who were offering to help the resistance, despite the associated danger. Even the chemist had taken to occasionally bringing soldiers to Edith for transportation.

As alone as Edith sometimes felt from time to time in this work, there were constant reminders that she was not alone at all.

A soft knock sounded at her door, and Edith sighed, wishing she had ceased her rapid thoughts and taken the chance to sleep.

"Yes?" she called, sitting up with a groan and rubbing at the soreness in her neck.

Lizzie poked her head around the door, her expression sympathetic. "Matron, I am so sorry, but we've had a new arrival."

"At this time of day?" Edith looked at the table clock, frowning. "How many?"

"Two."

Edith jerked to look at Lizzie in shock, startled by the idea of only two arrivals when a normal group was anywhere from three to ten soldiers at a time. One soldier was suspect, but two were not much better. If they were fortunate to have an excellent disguise, they might be safe enough to arrive in the light of morning without rousing much suspicion from the authorities, but the risk was still terribly great.

"They had the password, Matron."

Edith blinked, realizing she had not answered. "Are either of them injured?"

Lizzie shook her head, worry creasing her brow. "No, both seem very well."

Two soldiers without wounds arriving in the light of day.

Ought they be concerned for the safety of the others they were presently hiding?

Pushing up from the bed, Edith smiled at her most trusted nurse. "Where are they?"

"The front room of 149," Lizzie replied, her dark eyes darting across Edith's face. "You look so tired. You need to rest."

"I will," Edith assured her as they started down the hall. "Tonight, I will rest."

Lizzie exhaled in soft exasperation. "You said that last night."

Edith managed a soft laugh. "I will probably say it again tomorrow, Lizzie. Between our patients, our tasks, and the new clinic nearing completion, I fear I have little time to myself, and even less for rest." She bit her lip, frowning as they walked.

"What can I do?" Lizzie asked in a low voice when Edith did not go on. "To help you. To relieve some of the burden. Anything."

If only she could give up some of the burden without endangering anyone else. She would love to be free of this weight, to have fewer thoughts spinning in her mind, to have an unoccupied moment. To truly rest.

But the more she shared, the more people could be implicated should the world tumble around them. And she could not let that happen.

Edith paused a step, turning to face Lizzie fully. "If you would see that the next departing group is prepared and moved to the cellar, that would be helpful. Gilles will be coming before nightfall to begin dispersing them across town, and it would settle my mind to know all is ready."

Lizzie nodded eagerly and beamed as though she had been given the answer to all of life's questions. "Of course, Matron! I would be happy to!" She hurried off to do the simple favor asked of her, and Edith watched her go with a fond smile.

It was time to see to her new guests, though she was more than a little apprehensive. They had so many guests now, the challenge of housing and tending to them was growing more and more complicated. There had not been problems thus far, but how long could that last?

When would a problem appear?

And the question, she was afraid, was *when*, not *if.*

She entered the front room of 149, as directed, and saw two men within, both of whom were standing.

"Welcome to Berkendael Medical Institute," she greeted without preamble. "I am the matron here, Edith Cavell. How might we help you?"

"I am Monsieur Bonjean, and this is Monsieur Masson," one of them began. "We were told you could help us."

She gestured for them to sit, doing so herself, and folding her arms as she watched the pair of them. "And by whom were you informed?"

"Princess Marie de Croÿ," the other said. "We were told she wrote to you about two Belgians seeking guides to the Dutch frontier."

Edith thought back quickly, then eased into a more comfortable posture in her chair as gentle relief began to seep into her heart. "Yes, she did. I apologize; I am distracted." She tried for a comforting, if not consoling smile for them both. "Have patience, sirs. The passages are difficult."

Mr. Masson nodded in response. "We have heard as much and are prepared. I was unable to enlist, you see, and my home was separated from Belgian territory by trenches and barbed wire. I'd had enough and started on foot for Mons, suitably fitted by Princess Marie de Croÿ. I trust you know what that entails, madam."

Edith smiled and nodded, wondering if the man was intentionally distracting her from her anxieties with his story. If so, she was grateful for the consideration.

"Countess de Belleville guided me then," he went on, "and brought Mr. Bonjean into my company as well. Between the pair of us, we managed to reach Brussels, but I believe the next portion of the journey is the most difficult."

"It is, indeed." Edith pursed her lips, thinking through their options. "If you like, you may stay here tonight, and we can have our guides place you in houses tomorrow. If, however, you are eager to be underway, we do have a group leaving tonight for the other safe houses in Brussels."

The two men shared a look, Masson shrugging and gesturing for Bonjean to speak. "We'll join the departing group, Matron, if you truly do not mind."

"Not in the least," Edith assured them. "I perfectly comprehend the desire for a respite in a safe, secure environment. But first there are forms I must have you sign." She rose and gestured for them to follow her out of the room.

They quickly moved to her office, and Edith pulled out her operation consent forms.

Mr. Masson frowned as he looked at the paper. "Operation? I thought we were to receive help crossing the frontier."

Edith smiled at him warmly. "That, my dear sir, is the operation."

Both men returned her smile, signed the forms, and handed them to her at once.

After securing the forms with the rest, Edith started from the office, the two of them following closely.

"We will provide you with dinner before you leave," she told them as they walked. "It may be some time before you are collected, as we must wait for nightfall."

They moved to the cellar, and once the new arrivals were introduced to the others, Edith left them to the safety of the numbers there. It was not much, but at least the soldiers there presently were conscious of the danger they were in and kept the noise to a minimum. Even the probationers weren't aware anyone was in there, so accommodating were the soldiers.

Such consideration for quietness was a relief for Edith, as she could not often quell the louder groups when they were about. There were no hints that this place was any kind of prison. She had vowed not to act the jailer when she had offered her clinic to care for the wounded, and she meant it.

Edith moved to the ward, needing to look for herself on each of the beds and the nurses still tending to the patients there. She was feeling less and less like a nurse these days, which was unsettling at times. The Lord had called her to this, she was certain of it, but she was equally as certain He had called her to help these soldiers.

Somehow she had to be both a secret soldier and a healer, both defying authority and submitting to her training, and the pressure of being such conflicting things was weighing on her.

"Matron, do you need something?"

Edith smiled at Mania Waschausky, a beautiful and bright girl, who was also so dedicated that she had never once been caught flirting with patients or soldiers. "No, Mania, only having a look around. Has our Polish friend joined the others in the cellar?"

Mania nodded, though she bit her lip. "I found some bits of paper about his bed after he had gone down. It seemed odd to me." She reached into the pocket of her pinafore and pulled out the bits of torn paper, showing them to Edith. "I was going to take them to Sister Wilkins."

Edith held out her hand. "I'll take them, Mania, don't worry." She crooked her fingers in suggestion.

The ripped pieces of paper immediately fell into her palm. "Thank you, Matron." Mania smiled brightly, then returned to her work.

Edith glanced down at the paper, seeing clear script written down and nothing crossed out. Not a mistake, then. So why was it torn up?

She closed her fingers around the bits, walking down the aisle of beds and spotting Sister Taylor as well as Lizzie near the end of the row. "Sisters, would you come with me, please?"

Both seemed surprised but nodded and followed her back to Edith's sitting room.

Edith dropped the pieces onto a small table, rearranging them wordlessly until the message became clear.

It was German.

"What does it say, Sister Taylor?" Edith asked softly, reminding herself that it could say nothing and there was no need to fear.

Sister Taylor looked at Edith with wide eyes, then back down at the letter. "It says, 'The house is a nice one, but I cannot do anything that was required of me to do.' And that's it." She shook her head, her eyes moving to Edith's face. "Is he a spy, Matron?"

"Are we known to the enemy?" Lizzie whispered.

Edith stared at the pieces of discarded letter, her heart thundering in her ears. "I don't know," she said, her own voice sounding thin above the pounding. "I truly do not know."

CHAPTER 9

If there was a single word that could strike a chill into the heart of any person in Belgium, it was a single German word: *Verboten.*

Forbidden.

And at this moment, it was everywhere.

Absolutely everywhere.

On businesses, on fences, even the occasional wagon bore a sign with the word on it. In fact, the only place it seemed not to appear was the clinic itself.

Lizzie did not like to jump to conclusions, but the signs had begun to appear almost immediately after their mystery Polish soldier departed. The comfort was that he had decided not to do whatever he had been asked to do by whomever had put him up to such things. Lizzie hoped the soldier's change of heart was due to the kindness of the matron and the good care he'd received at the clinic. But enough had been told, it would seem, that signs had gone up across Brussels.

Not only a general *verboten*, but something rather specific.

It was now *verboten* to harbor English or French soldiers.

There had been warnings against such things before, but now it was as if the German officials knew what was happening, though they did not know enough to extend punishments or make arrests.

Each of the nurses and probationers had brought up the subject with either her or Sister Taylor in the last several days, and they were all feeling the same panic at the sight of those signs.

Edith was seen less and less by the nurses, and she was barely present even when she was there. She wasn't playing her piano anymore, and she looked so fatigued, so frail, so old.

Edith had never looked anything less than eternal and serene at any given moment, regardless of age.

But now she was starting to show the strain of attempting to manage several decades of work in only a few months. It was worrying, but the matron refused to admit that anything was wrong or that she was even remotely tired. Lizzie could not help her if she would not admit that she needed help.

She was keeping her concerns to herself for now, more to bolster the matron's image and reputation than anything else, but she was going to watch very carefully, do her best to step in where she could, and intervene if required.

"Sister Wilkins! Sister Wilkins!"

Lizzie bit back a sigh as Edith's ward, Pauline Randell, ran up to her, eyes wide. She was a sweet young lady when it suited her, but her devotion was rather like that of the dog, Jack—only to the matron. And lately, she had been rather prone to tattling to the matron about the smallest things, so heaven could only imagine what she needed to tell Lizzie.

"What is it, Pauline?" Lizzie asked, turning with a polite smile. "I am due to assist Sister Smith with instruction today."

Irritation flashed across the girl's face, but it was quickly replaced with real concern. "Sister, Matron has gone to inspect the new clinic building, but there's an officer of the police here."

Lizzie's heart stuttered to an awkward stop in her chest. "A German officer? Is it Governor von Lüttwitz?"

Pauline shook her head, her eyes going even wider. "He says his name is Mayer, and he wants to speak to the woman in charge. With the matron gone . . ." She trailed off, biting her lip.

"That woman would be me." Lizzie exhaled very slowly, desperate to rid herself of the shivers of apprehension racing across her limbs. "Where is he?"

"The sitting room of 149," Pauline told her, dropping her voice to a whisper as though the man might appear at any moment. "What if there is another official inspection?"

Lizzie's mind already raced with scenarios. "There very well could be. I will talk to him, see if I can keep him detained for an extended time. Go to Sister Taylor and tell her everything. Quickly and quietly, you understand. The fewer people involved, the better."

Pauline's head bobbed in an eager nod, and she dashed off.

They had three soldiers hiding with them at the present, though the discovery of a single one would get them arrested. She dared not trust Pauline with that information, but she hoped Sister Taylor would understand the significance of the message.

She reached the sitting room and smiled politely at the German. "May I help you, sir?"

The tall, severe-looking man with a dark mustache turned to her with the barest hint of a smile. "You are the sister in charge?" he asked in carefully practiced French.

"For the present, I am," Lizzie told him, trying to remain calm though her fingers seemed to tremble beneath her skin. "The matron is in Rue de la Bruxelles, examining our new clinic. We hope to move to the new quarters this autumn. Have you seen the site?"

"I have not," he replied, his tone polite, if a little curious as he lifted his lapel to reveal the telltale pin belonging to the German secret police. "My name is Otto Mayer, and I am a detective sergeant assigned to Brussels to help Lieutenant Bergan with maintaining order. Governor von Lüttwitz has sent me."

"I see." Lizzie folded her hands together, maintaining her smile and pretending not to understand the reasons for his visit. "Are you recently arrived in Brussels? You do not seem familiar to me, though we have been quite busy with our patients, so perhaps I am mistaken."

His brow creased slightly, no doubt wondering at her polite rambling. "Relatively, miss. And you are?"

Lizzie forced a light laugh. "Oh, of course! I am so sorry; my manners are shockingly lax at the present. Sister Elizabeth Wilkins. I trust you do not object to my being called *sister*, Sergeant Mayer. It comes from the tradition of nuns acting as nurses, you see, and the habit of doing so—"

"I know very well where it comes from, Sister Wilkins," he interrupted—impolitely, perhaps, but not harshly. "I would much prefer to get on with my business here."

Instantly, Lizzie nodded. "Of course, of course! You must be so very busy. What can I help you with today?"

His chin lowered, and his look became severe. "I am investigating, and I want to see this clinic."

That was unsurprising, and thankfully, the time spent in this ridiculously polite conversation had given Lizzie time to plan a few details. "Of course, sir. Perhaps we ought to start with the offices? We have several records that you may find both useful and informative."

"I would appreciate that," Sergeant Mayer told her, his expression unchanged. He gestured toward the rest of the clinic. "Please, lead the way."

If the man were truly an investigator, he likely already knew the layout of the clinic. Still, he had not barged in, demanding things or insisting she stay out of the way, so perhaps he did not know what to look for.

She could work with that.

They started down the hall silently, Lizzie walking in front of Sergeant Mayer, and doing her best to appear perfectly at ease when Jose appeared from the back of the house, whistling in his usual cheery manner.

"Good morning, Sister," he greeted in his accented French.

"German," Lizzie mouthed clearly, widening her eyes. Then she said aloud, "Good morning, Jose. Off on your errands?"

Jose nodded, his eyes showing he understood the situation. "Yes, Sister. I will return when they are done."

"Thank you, Jose." She smiled for him as he passed by, a burst of warmth in her chest, then she turned over her shoulder toward Sergeant Mayer. "Jose is Armenian, and he has been a wonderful addition to our clinic. We would be lost without him."

"Wonderful," came the unconcerned reply.

Lizzie returned her focus forward, biting back a nervous giggle. It was probably unwise to aggravate the man, but she was not doing so for spite. Jose and Sister Taylor needed time, and she needed a distraction, both of which were destined to get on the sergeant's nerves, should he realize what she was doing. But that would be the trick: doing all of this without him noticing.

Once in the office, Lizzie focused on being overly helpful to the sergeant. "Here are the office records of each patient we have seen in the last three months. Oh, and these are the attendance reports for each of our nurses, in case you need to know their whereabouts and educational status. Let me see . . ." She pretended to rifle through more papers.

She could hear papers rustling on the desk behind her but could not see how intently the sergeant might be looking at them, if he was at all.

"Ah, our food bills, which have not changed in some time," Lizzie announced, pulling those pages from the shelves and holding them toward the desk.

When they were not taken from her, she glanced in confusion at the man. "Did you not want them?" she pressed. "It may help."

With the reluctance of a child being asked to fetch eggs from a coop, Sergeant Mayer took the proffered pages and flipped through them without any interest whatsoever.

Lizzie returned to her task. "Plumbers' reports, should that interest you. Laundry lists. Prospective recruits for the coming term. Letter of reference requests from former nurses. Inventory—now this could be of interest." She pulled out the ledger and turned to the desk, setting the book down and opening it quickly, thumbing a few pages over. "There was something odd I noticed only a day or two ago. Here it is."

Sergeant Mayer leaned closer to the page, peering exactly where her finger was placed. "Lint?"

"Yes, sir," Lizzie confirmed, nodding vigorously. "We have used a remarkable quantity of lint in the last six months, more than we ever have in this clinic. We can hardly keep it in stock anymore, and yet the demand is increasing. Do you not think that odd, Sergeant?"

He frowned at the page, then looked at her. "What is it used for?"

Lizzie shrugged. "Binding of wounds and bandages, securing dressings in place, sometimes acting as padding for splints or bindings. It is unfathomable that so much should be used of late."

The man straightened slowly. "Do you not think, Sister," he ground out, "that such a thing might be required more because we are in a war? And you are tending more to wounds than to sicknesses?"

Lizzie pretended a dawning realization. "You may be right." She smiled at him, ignoring the glower he cast at her. "Would you have any interest in seeing our patient wards, Sergeant Mayer? We have several patients at the moment, both private and military."

"I would like that very much, Sister Wilkins, yes." He nodded firmly and nudged his head toward the door.

Lizzie led the way out of the room, feeling less nervous with each passing step, but not yet comfortable. She was detaining and distracting an officer of the law in a military government. She was offering up so much "helpful" but irrelevant information not only to prevent him from asking specific questions but also to present herself as fully featherbrained. A woman so flighty couldn't possibly be keeping secrets or hiding soldiers in the cellar, could she?

She could only hope her ruse would work.

"As you will see, Sergeant," she began, her voice taking on a more instructive tone as they entered the ward, "each of our patients receives the highest quality of care and attention. There is plenty of space between each of the beds for some sense of privacy, and our staff is particularly attentive."

She gestured toward a bed where Jacqueline was performing an eye washing. "Here, for example. This poor soldier's eyes were damaged by gas, and so require a flush with sodium bicarbonate every two hours. The irrigation is unpleasant, but we found it helps with the healing process."

Sergeant Mayer looked mildly disgusted and uncomfortable, but he said a few words of German to the soldier, who responded in pained tones, careful not to move while Jacqueline did her work.

"Now, our civilian cases are down in this ward, sir," Lizzie went on, gesturing. "I trust you will not object to seeing only a men's ward. The women's ward has patients, but they become much distressed by visitors who are not family. You understand."

"The men's ward will suffice," he grunted, barely a step behind her.

She nodded, leading him through the doors and greeting the man in the first bed. "Good morning, Mr. Maes. Your color is much improved. How are your lungs?"

They chatted for a moment in a peculiar blend of French and Flemish that Mr. Maes and other Belgians were accustomed to, then Lizzie moved to the next bed, greeting that patient and so on. After the fourth patient, Sergeant Mayer took her by the arm and pulled her away from the beds.

"This is all very well and good, Miss Wilkins," he muttered in a low voice, "but what I want to know is this: Have you any Tommies here?"

Lizzie widened her eyes and reared back. "Tommies? I can't imagine what you mean. I am not aware of any patients of that name."

His smile was less than pleasant. "Tommies, Sister Wilkins. British soldiers. Surely you know that."

"I have heard them called such, certainly," Lizzie admitted, keeping her expression as startled as possible. "But I cannot imagine why you would think there would be any of them here. We have not had any prisoners of the Germans in the clinic for some months, and even then, they were not here long. Surely they were returned with your officers, were they not?"

Sergeant Mayer's smile turned bland and thin. "Come now, Sister Wilkins. I trust you know better than that."

"Than what?" she asked with real curiosity, knowing full well she ought to change the course of the conversation as soon as possible.

His eyes narrowed. "Are there any Tommies here or not, Sister Wilkins?"

"Of course not, Sergeant," she told him firmly. "Why would there be?"

Her answer did not please, that was clear enough, and he gave a clipped nod in response. "Very well. You will come with me." He took her arm and all but marched her through the wards toward the entrance of the clinic.

"Where are we going?" Lizzie asked as her heart lurched into her throat and lodged there.

"Rue de Berlaimont," he replied, pulling her along roughly. "I have some additional questions for you, and I think it would be best if we do that there. Less chance for you to offer me useless information."

Lizzie swallowed hard and glanced over to see Jose and Sister Smith coming toward them, concern etched on both faces. "It's all right," she called to them. "The sergeant just has some questions for me. I shall be back soon."

Both nodded, and Sister Smith offered a tentative smile that told Lizzie her tactics had worked, and the message had been received.

The soldiers were safely away, and now, even if there was a full inspection of the clinic, no hidden men would be found.

CHAPTER 10

Edith would never forgive herself for leaving Lizzie in such a position. To be hauled away by the new sergeant of police for questioning after showing him around the clinic was bad enough, but now the man had returned with additional soldiers to search the place themselves.

It had been only one night since he'd interviewed Lizzie for several hours, and, apparently, he'd received nothing of importance from her.

Lizzie had assured Edith that all would be well and she was happy to do her part while Edith was away, but for Edith, it was too much to bear.

Lizzie had not been threatened, but Sergeant Mayer had suggested she be careful, which seemed to be a poorly veiled threat in itself.

At least there were no soldiers hiding in the clinic now, and nothing for the Germans to find in their search.

When Edith had returned from her inspection of the new clinic and learned what had taken place, she had burned a great many records and documents for safety. Lizzie had managed very well under the circumstances, but if Sergeant Mayer had taken it into his head to do his own searching, he would have found plenty to satisfy him.

Her most recent diary, addresses of safe houses, records of the men who had stayed, letters she had received from those safely returned home—all had been tossed onto the fire.

She would not risk her nurses, patients, and friends again.

She could not.

No documentation, however accurate, helpful, or sentimental, could ever compensate if she lost anyone under her care.

And now she could do nothing but sit with her nurses and wait for the inspector's verdict.

The sergeant had practically barged his way into the clinic that morning. Edith and the rest had put up no resistance, and Edith had asked only that her nurses be permitted to tend their patients in the wards. That had been allowed, though a policeman stood guard within each ward to ensure compliance.

Edith sat outside her office with Lizzie and Sister Taylor, waiting to be given the clearance to resume their activities. One policeman was in the office looking through papers while Mayer and the remaining two officers were roaming the place to search whatever quarters they liked.

While the soldiers were safely gone, Edith could not be sure there were no signs of them. After all, the few who had managed to get away yesterday might have left a thing or two behind in their haste to flee.

But the Germans would capture no one today, and that was enough for now.

Whatever happened, it was clear Edith would need to be more careful. Someone—perhaps their Polish soldier, perhaps someone else—had told the authorities some of what was happening in the clinic. Enough for suspicion, but not enough for arrests. It could have been the soldiers being too jovial at Chez Jules some weeks back. It could have been revealed by a soldier who had been captured at the border. It could have been any number of people who had whispered Edith's name or named the clinic as a place of suspicion.

Or it could have been Edith herself—perhaps her initial refusal of the general at the beginning of the occupation had planted a seed of suspicion that was now starting to bloom.

"How much longer do you think they will be?" Lizzie whispered beside her. "It's been ages!"

Edith shushed her gently, taking her hand. "I suppose we must be grateful the governor himself did not deign to come for the inspection. These men may shortly be done, and we may go on with our day."

"And our lives?" Sister Taylor murmured. "Surely we must be above suspicion when they continue to find nothing."

One would hope, but in times such as these, hope was often not enough.

It was a bruising thing to admit, but there it was.

"Very well, Matron," announced Sergeant Mayer as he and his fellow officers appeared, approaching them with politely distant expressions. "We have concluded our search."

"And?" Edith inquired patiently, rising to her feet. "Was it to your satisfaction?"

Mayer smiled slightly. "Enough. We found nothing of significance. Thank you for allowing us the search. Good day." He touched the brim of his cap and continued down the corridor, followed by his men, the other two joining them as they reached the door to the street.

Once the Germans were safely out and the door closed, Edith breathed a sigh of relief.

"*Allow?*" Sister Taylor snorted softly. "I did not realize we had been given an option in the matter."

"Why did he say *enough?*" Lizzie demanded. "That is not an answer as to satisfaction."

"But it will suffice," Edith murmured in a low voice. "Come, let us go about our work. I must send some letters." She entered her office, grateful to be able to take a moment to herself.

She would write to Herman Capiau, who, she hoped, had returned from his trip to Germany, and ask him to come.

She would write to Louise Thuliez, who was risking so much herself in saving soldiers and getting them to safety, and invite her to come as well.

And she would write to her mother. With everything becoming so perilous and uncertain, it was important to Edith to ensure that her mother did not worry. Of course, she had no guarantee that any of her previous letters had gotten through, but the act of writing itself gave Edith peace enough to settle her heart. If the letter was delivered to her mother at any point, perhaps Edith's words could do the same for her.

It was better than not knowing, at the very least.

She had no doubt that Herman and Louise would know how Edith's work could continue without endangering her staff. Everything was becoming so difficult, and it seemed that the number of men who needed help was increasing day by day. Guides were limited, safe houses were growing less safe, and now she was certain she was being watched, so each soldier who entered her clinic would need a convincing story or disguise.

Perhaps she would need to have Jack trained as Marie de Croÿ's dog, Sweep, was trained. He patrolled the grounds at Bellignies and would bark if he heard or smelled a stranger. Only when all was clear would the men cross the fields to the first safe house.

It was not a perfect system, as several of the safe houses had been raided and both hosts and participants arrested. Gilles and Charles never told the fugitive soldiers any information that might compromise the identities of those they worked with, and they did their very best to conceal the routes they took. They also shared their precautions with other guides working with them.

But was it enough? Would any of it be enough?

What could she do? The clinic was being watched. The governor's mistrust of Edith was growing as constant as the war itself, and she was not likely to be freed from his watchful eye any time soon.

Philippe Baucq had told Edith as much earlier in the week during a surprise visit. He had assured her the word had come from the town authorities themselves. There had been a suspicious number of individuals asking for help without the requisite password or information, and Edith was almost entirely convinced those had been attempts to catch her in the act.

But what was far less clear to her, and far more unnerving, was that she could not know who had suspected her or how her name had come up in such things.

Granted, she had not been trusted by the German authorities since the earliest days of the occupation, but she had endured very few confrontations with any of them. She rather thought they had all been getting on decently well, considering the circumstances.

Yet now the clinic was being watched.

As if she needed something else to contend with.

She had only just fully understood from Gilles and Charles what the crossings entailed. Bribes for people on both sides of the border could reach as much as a thousand francs. Poachers in the woods were growing more and more important to their success, and they could not always be trusted without funds for their trouble. Electrified wires at border fences required rubber strips to be wrapped around them before the men could crawl through. Some of the other guides and escapees had been caught at the border and shot, though she did not believe any of their particular guides and soldiers had suffered that fate.

But she could not be sure.

All she could know was the fate of those guides who reappeared to help the next group; she could not think further than that. Her prayers throughout the day were growing more desperate for the safety of those she was sending forth, and her thoughts at night more consumed with their success.

Her first two letters completed, she pulled out a fresh sheet of paper for the third and paused a long moment. This was one letter that did not require the careful coding that only the recipient would comprehend. One that did not need to be full of warning and hinting at actions.

Certainly, this letter needed to be cautious, given that the authorities were likely to read anything leaving the country, but there was no need for double meaning.

Ten months had passed since she had seen her mother, and Edith struggled knowing it would be longer still before they could be reunited. None of that could go into this letter, however. Her mother might read that as a farewell, and Edith would not give her any cause to fear such a thing.

For her mother's sake, she needed to write with clarity, peace, and comfort.

She could do no less.

CHAPTER 11

For the first time in the seven months since they had begun housing fugitive soldiers, Lizzie did not approve of one.

At all.

Which put her in the minority of people in the clinic, as the man seemed to be winning over nearly everyone. He did not hide with the same effort others did. He strode about a little too confidently. He did not appear to have been affected by the war at all.

But he was a Belgian, and there was something to be said for that.

His name was Gaston Quien, and he had approached the matron earlier in the week while she had been talking with some locals near a potato field. His friend, a Mr. X, had joined the conversation once Mr. Quien had ascertained Edith's identity. They had asked for shelter, and Edith had given it to them. Mr. X was apparently British, though he said very little, and he had been placed with the other English soldiers hiding in the attic.

Thankfully, the quiet Mr. X had left with a group Gilles had taken the next morning.

Quien, however, claimed to be ill, and he had a foot injury that rendered him unable to travel well, so he remained.

Yet, neither his injury nor illness stopped him from entertaining several of the girls at the clinic. He quoted literature, he attempted to be amusing, and he listened sympathetically to their concerns and complaints, whatever they might be. He was a handsome man, Lizzie would not deny it, but there was something in his manner that she did not trust. Could not trust.

Would not.

She had gone to Edith with her concerns, wondering if he might be a spy, like their Polish soldier had potentially been. But the matron had brushed off her worries and told Lizzie she was seeing spies everywhere. That might have been true, but would it not be best to suspect more people as spies than fewer?

The matron had not even flinched when Gilles had returned and told them that Mr. X had disappeared from the group before they had even reached the border. He had even gone so far as to claim that he thought Mr. X was a spy.

It was unnerving, to say the least, and that was before Quien and the cook's daughter had gone for a walk during the dimout the night before.

The pairing wasn't unnerving, only annoying.

What *was* unnerving was that a uniformed German soldier had appeared at the clinic during their absence, claiming he needed a room for his ill son. He had looked about the clinic as he had asked but made no move to inspect any part of it. Thankfully, Edith had apologetically informed him that they had no rooms to spare.

The clinic did have rooms, as it happened, but the timing of the soldier's arrival was too suspicious to ignore, even for the kindhearted matron. But, on the chance that his situation was as he described, she had given him locations to another clinic where he could take his apparently ill child.

Edith had said nothing after he had left, and she walked swiftly to her office.

Lizzie hadn't seen her after that, so she had no way of knowing if there was something she could assist her with. She was already taking on most of the tasks with the nurses and probationers, leaving the matron free to see to the soldiers and their details, but Edith had grown so reserved, even with Lizzie. She was not an effusive woman to begin with, so for her to become more distant and aloof was concerning.

Each evening at dinner, she had taken to looking about the room and setting eyes on each of the nurses and probationers present. No haste in the action, just taking note of each individual as though needing to assure herself they were there and were well. There was such concern in her face when she did so, and every discussion she had with Lizzie about the nurses and staff was filled with the same.

Her feelings toward them all had not changed, yet the matron was becoming as much of a mystery as the guests they housed.

Lizzie shook her head, moving toward the civilian ward. She hoped she would not see Mr. Quien within, if for no other reason than his absence would improve her mood.

She smiled at Jacqueline Van Til as she neared, pausing when the girl did not smile in return. "Jacqueline?"

Jacqueline bit her lip, looking down at a letter in her hand. "The matron asked me to deliver this to Monsieur Fromage," the nurse said quietly.

Lizzie's eyes widened. Fromage was the *nom de guerre* of Philippe Baucq. And if the matron was having it delivered by hand rather than by post, it was significant indeed.

"And?" Lizzie pressed, keeping careful composure for the sake of the girl's nerves.

"I am afraid," Jacqueline whispered, reluctantly meeting her gaze. "Between the German inspections and the many secrets we are keeping, I half expect not to return at all."

Lizzie put a hand on her arm. "Nonsense. You know full well the matron still goes out on her own to visit private patients and the new clinic, and she is never accosted. Several of the nurses still make rounds about Brussels."

"But not to Monsieur Fromage," Jacqueline hissed, a touch of panic lighting her tone. "Come with me."

"I have work to do, Jacqueline," Lizzie told her with a laugh. "A great deal of work."

"Please, Sister Wilkins," Jacqueline pleaded. "With you walking beside me, we might look more professional and seem less of a concern, and the task will be done so quickly."

Lizzie sighed, taking in the near trembling state of the girl. "Very well, get your cloak and I will fetch mine. We must make haste, though, as we still have patients to tend."

"Of course, thank you." Jacqueline rushed by her, no longer trembling and moving with far more confidence.

If joining her on this errand could truly lift her spirits, Lizzie would be happy to do so, even if it did cause her to fall behind in her work. After all, a walk to Mr. Baucq's home would be pleasant enough given the fine day. His wife and two daughters were delightful company, and it would be good to get out of the clinic for a while.

She and Jacqueline were soon walking down the quiet streets of Brussels. Mr. Baucq's home was not far, but it did require a bit of maneuvering through the city.

No sooner had they turned down a new street than an unwelcome yet familiar sight met their eyes.

Mr. Quien, quite alone, strolling along as though nothing at all kept him from doing so in broad daylight and without any concern for who might see. No disguise, no ailment, hardly even a hint that his foot might be injured.

"Ah, my delightful nurses!" he called out to them, startling Lizzie with the volume of his cheerful tone. "Will you join me for a glass of wine on this fine day?"

Lizzie felt Jacqueline stiffen beside her. "No, thank you," Jacqueline chirped, her tongue a trifle tight, but not cold. "We've a timely errand to run. Thank you for the offer."

He nodded in acknowledgment, smiling widely at them. "Next time, perhaps." He sauntered away from them, untroubled by their refusal.

What was he playing at?

"Why is he out in the middle of the afternoon?" Jacqueline whispered to Lizzie once they were out of earshot. "They all know the rules."

"I don't know," Lizzie replied in an undertone. "Perhaps he thinks he is able to do so because he is Belgian?"

Jacqueline shook her head firmly. "That shouldn't matter. We have had several Belgians, and none of them did this."

Lizzie bit the inside of her lip. "We'll keep on the Rue Royale. It is just a stroll, Jacqueline. Perhaps that is all."

"But you don't believe that," the younger nurse pointed out, and there was no hint of a question in her words.

There was no good way to reply. Lizzie felt it was her responsibility to behave as the matron would have under the circumstances, yet the truth was that she did not believe Quien was merely strolling about Brussels. She could not prove it was true, had nothing but her instincts that were untrained in detecting spies or villains. She could not directly accuse him of anything but being untrustworthy.

And that was more irritating than knowing if he was villainous.

She could not claim the man was a traitor just because she did not like him.

But if he was walking about Brussels without pain, then he ought to be able to leave the clinic soon, which would remove him from her life and be the end of it. She would report to the matron that she had witnessed him walking without any kind of limp, adjustment, or compensation. Surely arrangements could be made that would not require him to walk long distances.

She would suggest it during her evening conversation with the matron.

"Yvonne will be pleased to see us," Lizzie told Jacqueline. "She is always so curious, perhaps she will become a nurse."

Jacqueline smiled slightly. "I think Madeline might be more excited. She has a quick mind and loves to show off what she has learned."

"It will be good to see them." Lizzie inhaled a deep breath, releasing it slowly, taking in the scent of Brussels for her own pleasure. The air might have been tainted with both the constant addition of sulfur from the distant shelling and a hint of smoke from whatever fires were burning, but beneath all of that, it still smelled of home.

And if she could block out the rest of it, that was enough.

She and Jacqueline chatted as they walked, finally feeling at ease when they reached the Porte de Schaerbeek, close to the Baucq home.

Then Jacqueline suddenly yanked her to a stop, clutching Lizzie's arm. "Sister Wilkins! There he is again!"

Lizzie blinked, glancing down the way to see Mr. Quien again, who had yet to see them, walking in their direction.

"Quick!" Lizzie pulled Jacqueline behind the corner they had reached. Quien would only see them if he turned down their street, and she would have more questions for him than he could possibly hold for her.

But he walked by without incident.

Lizzie peered out after him, frowning when she saw him turn down a side street where a young woman waited.

She did not want to know what he was doing, why he was doing it, or what she ought to do about it. She simply wanted to see Jacqueline's errand done and return to the clinic.

"Come on," she urged Jacqueline, tugging her hand and darting across the sidewalk.

"Sister," Jacqueline murmured. "There is a man behind us. He was in the Rue Royale. I saw him when we hid. He waited for us to cross and then crossed behind us."

"What?" Lizzie glanced behind her, making a show of fixing the collar on Jacqueline's cloak, letting her eyes cast back just far enough.

A man was indeed following, his eyes fixed on them, his pace matching theirs.

Lizzie returned her attention forward, swallowing. "Perhaps he is one of the Belgian boys who has taken a fancy to you. It would be natural for one of them to wish to accompany you."

"Or you," Jacqueline pointed out.

"I doubt that very much." Lizzie had put on a brave face for Jacqueline, suggesting the most innocent explanation she could, but the truth was she could barely feel the ground beneath her feet.

Her lower half seemed to pulse and buzz while her upper half seemed to have lost all sensation entirely. It made no sense medically, though heaven knew she was trying to explain it to herself in some logical manner to keep from panicking.

"Let's pause by this shop window," Jacqueline suggested, gesturing toward it. "If he is someone we know, he may stop to talk with us."

Lizzie nodded.

They stopped and pretended to look at the wares within the window, but Lizzie was too focused on the reflection in the glass to notice whatever items lay beyond it.

As they stared, a shadow appeared behind them, moving slowly, then continuing past them without stopping or even looking.

Lizzie's heart seemed to be in her ears and throat at the same time, thundering like the distant shelling.

She glanced along the sidewalk behind them and found no one.

Her exhale of relief trembled more than Jacqueline had earlier.

"Right," Lizzie murmured, clearing her throat. "Let's go to Mr. Fromage now. Quickly."

Jacqueline nodded, and they started in that direction, though Lizzie noted that their one-time follower turned down a nearby side street. Again, without looking at them.

Please let that be the end of it.

They said nothing as they hurried on, needing to go only another block or two, when, impossibly, the man who had been following them was suddenly ahead of them at the next corner.

And he was speaking to a German officer.

"*Nefoedd helpa ni,*" Lizzie whispered, her feet stopping and her throat clenching as though she were being strangled on the spot.

"You never speak Welsh," Jacqueline managed beside her.

Lizzie nodded once. "We cannot go by them. They will see us going to Mr. Fromage's home."

Jacqueline released a slow breath. "I have friends nearby. We can go there." She nudged Lizzie toward the nearest bystreet, and they hurried away from the two men they so dearly wished to avoid.

If they were to meet Mr. Quien again, Lizzie would have to wonder if heaven and fate were against her.

But their race to the home of Jacqueline's friends was uneventful, and knocking at the door was a blessed relief.

She did not expect to be greeted by a woman with a drawn expression and streaming tears.

"Sophie?" Jacqueline inquired in dismay, taking her friend by the arms. "What is it?"

The young woman waved them both inside. "Everything is in commotion. Pierre and my father were arrested only three hours ago and taken away. The Germans would not let any of us go with them."

Within the house, distant wailing and discontented voices could be heard.

Sophie shook her head, another pair of tears escaping. "My poor husband. And Papa. I don't know how the Germans discovered what they were doing. It was only a few French soldiers, and everything was done with such care." She dissolved into tears and fell into Jacqueline's arms.

Jacqueline held her close, giving Lizzie a wide-eyed, terrified look.

Lizzie fought for some words of comfort, some message of consolation.

She found nothing to say.

Not one thing.

CHAPTER 12

Edith could not take one more inspection.

There had been at least five in the past few weeks, one of which hadn't even been by men in uniform. They had claimed to be civilians wanting to see about renting the place, since the nurses and staff would be moving to the new clinic in Uccle soon.

The men had poked around the entire place, every nook and cranny, and it wasn't until they had gone that Lizzie and Mania had told Edith the men had worn shiny regulation German army shoes. And that one man wore glasses made by a distinctly German manufacturer.

The inspection prior to that had been only a single officer looking around the clinic. He had been quick, but thorough, and after he had left, Edith had found an English soldier's cap sitting out in plain sight in the upstairs bath.

The most recent inspection of the clinic had occurred just the day before and had been so unexpected that Edith had not been prepared. As the telltale footsteps of German soldiers had drawn closer, Edith had rushed to burn the papers at her desk. Had she more time, she would have carefully stowed the documents, as per usual, but she had been foolish enough to look over the documents during the light of day. Nothing had been discovered, thanks to the fire, but her heart still pounded.

The more difficult and intense all of this became, the more she would need her organization and structure in place. She would have to devise better ways to keep track of their soldiers and the money spent in their efforts, but it was difficult to imagine paperwork becoming such a concern amidst everything else.

Paperwork and nursing, in fact.

Nursing, in a way, was becoming less of her focus, though it was all she knew. Even now, in the middle of a surgery, her mind was miles away at the border, though there were no crossings today. It was only due to her carefully cultivated habits in nursing that she was able to assist in surgery without much thought. She had always been so focused and composed on every task, and now . . .

"Retract a touch more, nurse," the doctor suggested as he turned slightly to better observe the opening. "I think I see it."

Edith obeyed, exhaling very slowly, very softly. The soldier on the table required her full attention, deserved no less, and she was distracted.

Unacceptable.

"Where was this one wounded, nurse?"

Edith swallowed. "Mons, I believe, Doctor."

He nodded as he continued to work on the injury. "There is some debate as to Mons. Nurse Cambridge told me a German officer informed her that nine officers of his regiment were killed, but not with English bullets. What do you make of that?"

"I should not like to speculate, Doctor," Edith replied softly. "War is a disastrous business."

"That it is." He sighed heavily. "I've heard from a colleague in Ypres. Chlorine gas is now being used."

Edith stared at him in horror, though he would not see it as he was focused on the surgery before them. "Chlorine?"

He nodded. "Burns the air passages the entire way down. Fluid fills the lungs, destroys the eyes, ears, throat. And then there are the skin burns. You may want to prepare your staff, should the usage spread closer to your clinic."

"They will be ready, Doctor," Edith assured him. "They have already seen more than they were trained to."

"We all have."

There was nothing else to say, and the two of them worked in silence, lost to their thoughts and morbid reminiscences.

Soon enough, the surgery was complete, and Edith had the soldier taken to a quiet corner of the ward to recover, leaving explicit instructions for his care once he woke. She ought to have sat with him herself, perhaps, and taken some time to think and reflect, but her mind was too occupied.

Philippe Baucq had chosen to take a group of soldiers to Holland himself, though Edith and the rest had begged him not to. The risks were too great, and he had his wife and daughters to think of. But he would not listen, and so he had gone.

He had taken Mr. Quien in the group, and there, at least, was some relief.

"Matron."

Edith turned and smiled wearily. "Yes, Lizzie?"

"I am so sorry to trouble you," Lizzie said with an apologetic smile. "Princess Marie of Croÿ is in your sitting room. I told her you were in surgery, but she begged to wait until you were free."

Edith's brows rose slightly. She knew Marie, of course—the woman and her brother were among the leaders of their little resistance band—but they had met on only a handful of occasions. Her brother had occasionally called at the clinic, but the princess almost never made an appearance.

"Did she say what she wanted?" Edith asked as Jack came trotting down the aisle of beds toward her, his tail wagging with enthusiasm and whacking against the legs of passing nurses.

"No, Matron. Not specifically." Lizzie's smile turned hesitant, her eyes showing both understanding and trepidation.

"Thank you, Lizzie," Edith murmured, patting her arm as she moved past her. "Are those men still pretending to work in the square?"

"Yes, Matron."

"The governor still thinks we do not recognize him in his poor disguise?"

"It would appear so."

Edith hummed a soft sound of irritation. "So they would have seen the princess arrive."

There was a slight pause. "Yes, Matron, I believe so."

Edith nodded. "Very well. I will go to her now." She made her way out of the ward, her heart ticking within her ominously.

The house was being watched, and the officials had seen the princess arrive. What else had they noticed?

She moved swiftly to her sitting room and opened the door, looking at the elegant woman with dark hair and bright eyes sitting within.

"I wish you hadn't come," Edith said gently, closing the door.

"I am evidently suspect." She gestured to the window in the room. "Those men cleaning the square in front? They have been there several days and are scarcely working at all. The governor himself is among them."

Marie looked out at them, sighing. She turned back to Edith, folding her hands in her lap. "I came to say that we must stop."

That was not what Edith had expected the princess to say, and she blinked, unable to conjure a single response.

"I have had search parties," Marie went on, "and dare have no more men brought to Bellignies."

Edith exhaled and sank into a nearby chair. "I also had a search party. Yesterday, in fact. I heard their footsteps from downstairs and only had time to throw my papers in the grate, pour some alcohol over them, and set them alight before the Germans came in and began searching the room. But all my records are gone. How shall I explain the use of his money to Dr. Depage?"

She put her face in her hands, groaning softly as the weight of her present situation pressed down on her painfully.

"Do not let that worry you," the princess encouraged, gently patting her knee. "If we all come through this alive, I will be your witness as to what you have done. But this shows we must stop now."

Yes, that was the answer. It would save her clinic from further observation and would allow her to return her attention to nursing, to teaching, to progressing the work of medicine in Belgium, as she had wanted to for years.

She looked up at the princess with a smile, feeling the release of her burden as a wave rolling through her entire frame. After so long in the face of danger, the idea of resting from such stress was heavenly.

Yet she thought of all the soldiers who had passed between each of their respective residences, all those they had helped reach the border, and how many more might yet be suffering in hiding, hoping for some way to get back to their country, their family, or even their army.

"Are there any more hidden men?" she asked, afraid of the answer, afraid to break this beautiful breath that had settled between them with the prospect of the end in sight.

The princess's nod seemed to happen in slow motion. "Yes. Mademoiselle Thuliez has found over thirty more in Cambrai."

"Thirty?" Edith looked away, swallowing hard.

Thirty men somewhere in Belgium, hiding from the Germans. Wounded or afraid or helpless, waiting for the next phase of their escape and hoping someone could help them.

How could she abandon them?

With a silent prayer for strength and peace, Edith looked back to Marie. "In that case, we cannot stop. Because if one of those men is caught and shot, it will be our fault."

Marie heaved a sigh rather unlike her usual composure. "I was afraid of that. Nothing for it, then."

"But truly, after this, I should not have more refugees," Edith said quickly, wincing as she admitted it. "The risks are too great for my nurses and staff. I may content myself with directing the guides and communicating orders as to means of passing into Holland. We cannot count on bribing the Landsturmen to look the other way while the men pass."

"Indeed not," Marie agreed. "The Germans are becoming more strict and more influential."

Edith nodded, rubbing her fingers together as she thought. "We will need to create contingencies for emergencies and the like. Perhaps when Mr. Fromage returns, he and others might have some ideas."

"Certainly, and some of them will have several." Marie smiled at her, the natural warmth of her manner on full display. "You have been a magnificent part of our scheme, Matron. Your help will never go unappreciated, I can promise you that."

The praise sounded too final, too lofty to be accepted, and Edith shook her head. "Hardly. I would have done more, if I were able."

Eager to avoid more praise, Edith rose from her chair and smiled. "I am afraid we will need to take some extraordinary measures for your departure."

Marie's smile spread into a wry grin. "I believe I can manage that. What do you have in mind?"

The directions were complicated at best and muddled at the worst, but they would save the princess from being followed by the men watching the house.

Edith gestured for her to join her by the window, pointing out at the street. "Go to the end of the road where a shop window will reflect the street behind you. Stand looking into this window for a moment or two. Then quickly turn down the road to the left and walk until you reach the pastry cook's shop. Look in the window there. Wait for the bell to sound that the tram will start, then turn and jump onto the tram as it moves off, no matter which direction it goes."

Marie's eyes were wide, and she blinked once. "That is complicated."

"I apologize," Edith murmured, her cheeks heating with embarrassment. "We must take every precaution for us both. We've learned this is one of the best methods for leaving the clinic without being followed."

The princess swallowed. "Of course. Do you have anything you need me to take?"

Edith bit her lip, then looked at her desk. "If you could try to post this letter for me, I would appreciate it. I cannot send anything directly from here anymore, no matter how innocuous."

"Of course." Marie waited for her to fetch the letter, then took it with a wide smile. "Next time I come, I'll send word first. And perhaps you might direct me as to a better way to arrive so I might leave with fewer instructions."

Edith chuckled and started from the room. "Someday, we will both be able to live in less complicated times and with fewer restrictions."

"One can only hope." Marie laughed. "There will be just a few guests coming from me shortly, and then we should be able to maneuver you into more of a conducting position. Would that be agreeable?"

Relief, that small and unfamiliar friend, returned to the center of her chest with a brief flicker of light. "Yes," she agreed with a sigh. "Yes, it would. And tell your brother I am sorry, but I have already put too much on my nurses. We are supposed to move to our new clinic soon, and with our being watched . . ."

The princess put a hand on her arm, silencing her. "You don't need to explain to me, Matron. Your Christian spirit does you credit, but even the Lord Himself would not sacrifice His disciples for a cause needlessly."

Edith hadn't thought of that, and she certainly would not like to be compared to the Savior Himself in all of this, but the statement was true enough.

"No," she murmured to herself. "No, He would not."

With a farewell wave, Princess Marie set off into the streets, blatantly ignoring the men pretending to work in the square.

Edith, however, stared directly at them, almost daring them to come ask her questions, accuse her of something, give her a reason to act out against authority. But they simply stood there, idle enough to look natural yet casting frequent glances at the clinic.

And they did not seem at all concerned that Edith was watching them.

Which meant nothing would happen. Nothing would change. Nothing would improve.

She did not like such dark feelings. She needed to read, to study, to lose herself in the word of the Lord so she might find her truer self.

Closing the door to the clinic, Edith turned back and began the return journey to her offices. A few of the younger probationers saw her coming and whispered to each other, their eyes going wide.

Edith raised a brow at them. "Surely you have some task you ought to be about. If not, I am sure I can find you something to do."

"Yes, Matron," they chimed in dull tones, scurrying away and averting their eyes quickly.

Why they should act that way around her, Edith could not say. The dark feeling in her chest returned, and she felt her shoulders slump. There was so much to do, and yet at the moment, she felt quite incapable of doing anything at all.

CHAPTER 13

"Soldiers!"

Lizzie gasped and whirled, her eyes wide as Mania ran to her. "What? Where? Another inspection?"

Mania swallowed hard and shook her head. "Not yet. Two soldiers, and they wanted to speak to the matron. They're in her office now!"

Lizzie's head jerked toward Edith's office as though she could see through the walls. Was the matron being threatened? Accused? Was her office being torn apart? There were no sounds coming from that direction that would indicate any kind of destruction.

Should the nurses move their hidden soldiers? Send them out through the back garden again?

How could she just stand there and wait for whatever potential disaster to strike?

Lizzie's throat went dry, and she struggled to swallow, to breathe, to think. "How long have they been in there?" she whispered hoarsely, turning back to the young nurse.

"Twenty minutes. Perhaps more."

That should have been time enough to come to whatever point they wanted to make with the matron, and if an inspection was to take place, it would do so soon enough.

What could she do? What should she do?

Inhaling and exhaling slowly, Lizzie fought for clarity of thought. "Right," she managed to force out, even as her heart pounded amid the fog of her mind. "We had best be about our usual work, then. Until we know more, we must maintain our efforts."

Mania nodded, her dark eyes wide. "Yes, Sister." But she made no motion to move, and Lizzie could not blame her for that.

The matron was beginning to appear so frail, so thin, so pale, and those who knew her best were growing increasingly worried about her health as well as her safety. Lizzie would have been hard-pressed to leave the vicinity as well.

"Is this the end, Sister?" Mania asked in a small voice.

Lizzie gave her a sharp look. "What makes you say that?"

"It's so quiet," Mania went on. "All of the nurses are asking. Word has gone around the entire clinic, and we all fear it. Will we have to close our doors? Have we been found out?"

"Until the matron comes out, we cannot be certain of anything," Lizzie reminded the younger woman, trying for the authoritative tone Edith wielded with such ease and grace. "It could be the soldiers are simply asking questions. It will not do us any good to speculate."

The statement was as much for herself as it was for Mania, or any of the other young nurses and probationers who might have been wondering.

But how could they know for certain?

Just then, the door to the matron's office opened, and the two soldiers came out, expressions stoic. They didn't look around or make any move to inspect anything. They simply walked toward the door to the clinic as though they'd completed the errand they had been tasked with and were moving on.

The matron slowly followed them out of her office. Her steps seemed almost shuffling, and she did not appear entirely stable as she moved.

Lizzie waited for the soldiers to pass, nodding at them in a show of deference she did not mean, and then rushed to Edith's side. "Matron? What happened? What is wrong?"

"What did they say?" Mania demanded, coming to her other side. "Are we to close our doors? Did they question you?"

Edith shook her head, her hands fumbling a little as she reached for them, eventually taking hold of each woman's forearm. "No. Nothing like that."

Lizzie covered the matron's hand, leading their trio to the nearby benches and sitting, afraid that Edith might actually crumple under whatever weight now lay upon her. "Then what?"

Other nurses began to appear, and some of the probationers as well.

"We saw the soldiers leave," one of them cried out. "What happened? What are we to do?"

Sister Taylor shushed the girl who had spoken. "Let the matron speak. Give her a moment to breathe."

Duly subdued, the others all looked at Edith expectantly.

The matron's hold on Lizzie's arm tightened imperceptibly, her fingers trembling. "It was nothing to do with . . . any of that," Edith eventually said in a wavering voice. "They only brought news."

"News?" Beatrice repeated. "News of what? The war?"

"Is it over, then?" someone else asked.

"We would have heard that in the streets, not from the soldiers," another retorted.

Sister Taylor huffed again. "Ladies, I said to let the matron speak, and I meant it! If you cannot endure with patience, we will send you all away and have notes sent to your rooms if there is something that concerns you!" She looked at Lizzie with wide, exasperated eyes, then turned a gentle smile to the matron, saying nothing further.

Edith's slender throat moved as she swallowed. "The *Lusitania* has gone down. Been torpedoed by the Germans. There were only seven hundred and sixty-one survivors." She paused, wetting her lips. "Marie Depage was on board."

A series of gasps resounded among the group like a wave.

"She . . . she did not survive," Edith whispered.

For a long moment, nothing happened. No sound, no breath, no movement from any of them.

Then the sniffling began.

Lizzie blinked as her chest seemed to hollow out, and tears slipped down her cheeks with that slow motion of lashes and lids. How could she have begun to cry without noticing? Yet the tears were there, and just as suddenly, all her emotions raced back into her with a pain that ripped at her soul.

She leaned against Edith, placing her brow at her shoulder as she cried in earnest, each moment she had shared with the beloved doctor's wife replaying in her mind as though in tribute to the life she had lived. Marie Depage had been so kind and respectful, so intelligent and bright, so driven to further the dreams she shared with her husband. Such a kind friend to each nurse and would-be nurse, and so loyal to Edith in all things.

How could such a bright, luminous person be taken without the bowels of the earth groaning in despair?

Tears and sobs rang all about them, every woman present having seen Marie as a sort of mother to them all before the war. It was unfathomable that she should be gone, and they all felt the devastating loss.

Lizzie raised her head, looking at the matron again as she sniffed through her streaming tears.

Somehow, Edith was still erect and dignified, though slow tears trickled down her pale cheeks. Her thin lips were pressed together so tightly, they seemed almost bloodless, and her delicate, strong chin quivered ever so slightly. But she did not crumple, she did not sag, she did not bend.

Dignity even amid crushing grief.

She was a marvel, this heroic matron of theirs.

"Grant me patience, O Lord, even now in this emergency," Edith murmured softly, her lips barely moving. "Help me, my God, and then I will not fear, how grievously soever I be afflicted." She swallowed, the sound audible. "O that I may bear it with patience, until the tempest pass over, and all be well again, or even better!"

Mania sniffled and wiped at her eyes. "What is that, Matron? I don't recognize it."

"*The Imitation of Christ*," Edith told her, another tear making the slow descent along her cheek. "I could think of no other plea that so perfectly echoed that of my heart. In the garden of the Lord, we have all been planted, and life brings harsh conditions, weeds, brambles. We must learn how to blossom, bloom, and take root despite it all. But oh, how choking such trials can be!"

The words seemed to settle on each of them like a benediction, not removing their grief or even displacing it, but giving it a voice that none of them expected.

But one that each of them needed.

"I think we all need some quiet time, my dears," Edith murmured, pushing to her feet as though she were nearing ninety rather than fifty. "Some reflection. And do not forget to give thanks to the Lord for having Marie in our lives." She looked at Lizzie, her eyes filled with a pain that her voice did not hold. "I must write to the doctor. Will you come with me?"

Lizzie nodded, rising herself and keeping hold of the matron's hand. "Of course, Matron." She walked back to the office with her, leaving the other nurses to converse softly amidst their tears.

Once they reached the dark office, Edith shook her head. "This is a heavy blow, Lizzie. How shall I bear it?"

How did one answer such a question from such a woman? Lizzie ought to have turned to Edith for guidance, not the other way around. She had spent hours of her lifetime sitting at the veritable feet of this woman, taking in every bit of wisdom and intellect she had the graciousness to offer, and now . . .

"The Lord will give you strength," Lizzie found herself saying. "And He will have His reasons."

That seemed to straighten Edith's spine, and her hold on Lizzie strengthened. "Yes. He will, won't He?"

She sounded so much like her old self that Lizzie nearly cried anew at hearing it. "He will, Edith." She swallowed hard. "He has to. Remember what you told me? Faith as a mustard seed can move mountains. But a seed must also be tended if it is to grow into a strong and hardy plant. You are a gardener of nurses, of patients, and of souls. But you are also a plant that must be tended to, and the Great Gardener Himself will see to that."

"I feel very much like a reed in the wind," Edith whispered. "Blown about to and fro, bending this way and that, close to snapping under the strain."

Lizzie bit her lip, the admission from her mentor piercing her heart. "Then you must rest and recover your strength. It will do your mind and body good."

Edith nodded and took in a breath that seemed to shake away the dark shroud that had hung over her. She smiled at Lizzie gently, tears lingering in her eyes. "Thank you, my dear friend. I think I will rest for a while. Will you wake me in an hour?"

"Of course, Matron." She escorted her to her rooms, then closed the door behind her, wondering if the matron would rest as she said she would, or if she would spend the time engaged in prayer. Lizzie had known her to do such a thing frequently, and while Lizzie might not find imploring with the Almighty to be a restful occupation, it was clear Edith did.

Whatever would best restore her soul, she supposed.

Lizzie moved back into the clinic, determined to see it returned to smooth running after a morning's disruption of such magnitude. The others might cry in their rooms or rest for a time, as the matron had suggested, but Lizzie could not. While the matron was recovering, Lizzie would act in whatever manner might best serve their cause, whether that be nursing or aiding their secret soldiers in getting away.

How long she spent organizing linens, making rounds to check on patients, looking over the schedule for dispensing medication, and any other odd tasks that could fill her time, Lizzie could not say. She had noted when an hour had passed and gone to wake the matron, as promised, who, as it happened, had been resting in her bed, but then Lizzie had gone back to keeping busy about the clinic, and time had ceased to matter.

It was much later in the day when she was rolling lint that she heard footsteps coming up behind her.

"Sister Wilkins, look who has come back to us!" an eager young voice called out.

Any number of faces flashed through Lizzie's mind as she turned, smiling in anticipation.

Her smile froze the moment it reached full spread.

Mr. Quien was walking toward her in the company of at least three nurses, though a fourth seemed to be following at a distance.

"Is it not marvelous?" one of the girls squealed, looking up at the man as though he might somehow end the war, stop world hunger, and marry her in one fell swoop.

"How . . . is this managed?" Lizzie asked through gritted teeth as she forced her smile to remain. "After all that trouble to get you safely away . . ."

Mr. Quien offered a wry chuckle, his smile just lopsided enough to make Lizzie squirm, recalling that day he had seemed to appear everywhere in Brussels. "Yes, it would seem to fly in the face of sense, no? But the French authorities in Holland have given me money to be an intelligence agent in Brussels, and recalling how warmly I had been treated, how could I possibly refuse? Especially when it could aid my poor country."

The sighs from the girls flocking around the man nearly caused Lizzie's eye to twitch in irritation. "So you have come to pay your respects?"

He had the wisdom to look sheepish. "Actually, I was hoping I might trouble the matron for a room in which to stay while I am here. I can pay for my lodgings this time."

Lizzie would certainly like to see him pay, but not with funds. If anything he had said was even remotely true, she would eat the lint she had just rolled.

"I will see what the matron thinks," Lizzie told him, casting a stern eye over those clearly eager to have him stay once more. "I am uncertain as to the availability of rooms or beds. Ladies, please take Mr. Quien to the sitting room and see him suitably settled; we must not disturb our patients."

"Yes, Sister," they all chimed in the same obedient yet eager tone, turning and tugging their guest along with them.

He would not spend another night under this roof. Lizzie would make quite certain of that.

As soon as he and the nurses were out of sight, Lizzie strode to the matron's office, knocking once before opening the door and shutting it quickly and firmly behind her.

Edith sat behind her desk, her white nurse's cap seeming to illuminate her features with an almost heavenly glow. "Lizzie?"

"Mr. Quien is back," Lizzie told her in a low voice. "He says he has returned as an intelligence agent for the French authorities in Holland, and he would like to stay here." She took two steps forward, shaking her head. "Edith, I am certain he is an informer, and I do not say that lightly. I beg you not to allow him to lodge here. For all our sakes, not to mention your own."

Edith's eyes had gone round, her lips pressing together. "Perhaps you are right," she said slowly, her brow creasing slightly. "It is rather suspicious that he is here. I will tell him we have no rooms available."

Lizzie could not restrain her sigh of relief and nodded. "Thank you, Matron. And, if I may—will you cease helping with the soldiers? Food is scarce. The meat is gone. Bread and salads are our staples. We cannot keep risking so much. *You* cannot keep risking so much. We need proper food with the money we have, Matron. Please. You have done enough."

Edith's pale eyes took on a faraway look. "Perhaps I have. I will consider that, Lizzie, and discuss it with the others. Perhaps it is time."

That was a less than convincing answer, but Lizzie didn't press the matter. So long as the traitor wouldn't stay with them again, she would be satisfied.

Edith shook herself, then looked at Lizzie again. "And please, do continue to call me Edith in private. It is long past due, I think. You are no longer simply my assistant, but my friend and a treasured confidante. Let's have no more distance between us." She moved around the desk and patted Lizzie's arm gently as she passed her, her slight but tender smile giving the smallest comfort.

But it would suffice.

CHAPTER 14

"You cannot be serious, Matron."

Edith smiled and gestured for the young Irish soldier to continue donning his costume. "I am entirely serious. Why should you not go in such a disguise?"

The chap laughed and held it out as though to show her something she did not already know. "It's a monk's robe!"

"Indeed, it is," Edith replied, clasping her hands in front of her as her heart swelled with pride at the excellent scheme. "And you will be from a silent order. What could be better?"

The lad exchanged rueful looks with his companion and tossed the robes over his clothes, tugging the thick fabric down his torso.

"Are you certain we won't be struck down by the Lord for impersonating His devoted servants?" the other soldier asked as he, too, put on his disguise.

"I am of the opinion," Edith mused, turning to her desk to grab a few finishing touches for them, "that the Lord has a sense of humor and that He does not mind the use of devoted likenesses for a worthy cause." She handed each man a small Bible, nodding at the improvement with the addition. "Perfect. Now, we must be on our way, or we will miss the tram we need."

She led the way out of the room and down the corridor.

"Are you certain you should be the one taking us, Matron?" one of them whispered in rapid French. "Surely there are others."

"I don't mind," Edith told him calmly, looking over her shoulder with a smile. "It is good to be actively engaged in something, don't you think?"

She turned back before they could reply, smiling to herself now.

The truth was that she was exhausted and, despite her conversation with Lizzie, was continuing to take in soldiers and help them escape, and it was completely consuming her life. Last week, she had helped a young Welshman to safety, and she hoped desperately he would make it back home.

She had begun hearing rumors. Someone had said Colonel Boger had never made it to England all those months ago and was even now sitting in a camp in Germany. Another claimed that he'd heard in Chez Jules of an entire group of soldiers and a guide being arrested at the border. Still another said the Princess of Croÿ had recently been ambushed and arrested on her return trip to Mons, though she had been released after questioning.

None of the information could be confirmed, of course. The princess could have told Edith the truth of the matter, if she had returned to the clinic after their last visit, but she had not, and communication had been limited.

Edith shook her head, stopping the worrisome train of thought.

Something was coming, and the pains Edith felt in her chest from time to time seemed to grow heavier in anticipation of it.

She could not think about that today. Could not think of any of it. She simply needed to see these men to their next destination, and then return home. There were more soldiers to come, courtesy of Marie de Croÿ, and she had ordered the rooms at the back of the clinic to be prepared for them.

Edith shook herself as she and her newly minted monks neared the tram stop, forcing her expression to be calm. Were she truly traveling with such spiritually minded men, she would naturally have an air of serenity about her. The soldiers were not the only ones in disguise on this venture, and she needed to play her part well.

Brussels was a large city, filled with citizens of several religious beliefs, so the sight of monks would not be uncommon. It would also keep strangers from interacting with them, which was part of the attraction of the costumes. And Edith traveled about enough to visit the new clinic or the surrounding hospitals, or to see private patients, even during the occupation and war, that her presence ought not to warrant anyone's notice.

The trick would be keeping all three of them free from suspicion.

They boarded the tram in silence, finding seats close enough to each other to remain in eye contact. It had been straightforward enough thus far, but she knew she'd need to keep her attention focused and her guard up. There would be no relaxing until the soldiers were safely delivered to their next point and she had returned to the clinic.

A pair of German officers boarded the tram at the next station, sitting separately and seemingly uninterested in those around them. Edith couldn't blame them; they were not a popular breed among the local Belgians.

But she still felt shocks race through her veins at the sight of them.

They were not looking at Edith, nor at the pretend monks sitting near her. All would be well.

Just then, one of the soldiers looked over at one of the monks sitting in front of her. Or, more specifically, he looked at his feet and ankles.

Edith glanced down as best as she could from her position and bit back a groan.

The Irishman had rolled the hem of his trousers, exposing his boots. Boots that were almost certainly army issued, and not from the Belgian or German army.

Had the German soldier noticed that as well? Was he even now drawing conclusions about this monk sitting near him on the tram? And if so, would he then cast his suspicions on the other monk? On Edith?

For a moment, there was nothing to do but sit and stew with anxiety, to weigh fears and alternate actions against each other, to consider the risk of changing their plans.

She ventured a look at the soldier again, feeling the wracking beat of her heart against each rib. His attention was still on the boots, and Edith's throat clenched in distress.

She needed to move before he could make a decision about them. Before his curiosity became a certainty, and before that certainty provoked him to action.

The tram was approaching its next stop. There was no time to wait.

"We must disembark," Edith whispered to the monk closest to her. "Follow me and stay close."

She did not wait to see if he acknowledged her statement. The tram began to slow, and she rose with as much grace and ease as she could manage despite her nerves. She made her way to the front, trusting that her two monks would follow with as much wordless obedience as their costumes would indicate.

Please, do not let us be followed. Please, let me get them away.

There was no time to think beyond getting off the tram, not even to figure out their next steps or how they would get to the contact who would take the soldiers further on. She only needed to ensure they were not followed.

Edith stepped off the tram and paused at a shop window to pretend to examine her reflection, waiting for the two others to follow. They did so, coming to stand near her with bowed heads and somber countenances.

No one else disembarked.

The tram left without incident, and she turned to her now smiling monks with a relieved smile of her own. "Now, dear brothers, let us find a safer way to continue your journey."

It was a bit of a walk to reach their contact, but a good walk in the Belgian air was a cure for a great many things, including a crowded mind and burdened heart. She had never met this particular contact before, nor did she know his name. She only knew they were to meet him inside a church. It was the perfect destination, given the disguises, and Edith would never complain about the opportunity to take refuge in a place of holiness.

They moved into the church pews, the monks settling into the first row, as was proper, while Edith took a seat about halfway into the nave. This allowed her to see the monks clearly and note whenever they were taken away, while keeping her separated from the situation.

They waited only a quarter of an hour or so before a man in dark clothing came up the aisle and moved to the pew where the soldiers sat, leaning close to murmur something to them that Edith hadn't a hope of hearing. Then the soldiers rose and followed him out through the transept, none of them giving Edith a second look.

That was that, then.

Edith exhaled slowly, closing her eyes in a long moment of prayer. Gratitude for their safety, for their success, for all of their endeavors welled up in her like an endless spring. She poured out her heart with such thanks, feeling her words inadequate compared to the blessings she had received.

Then she found herself praying with equal fervor that those two soldiers would make it to Holland—and then to England—safely.

She prayed that her nurses would be protected.

She prayed that, above all else, God's will would be done, and that Edith, as a frail but fervent servant of His, might accept what that will might be.

Only when her heart felt at peace once more could Edith bring herself to rise from the pew and, upon shaking legs, make her way out of the church.

The tram back to Ixelles was uneventful, and Edith took great pleasure in walking at a leisurely pace back toward the clinic.

But there was one stop she needed to make first.

She entered Chez Jules without any trepidation at all, smiling slightly for the owner, Mr. Jules de Cloedt. He nodded at her, his smile much the same.

The sight of her at the café might have seemed odd to others, but Mr. de Cloedt was accustomed to her visits by now.

Edith moved to a darkened corner of the bar. She sat for a moment, looking about her to make sure no one was watching, then she pried up the loose floorboard near her. Beneath it lay a few sensitive documents she no longer felt able to safely keep at the clinic.

Mr. de Cloedt did not mind her keeping such things here, given his admiration for her work and her actions. Some weeks ago, he had told her about the floorboard after a soldier had come in for a drink, talking about yet another inspection at the clinic.

It was a relief to have a safe place to keep her most sensitive documents. The Germans would not suspect this small café, should they happen to find anything of note in her clinic.

She retrieved two documents she had tucked in the hidden pockets of her skirts and added them to the pile. Tamping the floorboard back down with her feet, then running the tip of her toe along it to ensure it was perfectly in line with the others around it, Edith nodded to herself in satisfaction. She would recover these documents when it was safe to do so. Perhaps then she might also be able to properly account for everything and everyone she had been involved with during this confusing time.

She could only hope for such a resolution.

Sighing, she rose and tucked a loose strand of graying hair behind her ear, making a note to pin it back when she returned to the clinic. She must maintain her appearance for the nurses and the staff. Be professional and tidy—no matter what.

The clinic was only a hundred yards or so away from the café, and the approaching evening gave the building a softer light that matched her adoration for it. What a blessing the place had been to her. What a mission and a cause for her to have devoted herself to. She would never regret coming back to Brussels when the war broke out rather than remaining in England.

This was where she belonged. This was where she had been called to serve.

At the time, she could not have imagined all that she would undertake, but she had no regrets. All the stresses and the angst, all the infuriating measures that had to be taken, all the inspections by the authorities to try to catch her out—she would do it all again to continue to make a difference for those she had helped, whether medical or military.

There was a heady sense of satisfaction in that.

As she entered the clinic, she breathed a sigh of contentment, a feeling she had not experienced in weeks, perhaps months, and the burdens weighing on her shoulders seemed less daunting.

Lizzie came down the corridor toward her, smiling brightly. "Good evening, Edith. I am glad to see you back. Is all well?"

Edith returned her smile, nodding with warmth and affection. "All is well, indeed. Would you prepare the space for guests? We anticipate as many as ten, due to arrive either tonight or in the morning."

Lizzie's eyes widened, her throat worked, but she nodded. "Yes, I will see that all is ready. I thought . . ." She frowned, giving Edith a searching look. "I thought we were done with housing guests."

There was nothing to do but utter a heavy sigh at that. "Hopefully, we soon will be. But with inspections happening about town and other houses being unavailable, we are still one of the safest places. And there are so many more soldiers that need help. How can we close our doors?"

The concern and confusion left Lizzie's face, and her jaw tightened. "Yes, of course."

Edith put a hand on her arm. "Tomorrow, we may also start moving into our new clinic. Slowly, as all is not ready, but we can begin taking some of the equipment over. Perhaps in a few days, or weeks, we may send some of the senior nurses over. Would you ask Sister Taylor to oversee that?"

"Yes. She will be glad for the work."

"I think we are all glad for work these days," Edith murmured. "Anything to distract us from the ugliness of war and from our burdens as they are for the present."

Lizzie put her hand over Edith's. "We all manage to find bright spots, Edith. And those get us through."

Edith exhaled slowly, smiling further. "We do, don't we? Come, I'll help you to ready the space."

CHAPTER 15

There was not much excitement about the finer points of tending to injuries of the eye. The glazed expressions of the nurses listening to the lecture on it told Lizzie that quite clearly.

Many of them had already been treating eye injuries of soldiers in the clinic, eye washes and bandaging having become two of the more common tasks. But the matron was determined that the education of the probationers and nurses be well-rounded and complete, so the lectures continued. Exciting or not.

But even Lizzie wasn't that devoted to education on the eyeball.

She smiled at her long-suffering students. "I think that will do for this morning. Go about your duties, and we can resume class this afternoon."

The sigh of relief released by the entire room was almost laughable, and Lizzie shook her head as the nurses began to talk amongst each other in low voices, leaving the room with an efficiency that would have been useful about the clinic, should they have applied it thus.

Lizzie noticed a lone figure entering the classroom while the others departed. "Pauline?"

The girl hurried to her, so pale it was frightening to see. "Germans, Sister," she whispered, the words wobbling on her voice. "Two in the matron's office. Two standing outside. What do we do?"

Cold shivers raced up Lizzie's legs, freezing each toe within her shoe and reaching deep into the pit of her stomach before exploding into brutal sparks of icicles.

What do *we do?*

"Take two nurses," Lizzie ordered, her voice steadier than her body. "Any two who can keep calm. You know who they are."

Pauline nodded obediently, which felt like a miracle.

"You and they will talk with the soldiers waiting outside the office." Lizzie pursed her lips, thinking quickly. "I will take two nurses with me and escort our guests out before an inspection can begin and rid the place of evidence. If we work quickly, we should be able to manage it easily."

"Yes, Sister." Pauline bit her lip, looking far younger than her age would indicate. "God be with you." She rushed from the room, and Lizzie followed at a much slower pace.

Her own nurses would need to be carefully chosen; she would require those prudent in thought, calm in manner, and decisive in action.

And those who would not be surprised about what they needed to do.

Clearing her throat, she moved to the dining room where several nurses had gathered for lunch. She scanned the room quickly. "Beatrice, Mania, would you please come help me for a moment?"

The two nurses looked up from their meal, not particularly surprised by the request.

They came directly to her, and Lizzie wordlessly indicated for them to follow her. Once they were moving toward the basement, Lizzie finally spoke.

"There are two Germans in the matron's office," she said in a low tone. "And two more standing outside her office. Pauline has taken a few nurses to keep them occupied in conversation. We must get our guests out of the basement. Can you two take care of the evidence?"

As she spoke, the eyes of the two nurses grew wider and wider, and, for a moment, neither of them responded to her question.

She raised her brows. "There is no time—can you do it?"

"Yes, Sister," they told her, almost in unison.

Lizzie nodded. "Good. Go!"

They darted off, and she turned, heading swiftly for the basement, doing her best to stay as silent as possible. The last thing she needed was to attract the attention of the Germans near the office.

Get the soldiers out without the Germans being made aware— that was the priority.

Her steps lighter than her heart, Lizzie moved for the basement, relieved when the door opened on silent hinges. She began her descent.

Cautious eyes met hers, and she put her finger to her lips, looking at each soldier in turn. There were nine of them, which made their distribution that much harder.

They had arrived only that morning, which meant they had yet to have grown comfortable, which ought to help them now. She could trust that nothing incriminating would be left behind. She indicated the door toward the garden, and the soldiers began gathering up their things, slipping their arms into jackets, wordlessly communicating with each other in gestures and looks.

Lizzie ushered them all toward the door. "The house across the garden is vacant," she whispered. "You will be safe there. Wait for Jose to take you elsewhere."

She waited until they all nodded before stepping out of the door herself and looking up at the windows to ensure no Germans were watching.

As far as she could tell, none were.

She waved the soldiers out, keeping her eyes fixed on each of the windows, her eyes darting from one to the other as though she anticipated one of the shells of war to fly out of any single pane of glass to rain disaster upon them all.

The soldiers filed out one at a time, neatly hopping over the stone wall before jogging across the back garden and disappearing into the abandoned house. When the last soldier was gone, Lizzie returned to the basement, looking around to take stock of the surroundings. Would this area be suspect for housing soldiers if inspected?

She made quick work of folding blankets and tossing them haphazardly into a pile in the corner, rather as one might have done to raggedy and moth-laced materials used only for packing or work. It wasn't perfect, but she hoped it would at least represent a standard basement for a clinic of nurses.

Whatever that ought to look like.

Lizzie hurried back upstairs, hoping the other nurses had managed their tasks. She had not heard any heavy footfalls above her while she had gotten the soldiers out, nor while she had worked, which seemed a good sign. But she knew better than to believe all was safe.

Not until the Germans were gone, and all was quiet in the clinic again.

"*Verboten!*"

The sudden bellow from somewhere within the clinic made Lizzie jump, her eyes widening to an almost painful degree.

Then she was running, ears straining for any other sounds to direct her path. The shout had been too clear to have come from behind a door, so it could not have been the matron's office, which meant it was the nurses. Beatrice and Mania, and anyone else who might have been recruited to help them.

How could this have happened so soon after their guests' arrival? Less than a day, and already there was an inspection. Was there a spy among the soldiers? Among the nurses? Among their neighbors? Was there anyone they could truly trust?

How could she ever look at any person the same way after this?

She heard the sound of papers shuffling, and she moved to the nearest set of bathroom facilities.

A German soldier knelt on the floor near the bathtub, pulling out French and English magazines that had been shoved under there. Near the water tank sat a stack of sopping wet papers, the ink smeared in places, but, from where Lizzie stood, not enough to make the paper illegible.

She glanced to the side of the room to see Beatrice and Mania standing there, tears streaming down Mania's face.

Lizzie swallowed, trying for calm as she entered the room fully.

The German whirled on his knees to look at her, shaking the magazines in his hands in her direction. *"Verboten!"* he insisted.

Clamping down on her lips, Lizzie nodded once.

That seemed to satisfy him, and he swept up both the magazines and the stack of pages, marching out of the room.

Mania and Beatrice swarmed in on her the moment they were alone.

"Oh, Sister!" Beatrice said in a rush. "We were so careful. But he followed us and pulled everything from the water tank onto the floor."

"Have we ruined everything?" Mania asked with a whimper. "There was so little time."

Lizzie shushed them gently, shaking her head even as her heart seemed to ricochet off each rib in an anxious frenzy. "You've done as well as you could under the circumstances. Is this the only . . . ?"

Both nodded their heads, saying nothing further.

"Good." Lizzie exhaled, patting their hands and listening to distant sounds of destruction. "We had best go to the matron's office and wait until this is over." She inhaled slowly, straightening her spine. "Chins up. The matron would not want us to show emotional faces."

Beatrice and Mania did their best, but anyone with eyes would see their tears and their terror. Even Lizzie felt the same emotions quivering inside of her. She simply could not release them yet, not when there was still much to do.

No one was with Edith in her office while the soldiers searched it, apparently having no care for her belongings, if the sounds were anything to go by.

"I recognize one of the soldiers," Mania whispered as they walked. "He came to the clinic yesterday in plain clothing and asked about renting the place after we move to the new location."

Beatrice gave her a startled look. "Did he examine the place?"

Mania nodded, swallowing.

"So he already had an idea of where to check," Lizzie said calmly, bobbing her head in a nod she had no control over.

"I'm afraid so."

That made a little more sense, though it did not answer all of her questions. But would that explain what was happening with Edith's office at the moment? The German likely wouldn't have seen that when he was looking at the premises.

But then, the Germans had surprised her with their knowledge before. If there truly were spies among the clinic's staff, it was entirely possible that the Germans knew everything. Though, if that were the case, surely the nurses would have been arrested by now.

So what did the Germans know? And who had told them?

Lizzie, Beatrice, and Mania reached the matron's office and paused, the door slightly ajar. Lizzie could not see far enough into the room to note the particular state of things, but the sounds were enough.

A harsh voice spoke in rapid German, which Lizzie could not catch, then changed to halting French. "We will return another time," he grunted. "You may be certain of that."

The door was yanked open, startling the three nurses. Governor Lüttwitz's dark scoffing sound as he looked at their faces made Lizzie's stomach clench. He glanced over his shoulder into the office.

"Good day to you, Mademoiselle Cavell. A pleasure, as always." He gave a mocking nod and stormed from the room with his two cohorts, not sparing another glance in the nurses' direction.

Lizzie watched the soldiers collect the others who had come with them, and she waited until the Germans had all disappeared from the clinic entirely before rushing into the recently vacated office.

"Matron!" Lizzie gasped as she came to a stop, looking around Edith's room.

Disaster was too mild a description for the state of things. It seemed as though the place had been attacked by a whirlwind capable of unearthing every document and valuable in any corner of the room. Cups and saucers were smashed into tiny shards on the floor. All the pictures, including a family portrait, had been torn down from the walls. Even the floorboards had been pried up in places, the wood littered with stray sheets of paper, the writing upon them apparently as uninteresting as anything else in the room.

Lizzie looked over at her mentor, her own heart too heavy for words. In the midst of the disarray, Edith sat quietly and calmly behind her desk.

She seemed so small, so fragile and frail, as though she might break as easily as the teacups on the floor.

Yet she did not break—would barely even bend. She refused to crumble.

Amid disaster and destruction, she remained calm, composed, and dignified.

How could that be?

"Sisters," Lizzie said calmly to Beatrice and Mania, "would you go and find some things to help us tidy the room?"

"Of course, Sister," they murmured, skittering from the room.

Once they were gone, Lizzie knelt before Edith, taking her hands. "Edith, this must stop."

Edith did not so much as blink, her gaze resting somewhere around her knees.

"Ask permission to return to England," Lizzie pleaded, firmly rubbing her hands over Edith's in an attempt to draw her attention. "Or, at the very least, go into hiding somewhere in Belgium."

Edith's gray eyes finally lifted to Lizzie's dark ones. "Hiding?" she repeated. "Leave?"

Lizzie nodded firmly. "Leave, Edith. Please, ask if you can leave. This is enough."

Edith slowly shook her head. "There are two other English nurses here. How could I leave when they remain?"

"They are not giving what you are!" Lizzie sat back on her heels, exhaling roughly. "Look around you. This is not going to get better. You must leave, if only to protect yourself!"

"And why am I to be so valued above others?" came the simple, unconcerned reply. "Why should I flee when so many others cannot? No, dear Lizzie, I will not leave, and I will not hide. I will remain until the end."

Lizzie knew that tone all too well, just as she knew the slight lift of the chin that came with it. There would be no persuading her otherwise, come what may, for good or for ill. For the first time in her life, she hated knowing that. She wanted to fight Edith on this, get her away from all of this so she might return to the woman she had once been rather than seeming to shrink before her very eyes.

She had always looked up to the matron, but during these months of their new roles and working so closely together, Edith had become some combination of sister and mother to her, as well as a friend. It was Lizzie's duty to intervene for Edith's own good, when it was necessary, wasn't it?

But how could she argue with someone who would not budge? Edith's will was iron, and nothing Lizzie could say or do would convince the woman to think of herself.

Maddening, this self-sacrifice. Admirable, but maddening.

A weighted breath left Lizzie's lungs with the same futility her words had held. "Then will you at least burn some of the letters and sensitive documents? Give yourself the comfort of knowing the Germans cannot find them."

Edith blinked before nodding slightly. "Yes. That I will do." Her hands finally moved beneath Lizzie's, and the glossy look faded from her eyes. "Did our guests get away?"

Lizzie nodded and rose, hoping to pull Edith up with her, but the woman remained sitting. "They did. I've told them Jose would be around to disperse them."

"We must be cautious," Edith warned, looking up at her. "The Germans are leaving an inspector to watch us from inside a front room, but I do not know for how long. You must not show yourself on the streets but remain indoors as much as possible. Perhaps the inspector will leave once it is night."

"Then we will put countermeasures into place," Lizzie said simply. "Mania is on night duty; I will make certain she is aware."

Edith smiled at her, the emotion behind her eyes difficult to read. "You always know what to do, don't you, Lizzie Wilkins?"

Lizzie barked a startled laugh. "Hardly. I only try to think what *you* would do and go from there."

Finally, Edith rose and began to pick up the portraits from the glass-strewn floor. Her expression shifted ever so slightly from item to item, her affection for those in the portraits and her nostalgia for every item plain to see.

Lizzie bit her lip against a sudden rise of tears, her strength all but failing her now that Edith was up and about, on her feet, quietly cleaning up the destruction left by her personal foes. It was too much to bear, but Lizzie could not cry in front of her. Not over this.

"Excuse me, Edith," she squeaked, darting for the door. "I shall return in a moment."

She scurried down the hall, finding a small nook near the bathroom that had so recently been inspected, and sank to the ground, covering her face as tears ran from her eyes, her lungs squeezing and pressing every ounce of energy into her cries.

How much longer could they endure this?

How much longer would they have to?

CHAPTER 16

The knock upon Edith's door in the middle of the night was half expected. She had not been able to sleep, though she had managed a brief dozing a time or two. There had simply been too much excitement in the day that had passed and too much uncertainty about the day awaiting them for rest to be possible. Not even additional devotions in her scriptures and reading could send her to sleep, though she had taken respite in the solitude all the same.

She had taken to pouring her heart out in prayer in an attempt to relieve her soul of its weighty burdens, and there was a kind of rest to be found in that, at least.

"Come," she called very softly, rising from her knees as the door opened.

"Matron," the small, accented voice of Mania called. "I need you."

Edith came to the door, startled to see the girl in her nightgown and pigtails. "What is it, child?"

"I am sleeping in the garret room overlooking the street," Mania explained as they started down the corridor. "I offered to be sentry tonight when Sister Wilkins asked. I know that Jose only took two soldiers away and Pauline a few more, which leaves several uncounted."

Edith nodded, noting how the girl's voice dipped lower and lower the closer they got to the front of the house. "And?"

"And three of our English soldiers are headed this way from Chez Jules!" Mania breathed, her dark eyes widening. "The German inspector is asleep in the front room. If they ring the bell . . ."

If they rang the bell, the entire operation would be over, and every one of them would be arrested, the consequences of which were unimaginable.

"Get the door," Edith murmured, nodding her head toward it. "Before they get to it. Silence, you understand? Have them remove their shoes."

Mania nodded and did as she was bid, silently opening the door and immediately putting her finger to her lips, though none of the approaching soldiers could see it yet. When they caught sight of her, they all had the decency to look sheepish, despite their evidently inebriated states.

Again, Mania pressed her finger to her lips. *"Le Boche,"* she hissed, jabbing another finger toward the sleeping inspector in the adjacent room.

The three soldiers now appeared properly horrified.

Mania pointed to her feet firmly, and all three removed their shoes and entered the house with a shocking lack of sound.

Edith waved for them to follow her and moved toward the back of the house and her offices. When they were far enough from the inspector to be relatively safe, she whispered, "We must get you away. Are you ready to go now?"

Nods abounded among them.

Edith looked at Mania, still standing wide-eyed behind them.

"Go back to your bed, Mania. Appear as though all is normal. I will return shortly."

Mania gave a quick nod and rushed off, dark pigtails flying in the night air as she moved.

Edith looked at the soldiers, such young men who likely had no real idea of the danger they were in or the trouble their presence could cause. Men who had only wanted to serve their country but found themselves at a very different end of the war than they expected.

And now she had to get them out without any plan at all.

"Put your shoes back on, gentlemen," Edith murmured as her mind spun on options, her spirit crying out for inspiration. "We have quite a distance to go."

The streets of Brussels were the most silent she had ever heard them. There was no shelling in the distance, an eerie fact that somehow made even the breath passing her lips more resonant in the night. There were no birds, no trams, no German patrols monitoring the streets. There were only the four of them, making their way across the city in the dead of night.

They did not speak; disturbing the silence would surely mean discovery, and she would not do anything to risk that. The soldiers seemed inclined to do the same, wordlessly following her wherever she led them.

But where would she lead them?

Her usual options were not available at this time of night, especially without a plan in place. She would never make it all the way out to Bellignies, so the princess was not an option. The safest option was undoubtedly the home of Philippe Baucq. He would know exactly what to do with the soldiers and how best to help them get out.

More than that, he might even be awake at this hour working away on his printing.

It was three miles from the clinic to his home, and they had likely already walked half of that. Philippe was a good man, if a little more daring and outspoken than Edith would have him be. He'd endured as many inspections as Edith had, though the Germans were usually looking for something quite different in his home. His activities seemed to be more along the lines of building up a network of resistance, even if he was taking a particularly active role in some areas.

But it was clear he would not rest until Belgium was restored to her rightful and independent place in Europe, and there was something to be greatly admired in that.

The man was wholly devoted to his wife and daughters, as well as to his faith. He was a Catholic, as was common in this part of the world, but he truly lived his faith. Edith respected and admired that.

Any man who would put his trust in the Lord was a man whom Edith could work with and confide in.

And he would help her in this.

"Quietly now," she breathed to the soldiers behind her. "We're almost there."

They gave no answer but seemed to draw closer to her. The image of a doe leading timid fawns through an exposed meadow slipped into her mind, bringing an impossible smile to her lips. She might know more than they about their destination, but she surely had no additional insight into their circumstances. Still, she was their caretaker, and they were in her charge.

The house was before them soon enough, as dark and silent as the rest of the city. Edith rapped her knuckles on the front door, checking the street on either side of the house for any witnesses. None appeared to be seen, but she knew better than to entirely trust that. If there was anything she had learned during this time, it was that the Germans had ways and means to do whatever they wished.

It was only a few moments before the door opened, but she

counted each of her heartbeats that passed. A bleary-eyed Mr. Baucq appeared in a nightshirt loosely shoved into trousers.

"Mademoiselle Cavell?" he asked as he squinted at her, his voice roughened with sleep.

"Forgive me, Mr. Baucq," Edith said quickly. "I know the hour is inconvenient, but we find ourselves in a predicament at the clinic." She turned slightly to gesture to the soldiers behind her. "Can you house these men and get them safely away?"

Mr. Baucq was instantly alert, and his eyes darted to the men. "Yes," he said without hesitation. "Absolutely. Come in, gentlemen. Quickly, now. Make as little noise as you can. My family is sleeping."

The men filed in, murmuring words of thanks, though it was not clear if the gratitude was for Edith or Mr. Baucq or both.

Edith released a breath of relief when the soldiers were inside, and she smiled at Mr. Baucq. "Thank you. There is an inspector staying the night at the clinic, and I could not risk it."

"Of course, I am happy to do it." He paused, giving her a thoughtful look. "Be careful, Edith. You give too much."

She returned his look with a scolding one of her own. "No more than you give yourself, Philippe. And you with a wife and daughters."

He shrugged. "They know the dangers, and they accept them."

"Even the girls?"

He paused, and his smile turned sad. "They do now. I've spoken with Yvonne most recently. We went for a walk yesterday, and I told her that affairs were not going all that well for me. Truth be told, I fear my arrest is only a matter of time. I have caused too much trouble and not hidden it well enough. But I've told her she must maintain complete ignorance, and that nothing must get in the way of her education, especially her music. It is important that her life continues regardless of what happens to me."

There was a tenderness to his tone that eclipsed even his usual warmth for his daughters, but the finality in his voice broke Edith's heart and brought tears to her eyes. Such a good, loving family man did not deserve to be punished, and his sweet, lively daughters did not deserve to have their father imprisoned and named a villain simply for being a proud Belgian in a time of war.

"Surely it is not that bleak," Edith managed through the lump of emotion clogging her throat. "You must not give up hope."

"I don't," Mr. Baucq replied simply. "But I am prepared all the same. You had best hurry back to the clinic, or the inspector will wake before you return."

Sensing that was all Mr. Baucq would say on the topic of his impending arrest, Edith nodded firmly. "Yes. Thank you again. Good night."

She turned as the door closed and began the return trip to the clinic. Three miles to walk in the early morning hours, and too much time with her thoughts.

Had she done enough to keep her staff safe from punishment? She had made an effort to relay only the essential information to others while keeping the details to herself. She was the only one with whom others had communicated and worked with, so there would be no testifying about the actions of any other individuals. A few of the nurses knew Mr. Baucq, but they did not know exactly what he did or how involved he was in any of the illegal activities.

Would that be enough?

If Mr. Baucq was making preparations to keep his family safe, how long did she herself have?

What would her mother think? What would she know? Would she even be told? With the delay in the delivery of any post from Belgium, there was simply no way of knowing if her mother had received any of her letters of late, though Edith continued to write them. Would an official communication reach her with more efficiency than standard post?

And what of her nurses? If Edith were arrested, would they be permitted to carry on, to tend to the wounded? Would their work continue? Or would they be forced to return to their home countries? That would certainly assure their safety, but many of them were as dedicated to the nursing profession as Edith was and would wish to continue in it as long as possible.

But if the dangers in Belgium became too much, or the abuse from the authorities in retribution for Edith's actions became too much to bear . . .

Had her own subversive actions ruined the opportunities for the nurses and students she had taught and trained?

The more she thought on the topic, the heavier her steps became, as though her boots had been tied to blocks of cement or piles of bricks, and the lifting of each foot took every ounce of strength left in her frame. She had felt burdened before, but never as though her entire frame could become consumed by the earth, her body too feeble to bear any more.

What had she done? She had felt called to do it, just as she had about nursing or serving or tending to orphans, and had followed without second thought. Should she have had second thoughts? Third? Had her actions been blessed by the Almighty, or had it simply been her own pride leading her and giving her some success?

What had her motivation been? The glory of the Lord? The glory of herself? The glory of England?

She wasn't certain which it was, or if it was some combination of them all. Could she truly claim any victory in this? Any good works? Anything that ought to be attributed to her in any way? Did she want to have any of the actions attributed to her? Was that what she had been aiming toward from the beginning—something to claim for her own?

Had selfishness been the provocation into this world she had found herself in?

She hadn't thought so at the time, but looking back, she felt herself pause.

What was the truth? Where was her heart? Why had she done this?

Would any of it matter in the end?

How she managed to get back to the clinic, Edith could not say, but she arrived just as dawn was beginning to rise.

Mania answered the door, her expression tender and soft. "Oh, Matron . . ."

"Good morning," Edith greeted, her voice surprisingly rough. She stepped forward and wobbled, gripping the doorframe for balance, suddenly breathing with difficulty.

Mania caught her around the waist, steadying her. "The inspector has been awake for an hour or so, Matron," she breathed. "He has said nothing other than to demand breakfast. He is in the front room, reading the newspaper."

Edith nodded, barely hearing Mania's words as fatigue and weariness sank in. "Get him whatever he wants."

"Edith, come, let me get you to bed." Lizzie's voice found its way to her ears, and Edith felt herself being transferred into her friend's strong arms before they were moving again.

A faint sniffling registered in Edith's mind. "Are those tears I hear?" she asked, her words sounding far away.

"Yes, they are," Lizzie answered on a wavering tone. "I cannot bear to see you like this. You are so tired, so weak, and I feel so helpless. You must rest. I insist."

Edith nodded, her head feeling almost too heavy to do that much.

Lizzie said nothing else and continued to lead her to her rooms. She settled her into bed and pulled the covers up to her chin, rather as she might have done with a child. "Rest now, Edith. As long as you need to. I will see to everything."

Again, Edith nodded, her mouth opening to thank her assistant, but the strength to speak was beyond her.

"Don't speak," Lizzie said, her voice still clogged with tears. "Just sleep."

As though ordered to do so, Edith felt her eyes close on weighty lids, her body sag into the mattress of her bed, and sleep itself overtake her.

CHAPTER 17

"Where is the matron?"

No one in the room said a word. The nurses looked at Lizzie with wide eyes, unused to the firmness of her tone or perhaps the stern posture she held with her hands propped on her hips.

Lizzie raised a brow, looking around again. "Anyone? Surely someone has seen the matron, as she is incapable of fully disappearing despite her many gifts and talents. Where is she?"

Again, there did not seem to be any ideas among the gathered.

"Truly?" Lizzie put a hand to her brow, sighing. "When I last saw her, she was preparing for bed, and now she is not there. Someone had to see her go wherever she has gone."

A small group of young nurses looked at each other, one of them looking as though she might cry.

Lizzie stared at them hard. "Well?"

"She said she wanted to see the new clinic," one of them finally admitted, her voice almost childlike. "We begged her to stay, but . . ."

The bell at the front door rang, and the entire group of nurses jumped as though a German soldier had entered the room.

Lizzie felt something break within her at the sight. Once there had been such a response for the sounds of battle in the distance, the reminder of war and the dangers that could fall upon them all, but now something as small and simple as a knock upon the door —something that happened multiple times a day—could render the same reaction.

It was not fair.

Not to any of them.

"It will be all right," one of the nurses said. "There are any number of people who could be calling upon us here. The baker, for example."

"But every neighbor could be pointing their fingers at us," another said, looking toward the front of the building apprehensively. "How do we know they are not?"

They all looked at Lizzie for an answer, but she had none. The truth was that the neighbors could be telling the authorities anything about them. Could be relaying any amount of information. Could be betraying them at any moment. She would not have thought any such thing before the war began, but now . . .

Anyone could be a spy. Any of the soldiers who had come to them this morning could be spies. Nationality meant nothing— Polish soldiers working with the Germans, Belgians pretending to be French, Frenchmen being themselves but aligning themselves with the Germans. Even the Tommies could have been turned; there was no way of knowing.

She hoped the soldiers they had helped to escape were not spies. She hoped the ones that had arrived today were not spies, but she had not yet made her way to their rooms to meet them. She had gone to Edith to suggest they speak to the soldiers together only to find that she was not in her room.

Of all the days and times to visit their new clinic, she had to choose this day and this time?

A suspicious whining prompted Lizzie to look down at her feet. Her heart lurched when she saw Jack sitting there, peering up at her earnestly, his paws scooting toward her as he continued to whine.

Jack traditionally hated everyone except Edith, but here he was, sitting at her feet and clearly begging for comfort, for her to bring his mistress back to him.

Why had Edith not taken him with her? They were always companions on such journeys, but she had left him here this time.

Did that hold any meaning, or was it a simple change to routine and nothing more?

They were due to start moving to the new clinic this week, so perhaps Edith was simply seeing to her own preparations.

Lizzie would never forget the haunted, dazed expression Edith had worn when she had seen her that morning. How weak and unwell she had appeared. How childlike and helpless. For a woman who had always been a tower of strength and a pillar of hope, the image of her being so very diminished was heartbreaking, to say the least. There was nothing for Lizzie to do but tuck her into bed as though she were the ailing child she appeared to be.

The fact that Edith had not argued the point had been significant enough.

But now she was gone, after only having a few hours of rest.

If that.

For all of the matron's talk of lessening her load, it did not appear that anything had been lessened. In fact, she now bore weightier burdens that threatened to press her into the earth itself. Lizzie could not help the matron with things she did not know about, and the longer this had gone on, the more she realized that she carried very few of Edith's burdens.

She had been given additional tasks and responsibilities at the clinic, it was true, but none of them were things that would impact Lizzie's spirit or soul.

Edith had kept all those for herself.

"You seem lost in your thoughts, Sister. Anything the matter?" a man's voice said from the edge of the room.

Lizzie forced a smile, looking up while preparing some polite, nondescript answer that would never convey the whole truth.

Her smile froze, and her legs went numb from the knees down.

"Mr. Quien," she managed to force out in spite of the heat in her chest and a strange knot in her stomach. Icy shocks screeched into each finger, and each breath took every ounce of energy she possessed.

Why was he here? And how? They had not let him stay the last time, yet here he was only a few weeks later.

"Sorry," he said with the quick laugh the young nurses so adored. "I should have announced myself. I arrived last night, and the matron was kind enough to allow me a room."

The knot in Lizzie's stomach sank like a boulder. "She did?"

Mr. Quien nodded, smiling crookedly. "She did. Marvelous woman. So kind to an old friend."

An old friend, was he? Lizzie would certainly never see him that way, but she knew Edith had a kinder heart and thought the best of nearly everyone. It had to be the reason why she would allow the man to stay after she had refused him last time. Did she not believe Lizzie's concerns about him? Did she hope to be mistaken?

Had she simply answered the man's request without considering its ramifications due to the other matters occupying her mind?

Whichever it was, Mr. Quien was now within their walls, and Lizzie still did not trust anything about him. With all Edith had to contend with, pushing herself until the strain was literally engraved upon her countenance, this was not going to help matters.

The corners of Lizzie's mouth began to throb with the pain of maintaining her smile, but she would not give him reason to suspect her.

"And what are your plans?" Lizzie found herself asking, more to keep up polite appearances than anything else.

"After tonight?" Mr. Quien shrugged. "Making myself useful to my government. There are some connections I must make, and they will provide me with more permanent lodgings. I trust I may still be welcome to the occasional tea here?" He laughed with warmth, which, blessedly, kept Lizzie from having to answer. "It is good to be back, Sister. But, please, do not let me keep you from your work. Pretend as though I am not here."

He stepped back with a gallant motion that she instantly detested but would take advantage of all the same.

"Yes, thank you, Mr. Quien," she told him as she passed. "I must be about my work."

She rounded the nearest corner, though it would not take her in the direction she truly wished to go. She simply had to get away from him before her emotions betrayed her. Acting had never been one of her strong suits, which was not serving her well today.

She hadn't felt so unsettled since last week when a French soldier, Mr. Jacobs, had started taking too much interest in the work of the nurses and staff. He had struggled to obey the necessary restrictions and boundaries, and his eyes seemed to notice a great deal as he looked around. But he was a French soldier, and the other men with him seemed to vouch for him, so how could she raise concerns?

Besides, he was gone now, as were those he had come in with.

There was nothing suspicious now.

Other than Mr. Quien.

Lizzie could only shake her head as she made her way through the clinic. She had to figure something out, one way or the other, or danger would become their constant companion rather than a looming threat.

"Come, girls," she all but barked at a group of probationers standing about. "The matron expects us to be prepared to move to our new clinic premises. Begin cataloging our supplies and packing them securely. We will move the furniture as soon as we secure a cart."

They jumped at the instruction. "Yes, Sister," came their replies, each with an edge that spoke of the underlying strain upon them all.

Lizzie bit down on her lips hard to keep from offering an emotional apology to them and hurried through the ward to check on their few patients. Apologies were all well and good, but she could not let them see how worried she truly was. She had to go on as Edith would, which meant firm standards, strict behavior, and perfection in their work as nurses.

If she could cling to that, perhaps the threat she feared would not be so daunting.

Perhaps.

CHAPTER 18

"Your Highness, this is a welcome surprise."

Prince Reginald of Croÿ rose with his usual grace from the chair in Edith's sitting room, though his face was devoid of his usual congeniality. "Matron, I am relieved to see you today."

"Are you?" Edith blinked in surprise and gestured for him to sit back down. "Why should you be?"

His expression turned incredulous. "Matron, arrests are happening all over Belgium! Surely you have heard what befell Philippe Baucq and Mademoiselle Thuliez this week."

Edith nodded as she took her chair, her heart clenching as she considered her friends and the dramatic nature of their arrests. "Yes, and it is heartbreaking. In front of Madame Baucq and the girls, too. It will be all right, though. We have destroyed all the evidence, and in a few more days, we will be in our new clinic. The Germans will pay no more attention to us."

The prince did not look at all convinced. "But they have also arrested Madame Bodart. Did you know that?"

Edith had not heard that one, and she averted her gaze as a lump formed in her throat. Ada Bodart was a young Irish widow of an influential Belgian, and she had hidden several dozen soldiers during the course of their work.

"They used her son against her, Matron," Prince Reginald said in a low tone. "Asked him about houseguests staying with them, and the poor lad innocently answered. She was arrested not an hour later."

"Poor Madame Bodart," Edith whispered around her welling emotion. "And that poor boy. What a weight to bear."

The prince cleared his throat. "They will stop at nothing. I have left Bellignies to warn as many as I can, and then I am leaving the country. They cannot arrest me if I am not here. I encourage you to do the same."

Edith smiled sadly. "How can I leave? I have my nurses and my clinic, my patients. Am I to take them all with me?"

His brows slowly rose as he considered her. "You would sacrifice yourself for the sake of your profession?"

"It is no sacrifice to be found doing good works," Edith murmured, recalling the beautiful words of her morning devotional. "I have dedicated myself to this calling of nursing, just as I have recently dedicated myself to this work with you and our friends. Not all can say they have felt so brilliantly called to such things. How can I now bemoan doing so?"

The prince said nothing for a long moment, then shook his head. "It is a remarkable thing you do, Edith Cavell."

"I leave remarkable for the Lord, Your Highness," Edith demurred, mirroring his shake of the head. "And were I truly so noble, I might have encouraged more temperance in my manner, and that of my staff."

Prince Reginald chuckled. "Ah, yes, I did catch your young Pauline sticking her tongue out at the German inspector as she was moving items out of the Institute. He never caught her, of course, but the show of spirit was fine indeed."

Edith's exasperated sigh was touched with amusement. "Yes, Pauline has her own opinions about matters, and she does not hesitate to portray them. Perhaps I ought to have curbed such, but we do so adore Belgium."

"That we do, Matron." He offered a soft, knowing smile, and there was, perhaps, a touch of pity in its curve.

Edith did not mind. The prince was a good man and had given much in the service of Belgium and resisting the occupation of the Germans. That he was also a man of influence and means had perhaps added to his inclination to get involved with such work, but it also meant he had the ability to control some of his destiny. He could leave in anticipation of arrest, he did not have the same responsibilities to tie him in place, and he had connections in a vast array of places that could give him aid.

Where would Edith have found any of that, should she have also wished to flee?

But she did not wish to flee.

She would simply carry on as she had been doing, preparing her nurses and probationers for the world that awaited them, for the war they were in, and for the future of the profession. She would continue to guide the movement of furniture and supplies from their present lodgings to the new clinic. She would help those who came to her in need.

She heard a low laugh and glanced at the prince, uncertain when her attention had fallen from him to the carpet beside his chair.

His smile was far warmer now than it had been a moment ago.

"What?" Edith asked him, smiling a little herself.

He shook his head. "You will leave remarkable for the Lord, but I think you misinterpret how He brings about remarkable things. He must have the marvelous hands of mortals to do His work, and I think there could be no more capable hands than your own."

Edith felt her cheeks warm and swallowed the discomfort she felt by the praise. "Thank you" was all she could manage to say.

The prince waited a moment more, almost as though he anticipated further resistance from her, demurrals or arguments, something to give him additional cause to praise her further.

But she did not, so he could not.

When it was clear the conversation, such as it was, had ended, Prince Reginald rose. "I think I must bid you farewell, then, Edith Cavell."

Edith pushed to her feet. "I suppose you must. I pray that the Lord will see you and your sister safely away before all else collapses around us."

"Oh, Marie is not coming with me," the prince said quickly with a shake of his head. "She insists her place is here, and she will make a stand."

"She cannot," Edith protested, eyes going wide. "She cannot think she will escape this."

He shrugged his narrow shoulders. "I have made the same arguments, but nevertheless . . ." He took her hand in his and held it firm. "Goodbye, Edith. God bless you."

"And you," she murmured. She forced a swallow, as uncomfortable with farewells now as she had ever been. "May His grace and mercy be upon you all the days of your life."

The prince inclined his head. "Thank you, Matron." He gave her a final, tight smile and then moved past her out of the office and down the hall.

She did not follow him. The prince knew his way around the clinic well enough and would not expect her to stand on ceremony or formalities.

That was it, then.

Philippe was arrested, Louise was arrested, Ada was arrested, and the prince was fleeing. Others would undoubtedly follow his example when given the warning. But how many would be like his sister and choose to remain? How many, like her, did not have much of a choice to make? How many of them were truly in danger? How much was known by the Germans?

So many questions prickled at the edges of her mind, taunting her and testing her determination to rise above anxiety and fear. It would be easy to dwell on the possibilities that lay before her, each as dark and unhelpful as another, or to fret over imagined scenarios and plan her defense for when the time came. But she had no desire to curl up in her bed and wait for the end to come, whenever and wherever it may.

There was far too much work to be done for that.

Gaston Quien was back in Brussels. Edith had allowed him to stay at the clinic for a night, which could have been a mistake, but nothing dreadful had come from it. Pauline had seen him just the other day while out walking, and he had invited her and the cook's daughter to the café for drinks.

They had gone, of course, being the silly young girls that they were, but when Pauline had reported back to Edith that night, her eyes had been wide with uncertainty and fear. Mr. Quien had bought them drinks and flirted with them, and then had asked if Edith would get his friends to the frontier.

It was not that peculiar a question, considering they had helped Mr. Quien to the frontier once, but asking it in a café where there were German soldiers in attendance had not sat well with Pauline, and it did not sit well with Edith.

Mr. Quien had not been back to the clinic, which had been a sad thing for some of the nurses to accept, though Edith was grateful to have the distraction removed from their lives and had reminded her girls of the same.

Then there was the move to consider. They had done a great deal of work in recent days, moving some of the furniture and equipment to the new clinic. Some of the senior staff had begun setting up the lodgings and ensuring all would be in readiness. But there was still so much to move over, and, while trying to maintain their patients' care, as well as Edith's other activities, it was becoming quite the project.

She could hardly believe the new clinic was actually ready for them after having worked toward it with Dr. Depage for so many years. It spoke to the dedication they had both given to their professions and to the rise of the medical profession in Belgium. They would no longer be crammed into rows of houses and forced to transform a space into an environment appropriate for medical work. All would be at their disposal, and they would make their mark on the community of Brussels.

What remained of it, anyway.

And beyond that . . .

Well, she still had soldiers to deal with. The last of her most recent group would depart tonight, and God willing, she would not receive any more. Perhaps when they were settled into their new clinic she might renew her secret role, but for now, it was time to rest from such labors and return her focus to the training and education of her nursing staff.

She hoped such a respite would allow her heart to feel at ease once more. She had such pains from time to time, and she had done her utmost to keep such instances from the notice of her staff. Thus far, no one had seen her struggle or grimace in pain. Weary from her work, yes. Overwhelmed from all she did and endured, yes.

But in physical pain? Never.

Edith allowed herself a slow exhale, forcing the anxious air in her lungs to depart and then bringing in fresh, new air that might give her renewed strength.

Though she was concerned about the possibility of arrest, there was also a centering feeling of calm. Something without words and without explanation. It did not change her circumstances, nor the risks, but it kept her from despair, and that seemed quite enough.

"Matron?"

Edith turned with a smile to the young Belgian nurse standing in the doorway of her office. "Yes, Helen?"

Helen Wegels bobbed slightly. "Matron, there are three soldiers in the front room wishing to speak with you."

A sharp flash of heat lit her chest. "German?"

Helen shook her head. "No, Matron. They said they were English."

Edith's brows shot up. English? And they were calling on the clinic as though it were no more than a social visit? It was the middle of the day; it could put them all in danger. But perhaps they were French or Belgian and thought they might have more luck with staying at the clinic if they claimed to be English.

In a world where neighbor had turned against neighbor, and sometimes brother against brother, it was not too unreasonable a thought.

But she could not take on more guests now. Not yet.

She nodded at Helen and gestured for her to lead the way. Though Edith did not need her to walk the route with her, there was great comfort in having another person beside her, even if that person could not possibly comprehend Edith's turmoil.

"Thank you, Helen," Edith murmured when they reached the front room. "Return to your work, please."

The girl bobbed quickly and moved on.

Edith watched her go, swallowing her reservations and her sudden tension. She would not have more of her staff involved in these discussions and work than absolutely necessary, and the fewer faces the soldiers could recognize, the better.

When she could no longer hear Helen's footsteps, Edith entered the front room, pasting a polite smile on her face. "How can I help you, gentlemen?"

Three young and able soldiers rose from chairs, inclining their heads.

"Ma'am," the tallest of the group said. "We are English soldiers in need of hiding. We have heard that this may be a safe place for us. Might we take refuge here?"

Something about the careful cadence of his words sent a wordless warning into Edith's mind, a feeling that the man was no more English than she was German, though his accent was rather good. But a lifetime around Englishmen had taught her ears to recognize their natural way of speaking, and this was not it.

"I am so sorry," she told the three as a whole. "We are moving to new premises across town and are in no position to take in new guests. Perhaps you might call upon the chemist in town, Louis Séverin. He may be able to assist."

There was a pause as her words sunk in, and then the tall one smiled. "Thank you, ma'am. We will inquire of him."

The men nodded again and left both the room and the clinic in an eerily orderly fashion. Almost as though they were still marching in the ranks of their fellow soldiers rather than trying to escape to safety.

Curious.

But she had done her duty by giving them an alternative and a warm smile, and now she need not think on them more.

She set about her work, tending to patients on the ward and overseeing the work of her probationers and nurses. Then, of course, she went to see to the soldiers still remaining in her care. They were a good sort—quiet, obedient to her strict rules, and unfailingly grateful for the risks and care being taken.

Perhaps she should not have sent the other soldiers away. Who was she to judge them for claiming to be English when they could not have been, and to then mistrust them for such a claim? Would she wish to be judged on such superficial terms? She was, after all, an English nurse, and she had been forced to work twice as hard to prove herself worthy of trust by the locals when she had first arrived.

In truth, she ought to be ashamed of herself.

She returned to her office to engage in repentant prayer when Lizzie suddenly burst in. "Edith! A German officer is here. He wants to speak with us."

Edith bit the inside of her lip, feeling oddly calm. "Very well. See that he is brought in here."

Lizzie's eyes widened, panic evident. "Truly?"

"Truly." Edith gave her a soft nod. "Our guests are safe and quiet and will soon be gone. It will be well."

A crease appeared in Lizzie's brow. "Edith, Mr. Séverin has been arrested. Jose just returned from his errands and told me. It took place not half an hour ago."

That froze Edith's heart, and she placed her hands on the surface of her desk for stability. "God forgive me," she whispered, the knuckles of her hands turning white. "I have done this to him."

"What? How could you have?"

Edith shook her head, taking a breath and looking up at her. There was no time to mourn the consequences of her actions, however innocently taken. "Never mind. Bring the officer here, please. Quietly."

Lizzie pressed her lips together in a firm line, giving one clipped nod before turning from the room.

"The Lord is my shepherd," Edith whispered to herself. "I shall not want . . ."

She had nearly finished the entire psalm before Lizzie returned with the officer, which gave Edith enough composure to manage the interview.

The officer gave her a cold look as he entered, his hair slicked back, hat under one arm. "Matron."

She inclined her head, eyeing his uniform. "Captain. How can I assist you this evening?"

He sniffed a humorless laugh. "You could get out of my way, that would help a great deal. The governor sends his regards. He would have come himself, but he was bored by the prospect." He set his hat down and looked about the office before settling his eyes on Lizzie. "Have you received any correspondence from the British War Office, mademoiselle?"

"The War Office?" Lizzie repeated in confusion. "No. Never. Why should we?"

"Why, indeed," he answered, sniffing again.

Lizzie looked at Edith, agitated, and twisted her fingers together. "We have not, sir, I can assure you. We are not associated with the War Office in the least. We are a Red Cross establishment and know no particular nationality."

He waved a dismissive hand. "Yes, I know all the official lines, mademoiselle. You need not recite them to me like a schoolgirl."

Lizzie clamped down on her lips with a small whimper, gripping her fingers so tightly her knuckles turned white.

He looked at Edith. "I have questions for you, Matron. It would serve you well to answer them."

"Of course, Captain," Edith returned with all due deference. "I shall endeavor to do so."

For the next hour and beyond, he walked about the office almost aimlessly, his eyes never resting in one place long, and asked endless questions of them. How the clinic was run, what patients they were seeing, how they determined which probationers to accept, what their capacity for patients was, how many soldiers they had seen since the war had begun. On and on and on, every question that could possibly be thought of, he asked. Some were for Edith, others were for Lizzie, and with each question and each clipped response to their answers, Lizzie shook further.

Edith did not believe she would confess to their secret activities, but she did worry for a moment or two that her poor friend would collapse in a wash of tears.

That would not help their case at all. It was clear this officer had no sympathy or pity for them.

"The account books," he suddenly ordered, spearing Edith with a dark look. "Let me see them."

Surprised he had not asked to see them before, Edith obliged by producing the books and laying them out on the desk. She opened the pages to April of the previous year; she made no effort to turn to the most recent entries.

If he noticed, he gave no indication.

He looked at the dates and began flipping each page, one at a time, his eyes tracking down each and every column. The closer he got to the present day, the more intent his focus became. He said nothing to her or to Lizzie, gave no hint of what he was looking for or any insights he might have gleaned. He simply read as though it was some novel he had yet to finish.

He paused, cocking his head as his finger ran down the page. "Have you, by chance, another ledger of accounts, Matron?" he inquired with all the mildness one might have used to discuss the weather.

"No, Captain," Edith replied easily.

His eyes raised from the page and met hers. He smiled wryly. "No entries for three months, then?"

Edith's heart skipped a beat, and she swallowed. "So it would seem."

He returned his attention to the page. "What a way to manage business." He turned the rest of the pages, which were blank, and then closed the book and straightened. "I have seen enough. Kindly show me out, Matron, and I will leave you in peace."

"Of course, Captain."

She opened her office door and strode out, keeping her pace slow and even. He followed without any urgency or speed, apparently quite at his leisure.

What it must feel like to belong to the party in power, able to do as he liked without deference to anyone else? To terrify and intimidate the already oppressed simply by being present. To survey cowering figures without emotion beyond superiority.

There was nothing she would not do to end their reign of power. Nothing.

The realization tightened her jaw, and she stopped at the front door, gesturing with all the politeness she could manage. "Thank you for your attention, Captain."

He seemed to laugh and inclined his head. "My pleasure, Matron. Good evening." He left, and Edith closed the door firmly behind him.

There was silence for the space of four heartbeats, and then she heard a series of sniffles, whimpers, and sighs from various quarters of the house.

Edith looked around in surprise and noted several of the nurses and probationers appearing, each looking more distressed than the next. Lizzie came down the hallway from Edith's office, tears rolling slowly down her cheeks.

Only now, looking each of her nurses in their faces and seeing their eyes, could Edith fully appreciate the terrible strain each of them had been under for so many months now. Lizzie, in particular, who was not only Edith's assistant matron, bearing the entirety of the weight of education and training, as well as patient care, but who also knew the details of what Edith was engaged in and assisting her in it, knowing they could be arrested at any moment for such things.

Edith opened her arms, and two nurses rushed to her, reaching for the comfort she could offer. She held the distraught girls close, offering a consoling smile to the ones she could not reach, praying it would be enough.

"It is all right, my dears," she told them, using the warm, motherly tone she employed when she was called upon to comfort them individually. "All is well now, you see?"

But her words seemed to lack power, and there was no comfort to be found in them.

She could only sigh and walk with her girls to the dining room for supper. It would be another meal of carrots, thin soup, and bread that tasted like sawdust, but it was better than having nothing at all.

If only just.

Once in her position at the table, and all of her nurses in theirs, she smiled at them, and, as one, they lowered their heads.

"Almighty God, who has given us grace at this time with one accord to make our common supplications unto thee . . ."

CHAPTER 19

"Load up that wagon, if you please, and be quick about it! There are several other loads we need to take over, and the more time we waste, the longer it will take!"

"Yes, Sister Wilkins."

Lizzie did not enjoy being the hard taskmaster, but someone had to ensure that the move went smoothly and that all of the essential items made their way to the new clinic without incident. And it seemed that the nurses and staff were not entirely motivated to engage in such manual labor.

She could not blame them, all things considered. It was the middle of the afternoon and desperately hot, especially for a summer day in Belgium. Everyone was perspiring heavily, fatigued from hard work, and somehow there was still so much to do. It felt as though they were never going to finish the move, never get to the new clinic, and never be able to start over, as Lizzie had so hoped they would.

That was what the new clinic represented—growth, improvement, respect, renewal, and a firm stamp upon the community that had been hard-won by Edith and Dr. Depage. More than that, it was a glimmer of hope in this war-darkened world.

Yes, the Germans would still be in power when the move was complete, and yes, the Belgians were still being oppressed, but the nurses would be capable of so much more care and treatment at this new clinic. They would be better equipped to tend to the sick and the injured, as well as establish promising careers for themselves.

And perhaps Edith might be able to put the terrifying secret work to rest for good.

She had yet to have that conversation with the matron, but she hoped and prayed Edith would agree with her. After all, the last of their soldiers had gotten away last night, and there were no new ones arriving to take their place. With the move at hand, she doubted there would be more coming for some time.

Perhaps she ought to allow the move to take a trifle longer than expected to keep them all safe from such guests.

The moment she had the thought, a dreadful feeling of guilt rose within her. Of course, if another weary, war-torn soldier appeared at their door in need of tending, they would take him in, return him to health, and then deliver him to the safest place they could to protect him from the Germans.

They could not, and would not, turn one away.

But if they could avoid an entire group of such soldiers arriving all at once . . .

"We would like to look at the furniture, please," a heavily accented deep voice asked from behind Lizzie.

She turned with a smile, nodding at the three burly men approaching. "Of course! There are several pieces in front of the house, and quite a few within. What are you looking for in particular?"

The man in the center of the group curved his mouth in the

slightest smile. "A very great deal, mademoiselle." He suddenly pulled out a revolver and held it to her head.

Lizzie barely had time to gasp, her hands flying up in a gesture of surrender. "Please—take the furniture you want!"

"I am not here for tables and chairs," he growled. "Move." He pressed the tip of the gun harder against her, pushing in the direction he wished her to go. "Inside."

Lizzie nodded shakily, doing as he ordered. He gripped her arm and walked with her, the motions rough and jerky. Lizzie was grateful the other nurses had already gone inside to get more things for their borrowed wagon. No one else should have to have a gun pointed at their head.

Her captor forced her into a side room, holding his gun on her while the other two moved elsewhere in the house.

"Find her," the one with the gun ordered. "Bring her out!"

Lizzie swallowed hard. He could only mean Edith, and she would not be difficult to find.

This was the end of it, then.

"Sister Wilkins," a young voice called, "where would you like—?"

"Get over there," the gunman barked, overriding whatever Mania had been trying to ask, jiggling his gun to emphasize the severity of the situation.

Mania shrieked and started for the door, but the man quickly grabbed her arm, setting the gun to her brow.

"What did I say?" he demanded, hauling her back in and forcing her to stand by Lizzie. "Stay there!"

Lizzie took Mania's hand, holding her close to her side. "It's all right," she whispered, though her voice wavered. "We'll just do as he says."

Mania gave a jerky nod, burying her face in Lizzie's arm.

"Was that Mania I heard?" one of the English nurses asked from the hallway. "Have you seen a mouse, Mania?"

The nurse appeared in the doorway to the room and was quickly herded over to join Lizzie and Mania. Though she was more defiant than Mania had been, she also trembled from head to toe as she stood on Lizzie's other side.

Beatrice was next to join them, followed by Jacqueline, Helen, and another young woman. They outnumbered the man, it was true, but he was a German, and therefore held more power than just the gun in his hand. Any act of resistance or rebellion would be met with significant consequences for them all, and she would not wish for any harm to fall upon the heads of those in the room with her or the others within the building.

She could not risk it.

"Don't move!" the gunman bellowed, slowly panning the gun so it pointed at each of them in a menacing turn.

They stood there for what seemed an age, the sniffles and whimpers of the nurses huddled around Lizzie filling the room, and the sound of someone wailing in a nearby hallway echoing throughout the house. Pauline, Lizzie presumed. She must have somehow seen the gunman wrangle the other girls into the room and frozen down the corridor.

It was torment, this waiting.

Lizzie pulled her hands free of the others, her heart pounding in her throat, and inched toward the door.

She would never be able to wrestle the gun from their captor, and she would be foolish to try to handle such a thing, but if she could escape, perhaps she could find someone to help them.

She darted for the doorway, but he caught her arm before she could pass him. Rather than toss her back with the rest, he held her close, his eyes narrowing.

"You want to leave, do you? Well, there is an errand you can do, if you're a good girl."

Lizzie managed a swallow through a parched and scratching throat. "What is it?"

He chuckled darkly. "Go pack a bag for your mistress. She'll be needing some things. Do you think you can manage that?"

It was not an escape, but it was a chance to leave this room and, perhaps, find a way to help Edith.

She would take it.

"Yes," she whispered.

He raised a brow. "If you do not come right back here with that bag, mademoiselle, one of your darlings here will gain a bullet. Do you understand?"

Someone behind her made a sound of distress, and Lizzie nodded, her stomach tightening. "I understand, sir."

"Good. Go." He released her arm, shoving her toward the hallway.

Lizzie stumbled but managed to stay upright. She moved quickly down the corridor to Pauline, cupping her cheeks and kissing her brow. "It's all right. Stay here and stay quiet, and you will be safe."

Pauline nodded quickly, burying her face in her hands with a fresh set of cries, some of which, Lizzie hoped, were for effect.

Lizzie moved further down the hall, hurrying toward Edith's rooms. If the Germans had not found her yet, perhaps she was not so easy to find.

"Please be hard to find," Lizzie whispered to the not-quite-silent house.

The house had no response for her.

She was quick in Edith's rooms, her mind spinning in several directions. If Edith was being targeted, she would likely be taken in for questioning, perhaps held overnight, due to the lateness of the hour.

But she would certainly not be gone longer than three days at most. No one ever was when no blame could be found.

If she was arrested, however . . .

Lizzie shook her head, dismissing the thought. She would not allow herself to go there. They had been careful and cautious, and the matron had taken every precaution possible.

All would be well. It had to be.

Once she had the bag packed, she left Edith's rooms, anxious to find the matron herself before she would have to return to the side room with the other nurses. Lizzie could not bear the thought of putting them all in danger, but neither could she abandon Edith without attempting to intercede.

She did not have to look long.

She heard sounds of scuffling from a nearby corridor, and Lizzie hurried forward, afraid for what she might see and steeling herself against the pain it would cause. She rounded a corner and saw the two other men from the street, each of them with a hand on Edith's arm, and Edith standing rather calmly between the pair of them.

It was a chilling sight.

"Edith!" Lizzie cried, unable to help herself.

Edith turned toward her, a soft smile on her lips. "It's all right, Lizzie."

One of the men saw the bag in Lizzie's hand and nudged his head toward the corridor. "You first. Go."

Swallowing hard, Lizzie nodded and led the strange procession down to the room where the gunman waited. Her heart pounded in her throat, ears, and fingertips.

"We found her!" one of them shouted as they approached the room. "She was in the upstairs pantry, arranging flowers!"

The gunman gave a dark laugh. "What a waste!" came the called response.

Lizzie shivered at the gunman's tone, and she could hear the sniffling from the room. A pained whimper came from her right, and she glanced over to see Pauline, who was looking up at Edith in agony as the matron was led down the hall.

"Matron!" at least three of the nurses called as Lizzie and Edith reached the doorway to the room. "No! Matron!" Their cries became less clear, muddling together in their distress.

Edith looked at them all as a fond mother leaving on a voyage might have done. "Don't be so sad, my dears. Everything will be all right. I'll be back soon."

The nurses looked back with disbelief in their tear-filled eyes, but Edith held her head high, no sign of tears or sadness, no fear or trembling.

That alone brought slight smiles to a few faces, though it did nothing for the tears.

"Let's go," the gunman said, gesturing toward the front door. He looked at Lizzie coldly. "You, too."

"Is that necessary?" Edith asked, shifting her attention from the nurses to him.

He snorted softly. "If it was not, I would not be bringing her. Now stop talking. You'll be talking plenty later." Again, he gestured toward the door, and the men roughly hauled Edith along.

Lizzie bit her lip and followed, looking at the nurses and wishing she had the same calm Edith had managed. They returned her look with trembling lips and tear-stained cheeks.

There was no time to discuss anything or make any true farewells.

The gunman took Lizzie's arm, but without the same force as before, perhaps sensing that she would be obedient now that Edith was captured.

Two cars waited near the front of the house, something Lizzie had not seen before in her work of packing up for the move. Edith was taken to the first car and forced in, though she made no move of resistance at all. It seemed to amuse her captors to treat her roughly.

It was a disgusting sort of cruelty.

Thankfully, Lizzie was not manhandled as she was settled into the second car. To her surprise, the guard did not accompany her, leaving her alone with the waiting driver in the car.

Jack came from the house, howling pitifully after his mistress, and Pauline followed him, inconsolable and sobbing hysterically.

The cars started to pull away, and Pauline immediately began chasing after them, calling out wordlessly. One of the German guards caught up to her and grabbed her arm, pulling her back.

Lizzie swallowed her own wash of tears as she watched Pauline reach out for the cars with her hands despite her restraints.

She turned to face forward, closing her eyes as the car continued to move away from the clinic and further into the city. She had no doubt that Edith would be asked many questions, some of them very specific. But what questions would they have for Lizzie? What part did they believe she played? How much did they think she knew?

"Pardon me," Lizzie asked her driver in a small voice. "Where are you taking us?"

"Headquarters," he grunted. "The Kommandantur." He did not elaborate.

Was Lizzie supposed to know where that was? Were they going to the police headquarters or the office of the military authorities? Was there a specific group of individuals assigned to uncover the works of the matron and the others, or was this simply something that the authorities had taken an interest in? Was this some vindictive order of Governor von Lüttwitz, or were there others involved?

The car turned several times, and it was a moment before Lizzie realized they were being taken to the Rue de Berlaimont. That was encouraging as no one was ever held there for long. And yet there was something about the façade of the place that sent a chill through her, despite the brief glimmer of hope she felt.

Lizzie was taken from the car and led into the building, Edith ahead of her with another guard. For a moment, she had the faintest hope they might be questioned together, but then the guards took Edith down one hall and Lizzie down another.

There would be no shared questioning, then.

Lizzie would be on her own.

CHAPTER 20

Lizzie was taken to a small room with only a table, a set of chairs, and a narrow window high on one wall that let in a sliver of light. The guard indicated that she sit on the far side of the table, which Lizzie did.

She opened her mouth to ask a question, but he left the room before she could manage the air to produce a single word.

She was left alone for perhaps twenty minutes, if she was any judge of the passage of time, and then a uniformed officer entered the room. His face was familiar, but his name eluded her.

"Miss Wilkins, my name is Lieutenant Bergan," he began, pulling out the other chair and sitting down. "Perhaps you remember me."

"Of course," Lizzie replied, though she could not say where or how she knew his face.

Something about her response made his mouth curve in a slight smile. "Thank you for coming in today."

Lizzie raised a brow. "I was not aware I had a choice in the matter."

His eyes met hers. "True, but you are here nevertheless."

"So I am."

They stared at each other for a moment, the lieutenant watching Lizzie as though she were about to confess something, and Lizzie wondering what the man wanted to hear.

Regardless of his wishes, she was determined to disappoint him.

She would give him nothing with which to hang her, and nothing to help his case against the matron either. She knew full well where her loyalties lay, and she would go to her grave keeping them.

Another long moment of silence passed, and then the lieutenant cleared his throat. "Now, then. To business." He folded his hands across the table and leaned forward a little. "This will all go very quickly if you tell the truth. Have you been harboring enemy soldiers at the Berkendael Medical Institute?"

"No," Lizzie said simply. "None."

Lieutenant Bergan frowned, his brow creasing slightly. "Miss Wilkins, I am not a fool. How many soldiers have you been hiding in your clinic in the last few months? Twenty? Forty? Seventy?"

"None, sir."

"You were part of the organization that has been secreting enemies of Germany and getting them out of Belgium!"

"No, I was not."

The lieutenant's smile turned into a sneer. "We know what has been going on, Miss Wilkins. We know there have been soldiers at the Institute. You might as well admit you were harboring them."

Lizzie shook her head. "I cannot admit what I do not know, sir."

He snorted a soft laugh. "I've already told you what *we* know, Miss Wilkins. We've had Quien and Jacobs in your clinic, passing through as soldiers, and they have reported everything to us. Your confession will not be telling us anything we do not already know."

The temptation to curse the names of both men rose up in Lizzie, but she forced her expression to remain calm. She furrowed her brow as though confused. "I am afraid I do not know either of those men, Lieutenant. What are they claiming?"

Her answer did not meet with Lieutenant Bergan's approval, and he was not shy in letting her know it. The questions continued, each one along the same vein but rephrased in an attempt to prompt her confession. The lieutenant grew more and more impatient, which gave Lizzie an added measure of courage to continue disappointing him. They could not arrest her for something they could not prove, after all.

And she would give them nothing to prove.

She did not know Quien and Jacobs. She did not know anything about young men in the school. She did not know anything about forgeries, guides, soldiers, or border crossings. She was simply a nurse who tended to her patients and oversaw a good deal of the education of their nurses and probationers. That was all.

Finally, Lieutenant Bergan, both his uniform and composure in disarray, threw his hands up and left the room, slamming the door behind him.

Lizzie sat back in her chair, trying not to laugh. Of course, there was nothing humorous in the situation, but she had succeeded in giving the man nothing, and surely that was something to take delight in.

What exactly would transpire next, she dared not hazard a guess, having never been in such a situation before. She had been questioned before, it was true, but that had not been so pointed and direct as this.

No doubt the lieutenant had gone to get a superior officer to take over or assist. Or perhaps he would bring in a more intimidating figure of a man to frighten her. Perhaps he was going to let her sit a while and overthink herself into a frenzy, leading to a confession.

So long as they would not resort to some heinous form of torture, she would be able to maintain her denials.

Were their suspicions about her significant enough to warrant the use of pain as a motivator? She could not be sure, but the idea was an unpleasant one. Lieutenant Bergan clearly suspected she was part of the organization the matron was engaged in, but nowhere in his questioning had he given any indication as to what he suspected Lizzie's role to be.

Which told Lizzie that he did not know. Likely they were assuming her position as the assistant matron would have put her in a position to act in a similar capacity to Edith in all things, not just with educating the nurses and maintaining the clinic. They thought she would also be Edith's right hand in moving soldiers here and there.

How unfortunate, then, that Edith should have kept the involvement of anyone else in such activities to a minimum.

Lizzie's thoughts turned to Edith, and her heart ached. She had been questioned for hours and had said nothing. But what was Edith enduring in her interview? Were the questions just as leading? Was she being threatened? How was she holding up under the strain of it all?

The matron had been so calm when they had been taken out of the clinic, but Lizzie had seen the toll that all of this had been taking on her as the weeks had gone on. Edith was not as young as she had once been and her strength not as endless. She would never admit such a thing, even to Lizzie, but it had begun to show.

There was no telling what information they had with regards to Edith, or what sort of trouble she might be in with the authorities. For all of Lizzie's success with disappointing her interrogator, it might not be so simple for Edith. If the Germans had compelling evidence, denials would be difficult.

And Edith was unfailingly honest in her dealings with her fellow man. Would that affect her situation now?

Lizzie bowed her head and murmured a soft word of prayer on behalf of Edith, asking for strength to buoy her up and comfort to fill her heart.

The door to the room opened, and Lizzie straightened, anticipating another round of questions she would have to refute. But the officer only scowled and waved for her to follow him.

"You are free to go."

Lizzie blinked. "I'm what?"

He gestured firmly, not bothering to repeat himself.

She would not wait for him to change his mind. She leapt to her feet and followed him, hurrying down the corridor and keeping right at his heels.

Why would they release her? She had not given them anything, but then they had not asked her any questions about Edith or her activities. The questions had almost solely been about Lizzie and her involvement with things, nothing about what she had witnessed Edith say or do.

It would not have changed the disappointment of the lieutenant and his cohorts where her answers were concerned, but it was curious that they had not ventured there.

And now she was able to return home? Just like that? Surely it could not be so simple.

But no one was stopping them. No one gave the soldier questioning looks, and no one looked at Lizzie at all. She might simply have been touring the headquarters for pleasure instead of being there against her will.

They reached the front of the building, and the soldier indicated the door with a bare flick of his fingers.

"Thank you," Lizzie told him as she hurried toward the door.

He made no reply.

There was a car waiting to return her to the clinic, and she was not about to question it.

It was after sundown when she reached the clinic, and the toll of the day's events finally caught up to her. She felt weak and ill, almost shaking with fatigue. She was quite certain she would need a full day in bed, if not two, before she felt herself again. Whatever courage had aided her in the interrogation had fled on the drive home.

She entered the clinic with a heaving sigh and was met almost at once by a barking, bouncing Jack. The warmth of his greeting was astonishing, and Lizzie took a moment to stoop and stroke him, praising him softly for his attentions. An armed guard stood just inside the door, watching her interaction with Jack without emotion.

"Sister Wilkins!" a cheerful voice shouted. "You're back!"

The call seemed to reverberate throughout the clinic, and nurses began to appear from all quarters, swarming Lizzie with hugs and reaching for her hands while asking questions and welcoming her. The sound was like waves crashing into shore. Tears were on several faces, and Lizzie tried to spread warmth and comfort in return, but found she had none to give.

She had nothing to give.

Her knees shook and suddenly gave out, sending her to the floor, though her descent was gentled by the several hands clinging to her.

"What happened, Sister Wilkins?" one of the nurses asked.

"Did they ask you lots of questions?"

"Does this mean the guard they left here can go?"

"Were they abominable to you?"

"Why were you released?"

"I don't know," Lizzie whispered, managing an answer for that question only. "I don't know why I was released."

"When is the matron coming home?"

Cold enveloped Lizzie, more than she had ever known in her life, and she slowly looked at the young nurse who had spoken, the motion agonizing. "What?"

The girl seemed surprised to need to repeat herself. "When is the matron coming home?"

Lizzie wet her suddenly parched lips. "She . . . she has not returned?"

Several heads shook, some of them quite somberly.

Sister Taylor crouched before Lizzie, taking her hands. "You did not see her, then?"

"No," Lizzie murmured. "They took us to separate rooms. I don't . . . I don't know anything about her being held there or her release. I don't know anything."

"But she *is* coming back, right?" someone else asked.

Hot tears burned in Lizzie's eyes, and she shook her head. Her chest tightened as though death itself were clutching her heart. "I don't know," she managed to say. "I don't know."

She was beyond words after that, and, for quite a while, the lot of them sat there together, crying softly and waiting for their matron to come back to them.

Eventually, the guard cleared his throat. "Your matron has been detained. She will not return tonight."

The words sounded as a death knell, and, with more tears and sobs than before, each of them went to bed, though sleep was not likely to greet them there.

CHAPTER 21

Edith had been at the St. Gilles prison for a full day now, having been taken there after two days at the Kommandantur, but as of yet, no one was asking her a great many questions.

She could only hope that Lizzie had been treated well and released quickly. She could not bear it if Lizzie had been brought to this prison as well, enduring questioning that she would not be able to answer fully or possibly incriminating herself by inadvertently admitting to something that would sound more troublesome than it was. Lizzie had not been as involved in the process of hiding and shuttling soldiers as Edith had, not by half, and Edith would move heaven and earth to see that her friend and assistant would be released free from condemnation or suspicion.

But she had seen no one except her guards, let alone anyone she knew. Not even Governor von Lüttwitz, who, she would have thought, would have taken great pleasure at witnessing her in prison. Perhaps it was beneath him, though she had no doubt he would be gloating aplenty over his victory.

Now she was being walked out of the imposing St. Gilles prison with no indication of where she was being taken or for what purpose. She knew she was under arrest—that much was clear. She knew the Germans had questions for her. That was also rather evident. But otherwise, nothing monumental was taking place.

The building was an impressive relic of centuries gone by, a fortress sitting proudly among the growing and changing city around it. She ought to have known this would be her final destination. Whatever information the Germans had about her activities, it was enough to warrant detaining her indefinitely. No one was taken to St. Gilles for a short stay.

Was this what the others had endured with their arrests— Philippe and Louise, Ada and Mr. Séverin, and who knew how many others at this point? She had heard nothing while she had been here; it was entirely possible others had been arrested after she had.

It was all over, then. Or close to it. The end of their small but very great resistance.

She had no regrets in engaging in the endeavor. She would stand by her actions, come what may. She had the calm, peaceful assurance in her heart that she had done right, and that meant more to her than anything else.

Edith smiled softly to herself as she was placed in another car, loving the sight of Brussels in the morning light. Brief glimpse though it was, the daylight was a welcome refreshment after her days in the Kommandantur and the first night in her cell.

It did not take long after the car pulled away for her to know where she was being taken.

Back to the Kommandantur.

She was due to be questioned, it seemed.

She felt a brief flutter of nerves in the pit of her stomach that she was unprepared for, but she managed to take a few slow breaths, which seemed to settle her.

She would not give them names of others involved. Would not be the cause for someone else to be arrested. She knew full well what she had done, and she would not attempt to deny it.

This was not about her, after all. This was about fighting oppression, helping her fellow man, and furthering the work she felt called to do. She would have treated any of the prisoners in St. Gilles without a second thought. She would have extended the same courtesy to the men who had arrested her and those who would shortly question her. She would have continued to treat wounded soldiers, regardless of nationality, and seen each of them restored to health and activity, whatever that happened to be.

It was simply who she was.

The fact that she had defied the present authorities by expressly going against their orders was only her expression of standing by the correct principles with which she had governed her life.

There was nothing to be ashamed of in that.

Guards were waiting outside the Kommandantur as she was helped from the car, not as roughly as she had been handled in recent days. She would not go so far as to think it was respect or politeness, but perhaps her guards had been instructed not to raise indignation in her prior to her questioning. That would be more aligned with the authorities she knew, and if that was what they had wished and planned for, they would be sorely disappointed.

Edith had been indignant from the day the Germans marched into Belgium, but she had always known better than to publicly display it.

Which was why she had done the things she had in the manner in which she had.

She was led down a familiar hallway and taken to a small room. Rather than being left alone, however, this time there were already men waiting for her. Four, to be precise, though she recognized only one.

"Sergeant Mayer," Edith greeted with a nod.

His smile was more of a snarl. "Miss Cavell."

"Will Governor von Lüttwitz be joining us today?" she asked him, her tone innocent.

He snorted softly. "Of course not. He has more important things to do than question a prisoner."

"Of course." She looked at the others, wondering if she would receive introductions to them.

The tallest one gestured for her to sit, smiling as though this were simply an afternoon tea together. "*Setzen Sie sich bitte?*"

Edith pointed to the chair, and the tall man nodded. He began speaking rapidly in German, and Edith fought to catch a single word.

Thankfully, another man in the room began translating almost immediately. "Miss Cavell, I am Lieutenant Bergan, head of espionage. This is the chief officer of criminal investigation, Sergeant Pinkhoff. He will be translating my questions into French for you, as I understand your German is limited."

"That is correct, sir." Edith gave a nod to the other sergeant. "Thank you for translating, Sergeant."

Sergeant Pinkhoff seemed bemused by her thanks. "Mademoiselle."

"That," Lieutenant Bergan went on, as translated by Pinkhoff, "is Sergeant Neuhaus, who will record the proceedings today. And our operative, Otto Mayer, you already know."

"I do, yes," Edith confirmed, finally taking the seat indicated for her. She dipped her chin in a demure nod. "Please, proceed as you see fit."

The four men in the room looked at each other, then moved into position. Neuhaus sat at the far end of the table, papers and pen at hand. Bergan and Pinkhoff stood directly across from Edith. Mayer stayed in the corner of the room, apparently only there for entertainment.

Lovely.

"Have you been treated well since you've been brought here, Miss Cavell?" Bergan asked her through Pinkhoff. "Have you been made aware of the facilities at the canteen?"

Edith smiled without irony. "Yes, I have been treated very well, thank you. Everyone has been very gracious, all things considered. And yes, I was made aware of those facilities from almost the first moment. This is an excellent establishment, sirs. You are to be commended."

Bergan nodded when the translation from Pinkhoff came through. "*Sehr gut*," he grunted, which happened to be some of the German that Edith knew.

But if he was trying to make an effort for her behalf, it faded at once.

"We have a few questions for you," Bergan said through Pinkhoff. "Everyone has confessed already, so the only thing for you to do is confess also. Everything we wish to know from you we already know from others."

If that was the case, why were they asking her questions at all? Still, Edith gave him a slow nod of understanding.

"Did you receive the amount of five thousand francs from the hands of Prince Reginald de Croÿ?" Pinkhoff asked her, his eyes sliding to Bergan as the rapid stream of German filled the room.

"Not five thousand," Edith corrected without thinking. "Only five hundred."

The light of victory in the eyes of the two men sent ice into Edith's stomach. They did not know everything, and she had just given them something to use against both her and the prince.

Neuhaus jotted down the question and answer, though one quick look told her it was in German, not French, so she would have no idea if the translation were accurate.

She swallowed and drummed her nails on the surface of the table. She vowed to answer any question with carefully worded answers for the rest of the interview, unless they already knew enough of what they asked. She would evade and dodge and resort to vagueness in all things so as to give them no new information.

It was the only weapon she had left.

"Did you knowingly hide wounded British and French soldiers in your clinic and then help them to escape?" Pinkhoff asked.

"Yes," Edith confirmed. They would not care as much about the wounded soldiers as able ones, as she was head of a medical clinic and wounded soldiers were far more likely to be under her care.

"Did you knowingly and willfully direct able-bodied French and British soldiers—who had been brought to you in secret—to the Dutch frontier to escape?"

"I directed no one to any frontier," Edith told him with a slow shake of her head. "I've never been to the frontier myself."

Near-identical frowns appeared on the faces of both Bergan and Pinkhoff as the latter translated Edith's words.

"Do you admit to harboring able-bodied soldiers of England and France who were bound for the Dutch frontier by some other means?" Pinkhoff demanded, his tone still mild, but with a definite edge entering in.

"Some," she answered with a nod. "Those who required care."

He did not care for that answer and seemed to resent her for making him translate it to Bergan.

Bergan muttered something harsh in German under his breath.

Edith held back a smile, not wanting to appear uncouth.

Bergan snapped something at Pinkhoff, who leaned forward over the table. "How many soldiers did you receive from the engineer Capiau?"

So they knew about Herman, did they? Poor man. "About forty English soldiers."

"And from the barrister Libiez?"

"Perhaps six English and ten French and Belgian."

"From Prince Reginald de Croÿ?"

"Fifteen or so. English and French."

Neuhaus wrote rapidly, the nib of the pen scratching loudly against the page.

Pinkhoff and Bergan checked their notes. "And from Mademoiselle Thuliez—who worked with the prince in recruiting and collecting these derelict soldiers?"

Edith hesitated for a moment. If they knew what Louise had done already, they would know how tirelessly she had worked to help hundreds of soldiers to safety, not just to Edith's door.

"Miss Cavell?"

She straightened and lifted her chin. "Between eighty and a hundred English, French, and Belgian soldiers."

There was no surprise on their expressions, despite the staggering number, which confirmed her suspicions.

They already knew.

Why was she being asked these questions if they did not need them answered? Surely it was a waste of their time, not to mention hers. She had no great occupation or hobby in her cell, but it would have been better to be there than here.

Pinkhoff cleared his throat. "And you harbored these men until means were provided for them to escape. How long did they stay?"

"Sometimes a day," Edith answered. "Sometimes as long as three weeks. It varied for each circumstance."

"Would you kindly confirm these handover points for me?" Pinkhoff asked, handing over a sheet of paper.

Though it was in German, the location names were clear enough: St. Mary's church, the tram station at Place Roger, something relating to the Hôtel de l'Espérance in the Place de la Constitution, the clock of the school at Place Rouppe, the Cinquantenaire on Chaussée de Tervueren, and the Square Ambiorix.

Edith nodded as she read. "That all seems correct."

Pinkhoff looked up at her. "What others are there?"

Edith only smiled. There were several others, but if they did not already know them, she would not volunteer the information.

Her silence did not seem to perturb them, unfortunately. Pinkhoff took the paper from her and looked at Bergan for more instructions, which were not translated directly. Then Pinkhoff returned his attention to her.

"Before you took the soldiers to the pick-up point, would a guide or messenger come to you?"

"Yes," Edith confirmed. "To check arrangements."

"And they took the soldiers then?"

"Not always."

"And if you did not have room for all of the men brought to you?"

"I would take them elsewhere."

Pinkhoff smirked. "Allow us to offer some of those options you had, Miss Cavell. For where to take these men." He picked up another list. "To Mme Ada Bodart at 7 rue Taciturne and her subsequent address at 19 rue Émile Wittmann. To Marie Mauton at her boarding house at 12 rue d'Angleterre. To Philippe Rasquin at his coffeehouse at 137 rue Haute. To Mme Adolphine Sovet at her café at 16 boulevard de la Senne. Or to Louis Séverin, the chemist at 138 avenue Longchamp." He looked at her in triumph, his smile daring her to refute the names.

"That sounds correct," Edith hedged.

"It sounds correct because it *is* correct," he snapped, setting the paper down roughly. "How many of your soldiers wrote to you from the safety of Holland?"

Edith blinked. "I could not say."

"You do not know?"

"I have been much occupied of late."

"But you did receive notes of gratitude?"

Edith adopted an apologetic tone, despite the lack of apology she felt. "I may have. I really cannot recall."

Bergan barked something from his position, folding his arms, all politeness now gone.

Pinkhoff nodded at him. "Now, your revenue, Miss Cavell. Did you receive funds from Capiau, Thuliez, Prince Reginald, and the rest for the upkeep of these men?"

"Some. I would have to check my accounts for the exact amounts and from whom." She folded her hands in her lap.

The two men conversed in rapid German, with Sergeant Mayer stepping forward to join them. Neuhaus continued to write, which Edith found interesting, as she had said nothing to add to the conversation.

"I believe that will do for now," Pinkhoff announced, turning back to her. "Neuhaus?"

Neuhaus handed over the document he had been writing, and Pinkhoff looked it over, nodding. "Very good. Accurate and thorough. Now, Miss Cavell, it only remains for you to sign this as a true testimony of your actions." He slid the paper across to her, and Neuhaus brought over the pen.

Edith looked it over, blinking it disbelief. The lengthy document was entirely in German. How could she possibly know what they claimed she had said? Pinkhoff claimed it was accurate and thorough, but there had been so many lies throughout this endeavor. The Germans had used spies and underhanded means to glean information, and yet she was supposed to trust that this document was truth?

But there had been no monumental revelations in this interview, she had seen to that. There was a great deal she could have said but had not. Things the Germans did not know, or had not mentioned, that might have strengthened their case against all those Edith had worked with.

She knew full well there would be no justice for her, regardless of what she said or did not say. None of this was about justice or truth. It was about power.

Their power. And their need to exert it.

Picking up the pen, Edith signed her name quickly, then sat back.

Pinkhoff smiled at her. "Thank you for your cooperation, Miss Cavell. You will be returned to your cell at St. Gilles. We may do another interview in a few days."

Edith nodded, rising from her chair before Neuhaus could help her up in some show of faux gallantry. "Thank you, Sergeant."

"I hope you do not find solitary confinement too oppressive," he offered. "We cannot risk communication between prisoners, you understand."

Now it was Edith who smiled. "Not at all. I find the silence to be a blessed relief. Thank you for the opportunity."

Neuhaus opened the door, and Edith walked through, joined by her guards, who led her to the car waiting to return her to her prison cell.

CHAPTER 22

Be wise and good.

Edith's closing words in her most recent letter to the nurses lingered in Lizzie's mind as she walked toward the St. Gilles prison, clinging to the faintest hope that she might be permitted to visit her matron today.

Be wise and good.

Why did that sound like a farewell? She was not prepared to think of such a thing, and she prayed Edith had not intended it as such. Or that she was resigned to such a thing.

She would not allow Edith to be resigned to any finality. Not yet. This would all be cleared up sooner or later. It had to be.

She had read Edith's most recent letter to the others at the clinic just the other night, her voice fading in and out with her own emotions. To hear their matron ask them to remain devoted to their work and see the patients satisfied, to hear her encourage them in their studies and express that she wished for them to be prepared, to share advice about the new term—it was as though the matron had been sitting in a chair while the rest sat on the floor about her, speaking to them as she always had done.

And then Edith had spoken about learning and liberty, gratitude and patience, and that it was not enough to be a good nurse but they must also be Christian women.

Lizzie had been hard-pressed not to dissolve into tears at those words, her emotions warring with each other. Relief at hearing the sort of things Edith had always said. Agony for where she was and what she was enduring. Comfort from the words themselves, given by someone she adored. Despair for missing her so.

She could not now recall which nurse had done it, but once they had finished the letter, the windows had been closed, and the group of women had gathered around the piano. They had sung "La Brabançonne," the Belgian national anthem, followed by the British national anthem, "God Save the King," and there were no words for how stirring such an experience had been. Tears had flowed freely and without shame, embraces had been offered and received, and hearts had knit together in hope for their dear matron.

When a member of the clinic's supervisory committee had visited and given his opinion that Edith would be sent to a prison in Germany, their hope had been dampened but not diminished completely. Even if that was to be her fate, a prison or camp was not instant death.

That alone was cause for hope.

And hope was enough to propel Lizzie toward St. Gilles prison this morning, determined to see Edith, even though no one yet had succeeded in doing so.

She came to the entrance, as she had done so many times before, and approached the guard.

"Elizabeth Wilkins to see the prisoner Edith Cavell," she intoned with all the authority she imagined herself to possess.

The guard lifted a brow and held up a finger to indicate she wait. He turned and walked a few paces to where the hauntingly familiar form of Sergeant Otto Mayer stood.

The sergeant leaned closer to the guard as he spoke, his eyes moving to Lizzie. She caught the flash of recognition in his eyes, which turned her cold. She recalled all too clearly how he had grabbed her arm on one of his visits to the clinic. How he had demanded to know about Tommies. How he had so casually shown her the pin beneath his lapel to indicate his authority in the secret police.

There was no possibility he would permit Lizzie to visit Edith.

The guard nodded and returned to her, Sergeant Mayer at his heels.

"Sister Wilkins," the sergeant greeted before the guard could speak. "I would be happy to escort you to see your beloved matron today."

Lizzie blinked. "You would?"

"Of course," he replied with a kindness he had never shown previously. "And I will remain in the cell for the duration of your visit. You understand, surely."

Her heart gave an unsteady beat, and then she nodded. "Of course." She lifted the basket she held. "Do you need to see what I have brought for her?"

To her continued surprise, the sergeant shook his head. "I do not. The baskets from Miss Cavell's nurses have been regular enough to render a search unnecessary. I trust you have brought her bread, fresh linens, needlework, several letters, and perhaps yet more flowers?"

He was not entirely correct, but it was certainly close enough. "More or less," Lizzie grumbled.

Sergeant Mayer smirked at her. "Then let us be on our way. Follow me, please." He started down the long, clean, ancient-looking corridor without seeing if she would follow, his strides as easy as if he were merely strolling in a park.

To the victors the confidence, she supposed.

And the ease.

The kind Belgian deputy governor of the prison, Mr. Marin, nodded at her as she passed, and she smiled back. While the Germans controlled the place, Mr. Marin had retained his position, with what little power the government afforded him. He had been apologetic before when Lizzie or any of the other nurses had tried to visit Edith, and they knew the restrictions were not his.

At least she would see one friendly face besides Edith's here today.

There was no conversation from the sergeant, not even to continue his feigned politeness, but Lizzie preferred the silence, under the circumstances. She did not care to hear the arrogance in his tone, nor to see his condescending expression. It was bad enough the clinic had been without Edith for more than a month; Lizzie did not need her pain compounded by further communication between one of the villains who was to blame for it.

Sergeant Mayer stopped before an unmarked cell door and faced Lizzie. "Here we are," he announced unnecessarily. He pulled keys from his pocket and turned one in the lock, the loud clang of the metal echoing in the hallway.

"You have a visitor, Matron," the sergeant said as he pushed into the cell. He stepped back and gestured for Lizzie to enter.

A sudden bolt of fear and apprehension lanced Lizzie's chest, stuttering her steps. How would Edith appear after so long in captivity? Would she bear the evidence of brutal questioning? Would her usual calm and composure remain intact?

She stepped across the threshold of the cell, noting the whitewashed walls and cramped dimensions.

Edith stood by the narrow cot, hands clasped, expression not managing to hide her anticipation.

Lizzie's eyes filled with tears the moment they met Edith's. "Oh, Edith!"

Edith moved toward her before the words emerged. "Lizzie, my dear girl!"

They embraced, Edith's hold as tight as Lizzie's, and her too-thin frame trembled in Lizzie's hold.

"I have prayed daily that I would see you again," Edith whispered, her voice oddly choked with emotion. "Praise our Lord, it has come to pass!"

Lizzie could not speak and only nodded, clinging to her for fear that she might disappear the moment she let go.

Edith's hands rubbed Lizzie's back in soothing patterns. "It's all right, Lizzie. It's all right. Do not cry so. I am well, you see?"

It was so true to Edith's nature to turn from jubilance to comfort without a word, and experiencing it again was the most beautiful blessing Lizzie could have hoped for.

She nodded and finally pulled back, wiping at her eyes. "To see you again, Edith . . . It fills me with joy."

Edith took her hand, squeezing it with maternal warmth. "It seems the Lord knew what we both needed and has seen fit to bestow it upon us," she said, looking her over. "You look well."

Lizzie laughed. "I feel dreadful and have felt so since they took us away. You . . ." She frowned as she more fully took in the sight of her friend. "You look pale and rather thin."

The observation made Edith smile. "A daily walk without sunlight does wash one out so. Come, sit down." She gestured toward the cot and pulled Lizzie forward gently. "Tell me all about the new clinic and our dear girls."

Lizzie lost track of time as the two of them sat and talked of the nurses and probationers, the work taking place at the new clinic, the process of moving in and settling—all simple matters that hardly seemed important. Yet the discussion of them was a breath of much-needed fresh air. If this was what Edith wished to talk about, Lizzie would certainly comply.

Anything to make Edith's time more comfortable. Anything to give her solace. Anything to extend what time they had together.

After a while, Edith sighed softly. "How I miss them, and the clinic! I imagine the work you all must be doing, but I find I miss the evening chats most of all. Such lovely, quiet time with everyone. I should never have let those fade with the war. Consolation would have been needed then more than ever. But it sounds as though some of our nurses are no longer at the clinic. Is that the case?"

Lizzie had avoided broaching that topic, not wanting to give the matron anything else to worry about. Edith felt a responsibility to aid each nurse or potential nurse in becoming the best possible profes-sional in the field, so when they left of their own accord, she took it as a personal blow. As though she had somehow failed those in her charge.

Nothing could have been further from the truth.

"A few have left, yes," Lizzie admitted, keeping her smile fixed. "They couldn't . . . Well, it is very difficult without you there. The new directrice is very capable, and the committee did a marvelous job hiring her—she has let me continue in charge of the medical and teaching duties—but I am no adequate substitute for you, try as I might."

Edith covered her hand, smiling. "You are a marvelous instructor and more than capable of filling my place."

Lizzie shook her head firmly. "Not a jot. But many have re-mained, so we continue on and do our level best." She bit her lip, looking about the cramped cell. "How are you faring in here? It must be terribly lonely."

"Oh, I manage well enough," Edith assured her, smiling as though they chatted in a parlor. "We have daily walks, we are fed decently, and attentive men like Sergeant Mayer there ensure that I am never left to my own devices when outside of the cell."

Lizzie glanced at the sergeant, who watched the two of them with mild interest.

As though he knew nothing could be said that would change the situation.

As though he were only there to remind them both of their reality.

Which was certainly not needed.

"And," Edith went on, "the ample solitude allows me time to study and ponder the Word of God, which has been a blessing indeed. I am a plant in the garden of the Lord, after all, as you once reminded me. And to be so nourished in such harsh ground does feel miraculous."

That could not be all she felt. Edith was a calm, composed, oft-times serene woman, but surely she felt the pain of her arrest and confinement.

Lizzie squeezed her friend's hand. "But . . . ?"

Edith hesitated a long moment, then sighed, her shoulders slumping. "But I am weary, Lizzie. At last, the end has come. I cannot say I am sorry; this waiting, waiting, waiting, and this uncertainty has been a great strain on me, but I have done what was my duty. They must do with me as they will."

The words sounded too much like defeat for Lizzie's taste. Was Edith truly not going to fight the indignity of her arrest and imprisonment?

But as she processed the statements through her mind, she revised her opinion.

It was not defeat that rang from Edith's voice; it was resignation. A proud sort of resignation born from the consolation of her actions aligning with her conscience.

Lizzie was still not quite comfortable with hearing Edith use phrases such as "the end," but there was some truth to it: The time of her work against the Germans had indeed come to an end.

"When do you anticipate the trial?" Lizzie whispered, unable to give greater volume to her voice when the future was so formidable.

"The beginning of October, I believe," came the calm response. "I will write to request clothing for the occasion when I have certain dates." She glanced toward Sergeant Mayer in the corner. "I trust such a letter would be promptly delivered. Unlike others I have sent."

The sergeant shrugged. "I would think so, but I have no business with the running of the post hereabouts."

Edith shook her head and returned her attention to Lizzie. "I will not wear the uniform for the trial. I cannot stand as a symbol of the Red Cross, or the nursing profession as a whole, when I am viewed as a criminal."

"Surely it would help your cause," Lizzie protested. "You *are* a nurse, Edith. You are the Florence Nightingale of our era, and you ought to be viewed with such respect."

"I must be Edith Cavell and nothing more," Edith insisted with a familiar firmness.

There would be no arguing with that tone, no matter how Lizzie disagreed, and further discussion on the point would be useless.

Lizzie felt the burn of impending tears in her eyes. "We will do everything in our power to see you get a reprieve. Your family has written, and your brother-in-law is in communication with influential individuals to aid us. The American minister in Brussels has assured us that he is aware of the situation and will aid us. Apparently, Germany agreed that British civil subjects in Belgium are under his protection while the country is occupied. A Maître de Leval has been very good in reaching out to us on occasion to update us."

Edith smiled softly, but there was not much encouragement in the curve. "Very kind of them."

There was a moment of silence while Lizzie waited for Edith to say more, but Edith was doing nothing of the sort.

Lizzie sagged where she sat. "You don't believe it will do any good."

Edith's smile turned into one of almost pitying kindness. "I pray that it will, but I have accepted that my fate is in the hands of those who wish the worst for me. The Almighty knows the exact number of my days, and I will find no peace in wishing for more than I am granted. Only disconsolation and grief. So I will strive for patience and take comfort in knowing that I have lived my life in accordance with my beliefs."

Lizzie's heart began to race, her throat going dry. "You cannot give up, Edith. We must fight this! We need you back at the clinic. There is so much more you have to do!"

Edith slowly rubbed Lizzie's hand again. "I am not giving up, Lizzie. I will accept what is to be and move forward in faith, no matter what. Faith, Lizzie. The mustard seed, yes?"

"Then will you tell me not to fight on your behalf?"

The question spilled from Lizzie before she could truly decide if she wished to express it. She did not want to know Edith's thoughts on the subject. She wanted to go on according to her own conscience rather than sit idly by and wait for some impossible ending she might hate. She did not want to focus on the mustard seed. She wanted to march forward with a scythe into this miserable field before them. If she did not know Edith's thoughts one way or the other, she could continue to fight.

But if Edith wished for everyone to accept the unknown with the same aplomb . . .

"Of course not," Edith murmured softly. "It means a great deal that you would try for me."

Lizzie exhaled a heavy breath of relief. "Good. I cannot be patient and wait for the trial, Edith. I must do something, or I shall go mad."

Edith laughed a little. "I know, Lizzie. You must do what you feel is right."

"I shall, of course, attend the trial," Lizzie went on, turning her attention to the basket beside her.

"No," Edith said at the same time as Sergeant Mayer.

Lizzie looked between the two of them in shock, appalled that they would agree. "What?"

"I don't want you at the trial," Edith urged. "I don't want any of you there."

"None of you would be admitted as it is," Mayer grunted.

Lizzie huffed in irritation. "Then how are any of us to know the results and the progress?"

Mayer smirked slightly. "It will be made known. I trust you'll hear of it."

Was there ever a more maddening German than this particular one? It was all she could do not to stick her tongue out at him just as Pauline had done with the guard at the clinic.

Edith patted her hand, drawing her attention back to her. "Do not worry about the trial, Lizzie. We must believe in truth and justice, yes?"

"Not in this government, no," Lizzie muttered very low. "But I will listen to you and do my best not to worry. I doubt it would do me any good."

"Worrying usually does no good, but knowing such does not stop us from engaging in it." Edith's smile grew a little, and she looked at the basket beside Lizzie. "Now, what have you brought me today? Dare I hope there is another loaf of delicious bread?"

CHAPTER 23

Whatever Edith's fate happened to be, the trial beginning today would be its first step.

She had been escorted from her cell that morning with no fanfare. She had dressed in her blue coat and skirt, her best white blouse with a gold stud on the collar, a gray fur stole, and her hat with a tortoiseshell pin. She did not look like a nurse, which was the point.

She must be tried as a woman of England. Nothing more.

The bus containing all prisoners for the trial pulled up to the Parliament House with its majestic, three-story, terra-cotta roof. The imposing edifice drew Edith's eye upward immediately, though when she returned her gaze to the entrance itself, she noted the additional intimidation of large statues of discus throwers lining the gravel walkways.

"Out!" a guard ordered from the bus doors.

Edith shook herself and looked across the bus aisle to Louise Thuliez, who seemed calm, but her eyes were wide as she stared back at Edith.

Words failed her, and Edith could only smile in what she hoped was a comforting manner.

Then they were up and disembarking, walking silently down the gravel path into the building. German guards were everywhere, as were officers and military police with their spiked helmets. Among the stately, marbled halls hung portraits of celebrated Belgian politicians, which seemed a poignant reminder of the rich history being scrubbed out by the Germans.

Thick double doors at the end of the corridor were opened at their approach, and Edith blinked at the sudden bright ornateness that met them. The circular room was cavernous in its size and filled with red velvet-covered seats, most of which were embroidered with the proud Belgian lion emblem. The walls were covered with dark wooden panels. The ceilings were almost entirely decorated with gold, which seemed to illuminate the rest of the room.

The discrepancy between this room and the small, entirely white cell wherein she had spent the last ten weeks was startling to nearly every sense, and she could hardly note the faces of those in attendance for a full five minutes. When she did note them, it occurred to her that the audience was there more for the spectacle and the entertainment than to witness the due course of the law. Some had field glasses, which they used to look upon the prisoners being marched in, and the chatter among all was lively and light.

There was not a single familiar face among the crowd.

Edith and the other prisoners were marched to the front of the room with a guard between groups of them, the din of the room lowering in anticipation. She was near to Marie de Croÿ, but not immediately beside her. Jeanne de Belleville was close, while Louise was further down. Edith looked down the line of them, stunned by their number. She only knew a dozen or so by personal encounters. Not a one of them could identify the entire mass of conspirators, and this setting was the first time they had all been gathered.

And more still were outside these proceedings.

A German voice rang through the room, and everyone rose as five uniformed men proceeded from another room and into the seats set on a dais. Their ages ranged from mid-thirties to near sixty, each wearing an identical iron cross among their other heavy adornments. Two wore monocles, and each of them sported a mustache of varying size, some of which were great indeed.

All were imposing, and it was clear from their expressions there would be no mercy shown today.

Edith glanced behind her, curious as to where—and who—her lawyer was. She saw a handful of men with stacks of various papers and folders, though none seemed to give her a second look. Was one of these haggard-looking fellows charged with her defense? Were any of them?

She might not know until the time for her defense came. What sort of defense could even be given when there had been no communication with her at all?

The center judge spoke in German, which was then translated by a nearby officer.

"On this, the seventh day of October, in the year nineteen hundred and fifteen, we commence these criminal proceedings under the authority of Governor General von Lüttwitz, and, by further authority, Kaiser Wilhelm the Second. The prosecutor for this case is the Honorable Doctor Eduard Stoeber, who may now begin with his opening statements."

The judge then nodded at a handsome officer with a pomaded moustache and black hair, a glinting monocle propped in his right eye. The man stood, clearing his throat and opening a thick dossier before him.

"Honorable members of judgment, fellow officers in the law," the man began, according to the translator's words, "we are gathered today to relate the crimes against the German State of the following individuals." He held up his list, squinting slightly through his monocle.

"Philippe Baucq, of Brussels, architect. Louise Thuliez, of Lille, schoolmistress. Constant Cayron, of Brussels, student. Herman Capiau, of Wasmes, engineer. Edith Cavell, of Brussels, Head of Medical Institute . . ."

He continued on and on, his clear voice ringing as he pronounced each of the thirty-five names on the list, but Edith could barely hear anything after her own name was read. Something jolted within Edith as each name was read as if a hammer was striking a nail into a beam. If any of the other prisoners felt the same, she could not tell. It was all she could do to avoid looking at them. She could not show the fear that shook her stomach and her knees. She could only pray her expression did not betray her.

The judges seemed to be comparing notes on their lists of the accused, and then one gestured for Mr. Stoeber to proceed.

"I would like to begin with Mademoiselle Cavell," Stoeber announced crisply. "And I would ask that certain individuals among the prisoners be excused during her questioning."

Edith blinked, rising to her feet when her guard indicated she do so. Despite Mr. Stoeber stating only "certain individuals" ought to be excused, it appeared that most of the thirty-five prisoners were taken from the room. Some of them gave Edith apprehensive looks, even if they did not know her.

Why was she to go first? She had assumed they would proceed in the order by which the names had been read.

Edith was nudged forward to stand before the judges in a more prominent position, and she swallowed with some difficulty as she felt the eyes of all five men boring into her.

Mr. Stoeber moved to stand near her, his expression full of superiority and confidence, rather like a hungry lion surveying a herd of lambs.

It was all she could do to meet his gaze without flinching.

"Mademoiselle Cavell," the interpreter recited, as Mr. Stoeber rattled off in German, "from November 1914 to July 1915, you have lodged French and English soldiers, including a colonel, all in civilian clothes; you have helped Belgians, French, and English of military age, by furnishing them with the means of going to the front, notably in receiving them at your nursing home and in giving them money. Is this true?"

Flashes of memory from her repeated interrogations lit up her mind like a torch in an open field. Stoeber was just like those who had questioned her before, and she was determined to be as succinct and honest now as she had been then.

She had nothing to hide.

Edith nodded once. "Yes."

Those in the room muttered in low tones, but they were ignored.

"With whom were you concerned in committing these acts?"

The question was one she had expected, and, as with her interrogations, she would go only so far as to give the Germans the names of those they had already arrested. "With Mr. Capiau, Mademoiselle Martin, Madame Derveau, and Mr. Libiez."

Stoeber began to pace slowly in front of her, hands clasped behind his back, his dark eyes fixed on her. "Who was the head—the originator of the organization?"

Edith managed a calm, very slight smile. "There wasn't a head of the organization."

Stoeber stopped pacing and glared at her. "Wasn't it the Prince de Croÿ?"

"No," she replied with a short shake of her head. "The Prince de Croÿ confined himself to sending men to whom he had given a little money."

More muttering sounded from the audience and from the judges.

Stoeber frowned and continue his pacing. "Why have you committed these acts?"

Why? There was not time enough nor words in any language to adequately convey her reasons and her feelings, but now was not the time to make speeches nor to wax patriotic.

Prudence, her mind suggested.

Well, she still believed there was a higher duty than that, but she could be prudent in her honesty.

"I was sent, to begin with, two Englishmen who were in danger of death; one was wounded."

"In danger of death?" Mr. Stoeber repeated in disbelief. "Why would English soldiers be in such danger? If they would have been captured, they would have been sent to camps, Mademoiselle Cavell, not put before a firing squad."

"I believed they were in danger of death," Edith reaffirmed without fear, her cheeks beginning to heat with indignation. "In such times and such situations, would not the escaped enemy have been risking that?"

Mr. Stoeber scoffed. "Martial law does not carry the death penalty in such cases. Which you would know, if you were in any way acquainted with it." He shook his head and returned to his desk, picking up the thick dossier and flipping the first page. "Once these people crossed the frontier, did they send you news to that effect?"

Edith's face slowly began to cool. "Only four or five did so."

He nodded, and her attention was drawn to the judges as one or two of them began to make notes. What did they make of her? What did they believe they already knew? Were they as angered by her actions as every other German she had encountered thus far?

"Baucq and Fromage are the same person?" Stoeber asked, bringing her back to the present.

"Yes," Edith murmured softly.

"And what was Baucq's role?"

That was an odd question. Why was Philippe in this trial if they had to ask his role?

"I knew him very little," Edith admitted carefully. "I don't know what his role was."

Stoeber raised a dark eyebrow, which surely must have put the stability of his monocle at risk, yet it stayed in place. "Do you maintain what you said at the interrogation, concerning the people with whom you worked with a view to recruiting, that is to say with Prince Reginald de Croÿ, Baucq, Séverin, Capiau, Libiez, Derveau, Mademoiselle Thuliez, and Madame Ada Bodart?"

As she had already admitted as much, and they had each of them in custody, she had no qualms in replying, "Yes."

Again, the room buzzed, and Edith did her best to ignore the spectators, raising her chin.

"Do you realize that in thus recruiting men it would be to the disadvantage of Germany and to the advantage of the enemy?" Stoeber asked, his cold tone clear in the interpretation as well.

Edith's heart pounded hard just once. "My preoccupation has not been to aid the enemy but to help the men who applied to me reach the frontier; once across the frontier, they were free."

Her response did not seem to put off either Mr. Stoeber or the judges. In fact, Mr. Stoeber looked rather pleased with her. Or perhaps himself.

"How many people have you thus sent to the frontier?" he asked almost dismissively.

She swallowed. "About two hundred."

The room erupted into chatter and mutterings, which made her stomach clench, but she maintained her eye contact with Mr. Stoeber.

He smirked at her and nodded once. "Thank you, Miss Cavell. That is all." He indicated to the nearest guard that she be taken from the room, and she was escorted out.

That was all? That had been four minutes at most. She could not have said more than a hundred and fifty words.

That was all they wanted of her?

She was taken to an adjoining room where many of the other prisoners sat. They all looked as surprised as she felt that she had been kept so short a time.

Louise Thuliez was taken next, and she brushed her hand against Edith's as she proceeded toward the chamber to be questioned.

Edith sat and resisted the temptation to put her head in her hands. She would not regret what she had said, nor refute her own claims, nor wish for a chance to speak more. There had been no defense offered, but perhaps that was how the trial would proceed. Perhaps they were each to be questioned first and then have a defense when the prosecutor had completed his tirade against each of them.

If she had a lawyer to defend her. She had no doubt the judges would come harshly down on her simply because she was English, and any appointed defender could easily be of German nationality.

What a sorry defense that would make for her, indeed.

Louise was not kept long, and Philippe was escorted out. He seemed almost entertained upon his return and gave Edith a friendly wink.

"I should truly learn to mind my tongue," he quipped, making some of the others chuckle.

Edith smiled at his glib remark, amazed that she could feel truly amused by anything at this point.

Ada Bodart was taken next, followed by Mr. Libiez, Mr. Séverin, Mr. Derveau, and on until all of them had taken a turn. Whether or not the few prisoners who had not been excused from the chamber had been questioned during the interim, Edith could not say. Nothing was explained to them, nothing made clear, no expectations given.

Then it apparently was time for lunch, even in the court.

Thirty or forty soldiers came into the room, carrying a large cauldron of soup and their mess tins. They dished up a meal for themselves and paid no attention to the prisoners at all, which, while doing nothing for the prisoners' own hunger, did allow them to speak with each other, at last. Edith, for her part, sat silently, relaxing her posture, and trying desperately to not think too greatly on anything of importance.

The heat in the room was positively stifling, and there was no relief to be found.

A soldier drank the last of his soup, then eyed the group of prisoners, his brow furrowing. He approached Jeanne de Belleville. "Would you like some soup? I have finished and could dish some up for you."

Jeanne looked utterly delighted, if not astonished. "I would, sir. And if you can find a few rolls, I can pay you for the extra trouble. I have coin with me."

He smiled with surprising warmth, nodding. "I shall be back shortly." He looked at another soldier and barked something in German before he left.

Other soldiers offered their tins of soup to the prisoners, some reluctantly. Some soldiers continued to ignore the prisoners, but the general consideration was much appreciated. Mr. Libiez pulled some chocolate from his coat pocket and offered it to Edith and Louise, who took it with murmured thanks.

The soldier returned with the rolls Jeanne had requested, and she dropped a few coins into his hand in exchange. She immediately broke one in half and offered the halves to Edith and Louise.

They ate in silence, and a few soldiers came around with canteens of water, offering to pour some into the cupped hands of the prisoners. It was an odd sort of ministering to the afflicted, but it settled Edith's heart almost as much as her morning devotionals did.

But all too soon, it was over, and they were all brought into the chamber again.

Mr. Stoeber proceeded to call witnesses, first of which was Lieutenant Bergen. He eyed the group of prisoners with the same distaste one might upon seeing an intrusion of cockroaches and, according to the translator, expressed his beliefs that all the prisoners had been working together as an organization intent on destroying Germany by bringing soldiers to the enemy. He had a great deal to say about justice and the pure legality of the trial, which seemed to puff up both the judges and Mr. Stoeber, though none of them needed such assistance.

At long last, the man was done and dismissed from the witness box.

Mr. Stoeber bowed slightly to the judges. "The prosecution would now call upon Master Philippe Bodart to take the stand."

A gasp went up from the prisoners, all of whom turned to look at Ada, who had gone whiter than a sheet. The crowd in the chamber muttered, and even the judges looked slightly ill at ease.

But it was true. The boy of fourteen was led into the room by armed guard. Philippe was dressed in dark clothing, his dark curls almost flat against his pale face. He was slim for his age, perhaps too slim, and his fearful eyes flicked to his weeping mother.

He moved into the witness box and sat, shifting uncomfortably.

"Master Bodart," Stoeber began, striding toward him, "you do understand that, should you commit perjury while being questioned here today, you will be sentenced to ten years' hard labor?"

Philippe looked at his mother again, his eyes wide. "Y-yes," he answered, though it was clear he had not known any such thing before now.

Stoeber nodded as if the matter had been settled. "Did Mr. Baucq take copies of *La Libre Belgique* to Madame Bodart for distribution?"

"Yes."

"And did he," continued Stoeber, "while he was there, in your presence, say that he was trying to find a safe route to cross the frontier?"

Philippe glanced at Mr. Baucq, looking entirely tortured now. "Yes," he whispered.

Baucq groaned from his place and shot to his feet. "Please, sirs! The boy normally speaks English with his mother. He did not understand the French use of the word 'on.' He had confused 'someone is trying to find a route' with 'I am trying to find a route.' He did not understand, and he is only a boy, please!"

"Sit down!" ordered one of the judges, gesturing for a guard to force Mr. Baucq into his chair.

But Baucq sank down of his own accord, his head falling between his hands and his shoulders shaking with emotion.

It was a dreadful sight to see such a strong, vibrant man overcome with despair, whether for the risk to his own life or the injustice of a son being forced to testify against his mother and those with whom he had been acquainted.

Philippe Bodart looked as though he might break where he sat. He did not look up at any of them.

"Dismissed," Stoeber eventually said, waving his hand at the young man.

Philippe darted from the box and raced to his mother, who embraced him tightly, both of them weeping silently.

Edith could not bear to look at them. Could not look at Mr. Baucq. Could not look anywhere but at her own hands.

There was no justice here. No mercy.

CHAPTER 24

The longer Mr. Stoeber went on, the more oppressive the room felt. It was the second day of the trial, and it was as though he had been prevented from uttering a single word in the whole proceedings as yet. His present vitriol was both effusive and extensive.

They ought to all be condemned for high treason, he claimed. The German army had been exposed to great danger by their actions. He read excerpts from the prisoners' testimonies given during their interrogations and reiterated details produced or reintroduced the day before.

"All of this activity is akin to high treason," Stoeber said again, "and the law punishes it with the death sentence!"

The room went utterly silent. Even the judges seemed surprised, a few looking uncomfortable by the idea.

Death?

"Paragraph fifty-eight of the German Military Code supports the charge," Stoeber went on, clearing his throat as he pulled out the reference. "It reads: 'will be sentenced to death for treason any person who, with the intention of helping the hostile Power, or of causing harm to the German or Allied troops, is guilty of one of the crimes of Paragraph Ninety of the German Penal Code.' Which, gentlemen, you will recall specifies 'conducting soldiers to the enemy,' as our prisoners here have done."

He handed his book to an aide and faced the accused. "And now for my recommendations for sentencing."

Edith felt herself grow cold in anticipation.

"Philippe Baucq: death, plus one year and eight months imprisonment," he said simply.

Edith jerked to look at her associate, and he had paled several shades, his mouth gaping.

"Louise Thuliez: death, plus one year imprisonment."

A woman had been recommended for death. The room was abuzz with discussion, and the judges shifted slightly in their seats.

Stoeber was not bothered in the least.

"Edith Cavell: death."

A rush of air escaped Edith's lungs, and it took her a long moment to manage a single, worthless swallow.

Death. It sounded like a foreboding bell tolling in some desolate church tower.

She reminded herself it was only his recommendation and not her sentence in truth, but she did not know how much influence Mr. Stoeber would have on the court itself.

Death. Even the word tasted of bitterness.

Stoeber kept going, recommending death for a few others, imprisonment for some, penal servitude for others, but all was lost beneath the faint buzzing in Edith's ears and the sound of her own pounding heart.

She looked at the judges; none would meet her gaze.

She glanced down the group of her fellow accused, her mind

processing the images of them as though from a very great and emotionless distance.

Philippe Baucq had his chin in his hands as he leaned on the desk before him. Louise was flushed and perspiring, glancing around as though expecting to be woken from a dream at any moment. Jeanne's cheeks bore some color, but she looked dazed, her eyes unfocused. Mr. Libiez was pale and continually ran his hands through his hair and mustache. Mr. Séverin dropped the paper he had been holding and made no attempt to pick it up.

They had all expected punishment, but they had not expected this.

At last, Stoeber sat to the scattered applause of the gathering, though it was impossible to tell if they agreed with his words or were simply pleased he was finished.

The judges looked at each other, then the one in the center looked down at the pages before him through his monocle. "And now we may commence with the defense of the accused." He nodded at a nearby lawyer.

"Sadi Kirschen," the Belgian man announced as he rose. "Defense for Edith Cavell, Ada Bodart, Séverin, Derveau, Heuze, Demoustier, Cavenaile, Joly, and Pansaers."

Edith perked up at hearing her name, but then sagged when she heard the number of defendants her lawyer had. How could he possibly manage to appropriately defend each of them, even if he was the greatest lawyer in the world?

She had never seen the man in her entire life, and he now held her fate in his hands.

She could only pray he was sympathetic.

He began to speak in German, to her surprise, so she would hear her defense through the mouth of the translator. She could only hope he would be truthful.

"My clients," Kirschen said, according to translation, "are part of no organization. They are merely dedicated, devoted individuals striving to do what they feel is right in trying times." His Belgian accent rang perfectly in the chamber as though the room itself wanted to honor a son of its people.

"Take Mademoiselle Cavell." He gestured for her, smiling with a fondness she did not understand. "She is a nurse, gentlemen. She has devoted her whole life to nursing the sick and the afflicted, the wounded and the weary. Extreme circumstances have brought her to this place. She could not have refused the men who had asked for her help, any more than she could refuse to care for a patient. How could she not have taken in the British soldiers, given her own nationality? And she had been treating the German soldiers without discrimination, setting aside any personal feelings one might expect of her.

"This is because of her devotion to her profession, gentlemen. A psychologist would be better suited to try her than even expertly trained judges. A psychologist would understand how impossible it was for her, a woman whose nature it is to help others, not to do all in her power to aid the British, French, and Belgian soldiers she hid and protected. The first Englishmen who asked for her help were wounded. The lives of each man who came to her were in danger."

"Objection," Mr. Stoeber announced, pushing to his feet. "We have established there was no danger. It is not the case under German military law."

Mr. Kirschen turned to him. "Mademoiselle Cavell, like the other accused, did not know that. They could not know that, as they were not trained in military law, let alone German military law. They all believed that the soldiers were being threatened, and that the only way to help them was to get them over the frontier. Mademoiselle Cavell did not wish to damage the German cause. Can you prove that the men she aided enlisted again because of her help? Only that would make her actions liable to the death penalty. Not for giving the aid for which she has been known her entire career."

Mr. Stoeber had no response for that, and there was some discussion around them about Mr. Kirschen's words. Even the judges seemed to be considering the lawyer's statements.

"Perhaps," Mr. Kirschen went on, "she has exaggerated the number of men she helped reach Holland. A simple enough mistake, given the number of patients Mademoiselle Cavell tends to on a daily basis with her excellent team. If I had had the opportunity to see her notes and to speak with her before this trial, I might have been permitted to know the truth, but I have become her lawyer without this information. Be that as it may, this tribunal does not and cannot have the right to condemn a trained nurse to death."

"Hear, hear!" someone called out in a rough voice.

Mr. Kirschen gave Edith an encouraging smile before turning back to the judges. "I implore you, gentlemen, to recognize that Edith Cavell's life has been dedicated to the sick and wounded, that many German soldiers owe their lives to her care. If she is to be condemned of a crime, then at least let her sentence be mitigated to attempted treason, not treason itself."

A thrill of energy raced into Edith's heart, and she would have applauded had it been permitted.

Then Mr. Stoeber rose and came over to her.

She stood as he approached, her heart rate slowing.

He looked her up and down, his distaste for her evident. "What do you have to say for yourself?"

She allowed herself a slow, careful breath. "I have nothing to add," she announced simply and softly.

Stoeber nodded and returned to his desk, indicating that Mr. Kirschen go on.

He did so, moving his attention to his other defendants. His defense for them was no less fervent than it had been for Edith, and he had clearly been taking careful notes of their testimonies and statements, despite not having had an opportunity to meet with any of them. He asked the judges if death was warranted for any of the accused, given that they had not personally guided anyone to the frontier.

Mr. Kirschen finished his defense and sat, which prompted the next lawyer to rise and speak for his own group of clients. They were all much the same, and Edith found herself nodding at regular intervals. Those with open ears and kind hearts would believe the words of these good men defending them, would hear the truth in what they said. Surely there could still be clemency, especially now that all sides of the issue were being heard.

Edith had lost track of the defenses and who was being spoken of when she noticed Marie de Croÿ moving to the front of the room. Despite seeming frail in stature, her shoulders were pulled back and her chin high. The air about her was positively majestic.

Marie cleared her throat softly, looking around the room. "My lords, be merciful to those women whose death sentence is asked of you. My brother and I are the real culprits. It is we who, in undertaking the evacuation of French and English soldiers, led them into this affair. "

She shook her head, swallowing hard. "I take full responsibility for what I have done, but I must speak out for Miss Cavell in particular. What has been said about her is not true. She was not at the head of an escape organization." Her eyes met Edith's, and Edith wanted nothing more than to take the hand of her friend who was standing so nobly for her.

"She was brought into danger by my brother and me," Marie went on. "We sent the men to her. At first, it was I who sheltered and hid these men. And even when Miss Cavell told us she could not lodge any more, that her school would be in danger if more men were sent to her, we still sent others to her, and so did our confederates. The responsibility should fall on my brother and me. I am ready to take her place. I repeat, I am ready to take the place that falls to me."

Her voice faded, and there was no immediate reaction or response from anyone. The stifling room was filled with people, yet it was so quiet, a tree branch tapping against a high leaded window could be heard. Someone in the gallery cleared their throat. A pencil scratched against paper.

Perhaps the princess's eloquent plea had come too late, then. For any of them.

But Edith would never forget how her friend had spoken, had begged for clemency for her, and how, in spite of everything, she was ready to take the punishment meant for Edith.

Greater love hath no man than this, that a man lay down his life for his friends.

Warmth filled Edith's chest, growing with every beat of her heart until it threatened to consume her. No matter what happened here, no matter what justice was meted out, this had all been worth it.

Every sacrifice. Every risk. Every moment.

Marie moved from her position back to her seat, and only when she had sat once more did Mr. Stoeber move.

He stood, exhaled, and asked the court to hasten the rest of the proceedings.

They were only too glad to comply with his wishes.

The final defenses were made, and hurriedly so. There had been no luncheon break, not a single reprieve from the day's events and accusations.

The center judge rose, followed by his comrades. "Court is dismissed. Sentences will be communicated to the prisoners in prison. That is all."

The crowd rose, waiting for the judges to file out, while the guards came to stand by the prisoners, preparing to escort them out.

Edith glanced over at Mr. Kirschen, eager to thank him for his efforts.

He took a step in her direction, only for a guard to hold out a hand to stop him. Another took him by the arm, preventing him from getting any closer. His expression was still clear to see, and Edith offered him a smile of gratitude she hoped he would comprehend.

His brow cleared, and he gave her a slow nod, which she took to be acceptance of such thanks.

That was all she could hope for, under the circumstances.

The prisoners were led from the chamber and out of the building, loaded up into various vehicles, all bound for their cells again. Edith and Jeanne were put in the same van and quickly driven away. Belatedly, Edith recalled that Jeanne had also been recommended for the death penalty, and, in an instant, she felt a new kinship for the woman. She was one of very few who would perfectly comprehend Edith's fractured state of mind.

Jeanne took Edith's hand, though nothing was said between them.

Edith returned the pressure, taking comfort from the physical contact.

"I heard a rumor," Jeanne said loudly, leaning forward to speak with the guard in the van with them, "that, following the execution of that woman prisoner at Liège, no more women were being condemned to death. Do you know if that is true?" Her hold on Edith's hand tightened perceptibly.

The guard turned, frowning slightly. "I believe that is the case. I cannot be certain, but I think so."

Edith squeezed Jeanne's hand in return, thanking her silently for asking the question. Edith hadn't heard the rumor, but to know that perhaps death might not be her fate brought hope to her heart.

It was not far to St. Gilles, and they were unloaded from the van quickly and escorted into the hall of the prison.

A guard approached them, expression free of emotion. "I am informed that I may take you both to the prison yard for some brief exercise, should you wish it. As you have faced trial, there will be no need for hoods. If you do not wish to go, you will be returned to your cell."

Edith and Jeanne exchanged looks, then returned their attention to him. "I should like a walk, if you do not mind," Edith informed him.

"As would I," echoed Jeanne.

The guard gestured toward the yard, and hand in hand, the ladies walked forward, their fates now hanging in the balance—and entirely out of their reach.

CHAPTER 25

Rumors meant nothing.

Lizzie refused to believe that Edith would be condemned to death. It was not possible. There could not be a world without Edith Cavell in it.

She nodded to herself, as if that would be in any way comforting, and closed the book before her. She knew everything she could know about nursing rules on the sanitation of houses and how to incorporate those rules into rural nursing. It was a dull lecture, to be sure, but the exams were this month and even the dullest lessons had to be reviewed.

She walked into the classroom and arranged her things, waiting for the students to file in. The lecture would help pass the time while her heart and stomach tried to settle from Maud's revelation about Edith.

"Good afternoon, Sister," the first few of the students greeted as they entered, moving to the chairs.

Lizzie nodded to them. "Good afternoon. Please take your seats."

They did so, followed by the others, and soon the room was full. She smiled at the women, and they quieted under her attention.

"Today we will be discussing the health of houses and how rural district nursing must adapt," Lizzie announced.

The groan of agony from the room was fully anticipated, and Lizzie smiled wildly, recalling the same pain from when she had been a student.

"Yes, I know," she said, her tone only slightly apologetic. "But I must remind you that I do not write the exams for which you will soon sit, and therefore, I do not control the topics that must be reviewed. Now, who can recite the five essential points of securing health of houses?"

A reluctant hand went up. "Pure air, pure water, efficient drainage, cleanliness, and light."

Lizzie nodded firmly. "Very good. And how might the setting in which a nurse practices affect these points?"

The discussion from the girls was thorough, and soon Lizzie was not having to facilitate any of it. The students debated the values and restrictions of district nursing in the rural areas, then created possibilities for overcoming those restrictions. It was, perhaps, not entirely aligned with the forthcoming exam, but Lizzie was not about to hinder their conversation.

It was practical nursing they were discussing, and she would never begrudge preparing them for that. Or having them prepare themselves.

"Nevertheless," Lizzie broke in loudly when the discussion began to grow heated, "we can all agree that the observation of these basics is the surest way to safeguard against infection. Yes?"

Nods went around the room, and things began to settle.

A faint clearing of a throat drew Lizzie's attention, and she saw Helen standing in the corridor, waving her over.

Lizzie frowned but turned to the group. "Anna, would you take over for a moment?"

"Of course, Sister," one of the senior students replied, rising and coming to the front.

Nodding her thanks, Lizzie moved out to the corridor. "Helen? What is it?"

Only then did she notice tears on the girl's cheeks and a faint tremor in her jaw. Further down the hall, Helen's father waited, turning his dripping hat in his hands, brow furrowed.

Lizzie walked toward him. "Monsieur Wegels? What is it?"

He looked at her, expression drawn, shaking his head. "Poor nurses, poor child."

Her heart stopped in her chest. "What is it?"

"I heard from a Belgian warder that the prosecution asked for death for Mademoiselle Cavell," he murmured, his voice croaking. "And for the Princess de Croÿ, the Countess de Belleville, and more. They asked for death."

"Yes, but will they get it?" Lizzie demanded even as her toes began to lose feeling.

Helen came to Lizzie's side. "Yes. Monsieur van Halteren came to tell us just as Father did. The sentence has been handed down. The matron has been condemned to death, Sister."

The world seemed to still and fade in the same moment, all sound and color dimmed. A frigid air enveloped them.

She was . . . She had been . . .

It was not possible. It could not be.

Yet no one would be so cruel as to report this in error.

It must be true.

Lizzie could not breathe, could not feel her heart doing anything remotely resembling a beat, could not understand why her lips were tingling as though filled with a dozen angry bees. Heat raced into her chest, twisting every rib in her body with acute ferocity, while her palms and hairline began to perspire.

What was this? How could this be true? They could not think . . . They could not truly believe . . .

They would kill her? Over helping some soldiers?

What sort of justice was that? What world was this? Where had humanity gone?

What was the point of anything now?

"When?" Lizzie heard a soft voice say, only realizing shortly after the question caught the air that it had been her voice to utter it.

"Tomorrow morning at five o'clock," Monsieur Wegels told her. "But possibly as early two o'clock."

Helen made a soft keening sound, bringing a handkerchief to her mouth.

Tears threatened Lizzie's vision, burning at the corners of her eyes and dotting her lashes without falling.

She could not let them fall. Not yet.

"No," she muttered, shaking her head firmly. "No. Something must be done, and so help me, I will see it done!" She turned on her heel and marched deeper into the clinic. "Sister Taylor! Sister Taylor!"

Sister Taylor and Beatrice Smith appeared from the offices, concern etched on their faces.

"Lizzie?" Sister Taylor asked, coming toward her quickly. "What is wrong?"

Lizzie swallowed hard. "The matron has been condemned to death. I am going to the prison to see what can be done—see her, if I can. And if I cannot, I will go to Reverend Gahan. He will know what to do."

"I'll come with you," Beatrice volunteered, her jaw tensing.

Sister Taylor took Lizzie's hand, gripping hard. "I'll remain here and ensure that all runs smoothly. Send word as soon as you can."

Lizzie nodded and looked at Beatrice. "We will go to the prison first. Mr. Marin was kind to us before. Perhaps he will be kind again."

"It is worth a chance," Beatrice agreed. "I will get our coats." She rushed off.

Sister Taylor kept a firm hold on Lizzie's hand. "Are you strong enough for this? Can you face what might well happen?"

Lizzie blinked hard, looking away but holding fast to her hand as the hovering tears now shamelessly fell. "I don't know. But I must try, mustn't I? For the matron, I have to be strong. I have to fight. I have to do all in my power to make sure she comes back to us. And if I cannot . . ." Her voice broke, and she clenched her teeth to keep from crying completely.

"And if you cannot, then you have to go on."

Lizzie nodded, her breath hissing through her teeth.

"I would embrace you, my dear, but I fear that would only make things worse." Sister Taylor cradled Lizzie's hand in both of hers, creating a warmth that almost reached past her elbow. "We will pray for our matron, and we will pray for each other. I believe miracles can and do happen when God wills it. And if anyone was ever deserving of a miracle, it is our Edith Cavell."

Truer words had never been spoken, and yet hearing them created a new burden that sat squarely upon Lizzie's shoulders.

Was she going to attempt to bring about a miracle? Call upon divine intervention to prevent a fate that was too terrible to contemplate?

Divine work that perhaps mortal boots on the ground could assist in.

"I will not stop trying," Lizzie vowed, returning her attention to Sister Taylor. "I will exhaust every possibility."

Sister Taylor nodded and offered a smile, even as her eyes brimmed with unshed tears. "I know you will. And if you see our matron, give her all the love in the world from us."

"I will."

Beatrice returned then, coats in hand, and gave Lizzie hers. "We'd best be off. The prison is a decent walk, and there's no time to waste."

They left, hurrying down the streets of Brussels in the pouring rain.

Lizzie could barely feel the drops as they splattered on her shoulders and face, her feet clattering against the pavement, while the odd echoing of splashing in puddles rang in her ears.

Surely, Lizzie and Beatrice would be allowed to see Edith now that her sentence had been pronounced. What could be the harm in such a visit? The trial had been held, the proof set out, the punishment decided. Would it affect any lasting matters to let the prisoner have a few moments of comfort and consolation?

If Beatrice had any thoughts on the subject, she kept them to herself. She walked silently beside Lizzie, her arms swinging with a determination that would have rivaled any soldier as she kept pace with Lizzie's haste. Her face was devoid of emotion, and she exuded confidence and strength.

Being in her company bolstered Lizzie, and she would need such bolstering to see the rest of the night through. If the execution were to be in the morning, there was not an instant to lose if they wished to change anything. It was late afternoon now, and time would pass swiftly enough without the progress of the sun to remind them of their dwindling hours.

The domineering edifice of St. Gilles prison was soon before them, and it seemed more menacing and darker on this occasion than Lizzie could have imagined.

Lizzie faltered in hesitation, her fear rising in startling waves, but Beatrice marched forward and banged on the door.

To their surprise, Mr. Marin himself answered.

Hope immediately flared within Lizzie's chest. "Mr. Marin," she greeted, taking a few steps closer. "We've heard that sentences have been pronounced on our dear matron. Is that so?"

Mr. Marin smiled sadly at her. "I do apologize, Sister. I am afraid the death sentences have already been made known to the prisoners. Edith Cavell and Philippe Baucq are to be shot this morning."

Lizzie's legs buckled, and she stumbled into Beatrice, who caught her and held her upright.

"What can we do?" Beatrice asked in a clear voice.

"Can we see her?" Lizzie pleaded in the same breath.

Mr. Marin shook his head. "Only those in religious orders may speak with the condemned now. I am sorry."

Lizzie clamped down on her lips hard.

Beatrice rubbed Lizzie's arms. "What can we do?" she asked again, more firmly.

A faint flash of hesitation crossed the deputy governor's face, and he seemed to glance over his shoulder without actually doing so, then leaned close.

"Go at once to the American Legation's lawyer, Gaston de Leval, at his house in the Avenue de la Toison d'Or," he whispered, his eyes widening. "He may have power to intercede or may know where such power lies."

Lizzie inhaled sharply, the light of hope filling her lungs. "Thank you, Mr. Marin. Thank you so much."

His dark eyes slid to hers. "I do not know that anything can be done."

"I know," Lizzie assured him, borrowing Beatrice's strength for the time being. "But you have given us a possibility, and that is more than we had before."

CHAPTER 26

Death.

Such a strange word, so short and brisk, a mere five letters, and yet it had the power to destroy life and hope and will.

Death was familiar to Edith as a nurse, and it was not always the dreaded beast people imagined. For some, death was a blessed relief from pain and agony and anxiety. Death could be peaceful and calm, a simple reunion with heaven. There was still mourning, as the love once shared in life turned to grief at separation, but death was not always so tragic.

But then there was the darkness of death brought on by war and suffering and tragedies no mortal could explain. The death that brought the despair of lives cut short, farewells not given, words left unsaid. The agony of inexplicable circumstances and the refusal to accept the reality.

Death was so multifaceted, so complicated, for such a simple thing.

And the prospect of death . . .

Well, that depended entirely upon the person for whom death would come, and what they might make of it.

Edith was going to die. By firing squad, if the military prosecutor was to be believed. He had taken great pride in calling them all together and reading out those who would die.

Philippe Baucq. Louise Thuliez. Jeanne de Belleville. Louis Séverin. And the Prince de Croÿ, though he had evaded German custody and therefore was not present to hear his fate. Their dates of death had yet to be determined, but they were just as certain as hers.

"*Todesstrafe*," the prosecutor had pronounced, the word colder than its translation, the man's tone edged with cruel victory.

Philippe had blanched a near-perfect white and sunk to his haunches, running his fingers through his hair. Louise had turned away, so Edith did not know her reaction. Jeanne was impassive, except for the tear that had run down her cheek. Mr. Séverin had barely reacted, though he had leaned against the wall.

And Edith . . .

She could only stand where she was, letting the slow chill of the very real end of her mortality creep upon her. It was rather strange, feeling as though she were somehow inhabiting her body and yet hovering just outside of it.

"Mademoiselle," a soft, low voice murmured near her.

She started a little, looking at kind Mr. Hostelet, who had been sentenced to imprisonment for up to eight years.

He smiled gently. "Will you not make an appeal for mercy?"

Edith shook her head, finding the thought a sweet one, but without merit. "It is useless. I am English, and they want my life."

"No, mademoiselle," Mr. Capiau urged, coming toward her. "You must try something. The English have power and influence, and they will not allow the Germans to shoot a woman!"

Again, Edith shook her head. "They wish me dead *because* I am English."

A third figure joined their group, and this one startled them all. He was a young German soldier assigned as their guard, but his expression was utterly tormented. "Never . . . say . . . die, *fräulein*," he whispered, his English rough, broken, and beautiful to Edith's ears.

Had she treated this man in her clinic at some point? Had he been the recipient of care from her capably trained nurses? Or was he, like so many, fatigued by war and hatred and clinging to whatever goodness he could find in the midst of it?

What a beautiful reminder of the blooms of the garden of the Lord, regardless of which nation the particular plot of ground sat.

Tears filled her eyes, and a lump formed in her throat. "It is useless," she told them all in French, even as she smiled with gratitude for each of them.

Slowly, all of the condemned started the path back to their cells, their steps as heavy as the burden of their fate.

Edith looked up in time to see a pastor standing nearby, watching them with great concern. "Good evening, Pastor," she greeted, unable to infuse the proper joy into her voice at speaking with someone in religious orders.

He immediately extended a hand to her, his expression filling with a kind light. "Mademoiselle Cavell, I am Pastor Le Seur. You have my greatest sympathies."

His German accent grated just enough to make her smile forced. "Thank you. How much time will they give me? Before . . ." She tilted her head in suggestion, unable to complete the sentence.

The pastor tsked sympathetically. "Only until tomorrow morning, I am afraid."

Heat rushed into Edith's cheeks while her feet suddenly became blocks of ice. That soon? It was hardly time to settle her soul, let alone her affairs.

Tomorrow?

Her eyes filled with tears, and she looked away. She would not cry in front of him, or in front of anyone.

He squeezed her hand. "Might I offer you my services as a pastor, mademoiselle? I am at your disposal at any hour of the day or night."

Edith shook her head quickly and firmly. "No, but thank you."

"Can I not show you some kindness?" he pleaded, his gentle tone forcing her attention back to him. He appeared nearly as tormented as the condemned prisoners, and yet he was affiliated with those who had brought this upon them.

The discrepancy was disconcerting.

"Please," he went on, covering her hand with both of his, "do not see in me now the German, but only a servant of our Lord and Savior. A servant who places himself entirely at your disposal."

The emotion she fought to hold back returned as a lump in her throat. "Would it . . ." She paused, clearing her throat roughly. "Would it be possible to inform my elderly mother in England, so that she might not learn of this through the newspapers?"

He nodded immediately. "Yes, of course. I give you my word. I will write to her myself." He gave her a searching look, as though waiting for her to ask more of him.

She could not, and would not, ask for more. She believed him to be a man of faith, a man dedicated to his religious orders, but he was yet a German and he was not Anglican. She would not be especially comfortable receiving ministration from him, no matter how kindly and sincerely offered.

"Mademoiselle," Pastor Le Seur said slowly, lowering his voice, "I know Reverend Gahan very well. He is a most pious Irishman, and I know he has been able to continue his religious duties during this occupation. Would you wish that he come to you to enable you to partake of the Holy Sacrament?"

Air rushed out of Edith's lungs in a massive gust of relief that she had no power to contain. She felt as though all of her worldly burdens were suddenly lifted from her shoulders. "Yes!" she whispered, now clasping the pastor's hands in return. "Oh, yes, please!"

A light of remarkable joy entered the pastor's eyes and expression, and he nodded. "I will write to him now and ask him to come. Please, my child, be at peace."

Edith nodded, beyond words now.

"And also . . ." He hesitated, his brow wrinkling in concern. "It is my duty to stand by your side at the last."

Her relief began to fade, but no burdens returned. She nodded, swallowing hard. "I understand, Pastor."

"I could try to see if Reverend Gahan might be permitted to do so, but I do not think—"

"No," Edith said quickly, cutting him off with more sharpness than she intended. "No, it would be much too heavy for Mr. Gahan. He is not accustomed to such things."

Pastor Le Seur gave her a sad smile. "Ah, Mademoiselle Cavell, I am not accustomed to it either." He paused. "I should like to come and fetch you here, instead of meeting you first outside on the Tir National. Would that suit you?"

Oh, what a blistering thing to consider. Would she prefer to meet with a man of God in prison or in the moments before meeting her end? It was a ghastly prospect.

Still, she knew what would settle her heart the most.

"Yes, Pastor," Edith murmured with a soft nod. "I would prefer to meet you here. Thank you for that consideration. It is most generous."

He held her hand more tightly. "God is generous, mademoiselle, as you know well. I merely strive to follow Him and walk in His ways."

She had to smile at that. "As do I."

He returned her smile. "May the grace of God go with you, Mademoiselle Cavell, and may His light shine eternally upon you."

Edith shook his hand, now heartily embracing the consolation he provided, despite their differences in rites and particulars. "And you, Pastor. Thank you." She nodded and released his hand.

As she walked down the corridor toward her cell, the hope of seeing her friend and reverend in a few hours was enough to nearly banish the gloom of what was to come.

It was several hours before Edith heard any sounds beyond her cell door, though the exact number of those hours was impossible to calculate. Time ceased to follow its usual rhythms in her cell, no matter what any working clock might have shown.

But when those sounds reached her ears, Edith rose from her bed in eager anticipation.

The heavy latch on the door creaked as it slid out of the way, then the door groaned as it swung open. The familiar sight of the tall, dark-haired reverend with his high brow and kind smile was as much a balm for her soul as reading her Bible the few minutes before had been.

"Reverend." Edith greeted him warmly, coming forward with her hand extended. "I was not sure if you would be permitted."

He met her in the cell and took her hand firmly. "Miss Cavell. I was given a special passport to come, and I am so grateful for it."

"So am I." Edith smiled and gestured toward her small cell, the shame of it being her present home to which she would welcome a man of God not lost on her. "Please, sit."

He took the wooden chair near her bed and moved it closer, while she sat upon the bed itself. There was a shadow of sorrow in his eyes, a tender regret she understood all too well. They had known each other for several years and had worked closely together during their mutual years in Brussels, and for this to be their final meeting was heartbreaking.

Edith sighed a little. "It is good of you to come."

Mr. Gahan's brow creased in surprise. "How could I not? Not only do I feel this my calling, Miss Cavell, but as your friend, I could not do anything less than bring you comfort and consolation at this time."

"Yes, I suppose you are right." She glanced down at her hands, folded in her lap, her fingers somehow not trembling or lacing with each other. "I had expected it would end like this."

"Had you?" he asked, his surprise evident.

Edith nodded. "My trial was conducted fairly, and my sentence was, under the circumstances, what I expected." She raised her chin, her mouth curving in a smile as the familiar comfort of heaven filled her heart. "I am thankful to God for the absolute quiet of these ten weeks' imprisonment. It has been like a solemn fast from all earthly distractions and diversions."

Mr. Gahan shifted in his seat, leaning forward and resting his elbows on his knees. "Not all would see it that way, I think. What a blessing your perspective must be for you."

She shrugged a shoulder lightly, not finding anything within herself to praise. "I have no fear, no shrinking. I have seen death so often that it is not strange or fearful to me. Life has always been hurried and full of difficulty, so this time of rest has been a great mercy. Everyone here has been very kind."

"Have they?" Mr. Gahan murmured softly and without judgment.

Edith dipped her chin in another nod, the tangled thoughts and words pressing on her chest and needing to get out. She paused, letting her breath work at the knotted mass of them. "This I would say, standing as I do in view of God and Eternity," she began, choosing each word with great care. "I realize that patriotism is not enough. I must have no hatred or bitterness towards anyone."

There was a long stretch of silence, and she chanced a glance at Mr. Gahan, who seemed to have a new pride in his expression. "Well said, Miss Cavell. Well said, indeed." He sat back, rubbing his hands together as though to warm them. "Shall we proceed with Communion?"

"Yes, please." She glanced around, looking for something to be used as the table but not finding any success.

"Here," Mr. Gahan suggested, rising from his chair. "This will work." He moved to sit next to her on the bed, pulling the chair between them and then reaching for his case where the necessary items lay protected.

He placed a white linen cloth over the seat of the chair, then set the small vessels upon it, filling each with the bread and wine. When this was done and all was set, he bowed his head. Edith did the same.

"Almighty God, Father of our Lord Jesus Christ, Maker of all things, judge of all men; We acknowledge and bewail our manifold sins and wickedness, which we, from time to time, most grievously have committed, By thought, word, and deed, Against thy Divine Majesty, Provoking most justly thy wrath and indignation against us. We do earnestly repent, and are heartily sorry for these our misdoings; The remembrance of them is grievous unto us; The burden of them is intolerable. Have mercy upon us, Have mercy upon us, most merciful Father; For thy Son our Lord Jesus Christ's sake, Forgive us all that is past; And grant that we may ever hereafter Serve and please thee In newness of life, To the honour and glory of thy Name; Through Jesus Christ our Lord. Amen."

"Amen," Edith murmured.

"Hear what comfortable words our Saviour Christ saith unto all that truly turn to him: Come unto me, all that travail and are heavy laden, and I will refresh you. So God loved the world, that he gave his only begotten Son, to the end that all that believe in him should not perish, but have everlasting life.

"Hear also what Saint Paul saith: This is a true saying, and worthy of all men to be received, that Christ Jesus came into the world to save sinners.

"Hear also what Saint John saith: If any man sin, we have an advocate with the Father, Jesus Christ the righteous; and he is the propitiation for our sins.

"Lift up your hearts."

Edith nodded. "We lift them up unto the Lord."

He solemnly recited the prayers of the sacrament and broke the bread in pieces, laying them in the vessel. Then he blessed the small chalice of wine.

He paused the prayers to take a piece of bread for himself, then offered one to Edith. "The Body of our Lord Jesus Christ, which was given for thee, preserve thy body and soul unto everlasting life. Take and eat this in remembrance that Christ died for thee, and feed on him in thy heart by faith with thanksgiving."

As Edith chewed, Mr. Gahan set the bowl down and picked up the chalice, sipping a little before extending it to her. "The Blood of our Lord Jesus Christ, which was shed for thee, preserve thy body and soul unto everlasting life. Drink this in remembrance that Christ's Blood was shed for thee, and be thankful."

Edith sipped, then handed the chalice back to him. He set it upon the chair and covered the Communion with another square of white linen. He rested his hands upon the linen, then pulled his hands back, folding them deferentially in prayer.

"Our Father," he began, Edith joining him in recitation, "which art in heaven, Hallowed be thy Name. Thy kingdom come. Thy will be done, in earth as it is in heaven. Give us this day our daily bread. And forgive us our trespasses, As we forgive them that trespass against us. And lead us not into temptation; But deliver us from evil: For thine is the kingdom, The power, and the glory, For ever and ever. Amen."

Her eyes burned with tears, and she bowed her head even further.

"Almighty and everliving God," Mr. Gahan prayed, "we most heartily thank thee, for that thou dost vouchsafe to feed us, who have duly received these holy mysteries, with the spiritual food of the most precious Body and Blood of thy Son our Saviour Jesus Christ; and dost assure us thereby of thy favour and goodness towards us; and that we are very members incorporate in the mystical body of thy Son, which is the blessed company of all faithful people; and are also heirs through hope of thy everlasting kingdom, by the merits of the most precious death and passion of thy dear Son. And we most humbly beseech thee, O heavenly Father, so to assist us with thy grace, that we may continue in that holy fellowship, and do all such good works as thou hast prepared for us to walk in; through Jesus Christ our Lord, to whom, with thee and the Holy Ghost, be all honour and glory, world without end. *Amen.*"

"Amen," Edith whispered around the lump in her throat.

She had never sat in a shortened Communion service, so she simply waited in solemn reverence for anything else Mr. Gahan wished to add. But the most important part of it—the Communion itself—had taken place, and for that she would be eternally grateful.

She heard Mr. Gahan exhale, and then, in a soft voice, he began to recite something which took her quite by surprise.

> *Abide with me; fast falls the eventide;*
> *The darkness deepens; Lord with me abide.*
> *When other helpers fail and comforts flee,*
> *Help of the helpless, O abide with me.*

Edith began whispering the words with him, opening her eyes and staring at nothing in particular. It was her favorite hymn, the one that seemed to touch her heart and soul in a way none of the others could. She had always been sensitive to the power of music in worship services, but this particular hymn . . .

Could Mr. Gahan know how much this meant to her?

They continued to recite together:

> *Swift to its close ebbs out life's little day;*
> *Earth's joys grow dim; its glories pass away;*
> *Change and decay in all around I see;*
> *O Thou who changest not, abide with me.*
>
> *I need Thy presence every passing hour.*
> *What but Thy grace can foil the tempter's power?*
> *Who, like Thyself, my guide and stay can be?*
> *Through cloud and sunshine, Lord, abide with me.*
>
> *I fear no foe, with Thee at hand to bless;*
> *Ills have no weight, and tears no bitterness.*
> *Where is death's sting? Where, grave, thy victory?*
> *I triumph still, if Thou abide with me.*
>
> *Hold Thou Thy cross before my closing eyes;*
> *Shine through the gloom and point me to the skies.*
> *Heaven's morning breaks, and earth's vain shadows flee;*
> *In life, in death, O Lord, abide with me.*

Edith took a slow, almost steady breath.

In life, in death, O Lord, abide with me.

He had done so in life, and now death was upon her. The wishes, the pleas of the song were now acutely the pleas of her own heart.

Mr. Gahan shifted on the bed, turning toward her. "How can I bring further solace to your soul, Miss Cavell?"

Edith lowered her eyes to the floor, an odd tingling beginning in her chest. "I am concerned about my sinfulness and unworthiness. How can I be sure that heaven will welcome me after death?"

He nodded in understanding, his gentle smile spreading. "If you will recall the words of our Lord to the thief who was on the cross near him, you may find your answer. The thief pleaded, 'Lord, remember me when thou comest into thy kingdom.' And the Lord replied, 'Today shalt thou be with me in paradise.' The thief, who had been through trial and accusations for his sins, and also condemned to the cross, was forgiven and promised a place with the Lord. If he, who was a criminal, could be forgiven of all, why should not you receive the same? The Lord is almighty to forgive and to save, Miss Cavell, and to admit all His pardoned ones into His blessed presence and rest."

Edith laced her fingers together and brought her joined hands to her lips, letting the joyous words sink deep into her soul. She murmured a breathless and fervent plea that what Mr. Gahan had said might be so, then lowered her hands to her lap.

"This promise," Mr. Gahan urged gently, "covers all the need and ends all anxiety, does it not?"

"Yes," Edith whispered. "God is most gracious with us."

"He is, indeed." He held out a hand, and she placed hers safely within his palm. "What else can I do for you at this time?"

Edith swallowed, thinking on the details that ought to be considered before her death occurred. "Would you be so good as to send out these messages I have written to friends and loved ones?" She gestured toward a small but tidy stack of letters near the pillow of her bed. "I have been much occupied with writing while waiting for your arrival, and I am not certain that . . . Well, it would console me to know that you will see them posted." She reached for them and offered the stack to him.

"Of course, I can see that done," he affirmed quickly, taking the letters. He gave her hand a gentle squeeze. "We shall always remember you as a heroine and as a martyr."

"No," Edith protested, a new edge entering her voice. "Don't think of me like that. Think of me only as a nurse who tried to do her duty."

That was all she wanted to be in the memories and minds of those who knew her. She had not done anything of particular note, had not engaged in great and daring deeds, had not done anything to rise into the noble ranks of heroism. She was simply Edith Cavell, a dedicated nurse and devoted Christian.

Such a description would be far more fitting for her eternal reputation than anything else.

They sat together in the quiet for a few more moments before Mr. Gahan released a soft exhale. "Perhaps I had better go now, as you will want to rest."

She nodded and rose, feeling steadier than she had in some time. "Yes, I have to be up at five."

Mr. Gahan rose and moved to the cell door, Edith following. He turned and held out his hand again. "Goodbye, Miss Cavell."

Somehow, she could smile in response and truly mean it. "We shall meet again."

"Yes, we shall," he replied firmly, shaking her hand with a confidence only those with the certainty of their faith could possess. "God be with you."

"And with you, sir."

Mr. Gahan nodded, the tender light still in his eyes. He tapped on the cell door, which opened with the same disturbance of sounds it always did.

Edith watched him exit the cell, and she felt air leave her lungs when the door closed firmly, decidedly, behind him.

"God be with you," Edith whispered again in the silence of her too-empty cell.

CHAPTER 27

It was astonishing what one could manage through tears, and how one's legs could remain steady in spite of them.

Such a wry thought to have while standing in front of Maître de Leval from the American Legation, but in the face of his stunned silence, Lizzie could not blame herself for thinking it.

"No," de Leval murmured, shaking his head uncertainly for what might have been the dozenth time since their arrival. "No, I have been following the case very closely, I can assure you. Not an hour ago, I heard from the secretary's office at the Politische Abteilung that judgment had not been pronounced and was expected tomorrow."

"Sir," Beatrice interjected with a firmness Lizzie envied. "We have heard it directly from the deputy governor of the prison himself. He is the one who told us to come directly to your home! I can assure you, it is true."

Maître de Leval ran a hand through his hair, muttering to himself. "I had feared swift judgment, but not so swift as this." He shook his head once more and reached into his desk drawer. "I have been drafting a clemency appeal in the name of the United States minister, Mr. Whitlock, and I will add this information to it. The situation is far more serious now than can possibly be imagined."

He scribbled additional lines to the document, then pushed up from his desk and rounded it. "Come, we'll go to the Whitlocks now. It is just in Rue de Trèves."

He snatched his coat from the rack and practically tossed it about his shoulders.

He gestured toward the door, and Lizzie turned, hurrying forward.

"Can the minister do something to stop this?" she asked as they moved back out into the rain.

"If anyone can, it is him," de Leval told her. "He knows everyone, and America is not in this conflict yet. Perhaps he might appeal as a neutral party on her behalf."

Lizzie frowned, not seeing how the United States minister could be considered neutral when all British citizens could go to him for aid while living in Belgium. Everyone would know he had care over them, so he could hardly be truly neutral where Edith's fate was concerned.

"You have tried to intervene before this?" Beatrice asked as they continued toward the American Legation.

"Oh, yes," he said. "I was going to attend the trial but was advised it would do more harm than good. We have been sending many letters and telegrams to get information and to protect Miss Cavell but have received hardly any responses. We've been in constant communication with the Foreign Office in London, acting in all ways possible politically, but . . ."

Lizzie swiped at her still streaming tears, now mingling with the rain upon her cheeks. "But?"

Maître de Leval glanced at her. "But no progress has been made. As is ofttimes the case with politics."

"Politics are going to see my friend and matron murdered?" Lizzie cried in outrage. "What of humanity and decency?"

"My thoughts exactly, Miss Wilkins," he responded with maddening calm. "Which is why we are going to be bursting in on Mr. Whitlock—and hopefully quite a few other people tonight."

Bursting anywhere sounded marvelous at the moment, and Lizzie was not afraid to admit it. She would pay any price if it would help Edith out of her unjust fate at dawn.

They arrived at 74 Rue de Trèves shortly thereafter and were informed that Mr. Whitlock was ill and in bed.

Maître de Leval, thankfully, would not be put off and instructed Lizzie and Beatrice to wait downstairs with Mrs. Whitlock and the Legation secretary, Miss Larner, while he went to discuss the matter with Mr. Whitlock, regardless of his state of health.

Lizzie sat uneasily in her chair, fidgeting as she waited for Maître de Leval to come back downstairs. Waiting when every minute mattered was maddening, and she was not good at waiting before tonight.

Mrs. Whitlock offered them tea and then sherry, when the tea was politely declined, but Lizzie refused that as well. She did not want to settle, did not want to be set to rights, did not want to calm the anxiety raging within her.

It was the only thing keeping her from crumbling at the moment.

After what felt like an age, Maître de Leval trotted down the stairs, his expression unreadable.

Lizzie was immediately on her feet. "Well?"

De Leval turned to a nearby staff member. "Send for Hugh Gibson immediately. He is believed to be dining out, but he must present himself here at once. See if he can also find the Marquis de Villalobar to join him."

Without waiting to see if his order was obeyed, he turned to Lizzie and the others. "Mr. Whitlock and I have composed a telegram to be sent to London, and, as he is too unwell to join us on our demands, he suggested Mr. Gibson, his First Secretary, accompany us tonight to personally present the pleas to the necessary parties." His lip curled in a wry smile. "He is known to have a fiery temper."

"Good," Beatrice grunted, to which the other ladies nodded.

"It is unfathomable that they should find it acceptable to kill a woman," Mrs. Whitlock insisted darkly, seeming to shake slightly. "And so soon after trial, too."

"And those are the points we intend to make," de Leval agreed. "We have drafted a letter to be presented to Baron von der Lancken, who is our political liaison with the German military."

Mrs. Whitlock nodded and walked away, undoubtedly to request something else be brought to them for their comfort while they waited.

Lizzie watched her go, then leaned closer to Maître de Leval. "Mr. Whitlock will not go himself?"

He shook his head sadly. "He truly feels too unwell to do so. I am disappointed, as his presence would do more than his words, but I cannot argue further."

She nodded, feeling her own disappointment sink in. But if the minister thought Mr. Gibson would be sufficient, she had no course but to believe it as well.

The silence in the reception room was deafening, only the faintest hint of the distant rain outside audible. The dim light of day faded fully into night until only the lights of candles all around them enabled them to see. Lizzie glanced around the room, marveling at the golden American eagle that hung above them. Was such a sight motivating or imposing? Or both?

Did not the eagle represent freedom and independence? She desperately needed such a result for Edith. She took advantage of the quiet to pray fervently for it.

How long they waited for Mr. Gibson, Lizzie could not say, but the moment he strode into the room, his expression stormy, hope blazed to life within her.

"Where do we go first?" Mr. Gibson demanded, wiping at the rain that had splattered across his face.

Behind him stood a well-dressed, stocky, bald man—Marquis de Villalobar, Lizzie surmised.

If Maître de Leval was shocked by the bold manner of Mr. Gibson's arrival, he gave no indication. Instead, he nodded briskly. "Politische Abteilung. Von der Lancken is the best bet."

Gibson returned the nod and turned on his heel. "Best be off!" he called behind him.

Maître de Leval gestured for Lizzie and Beatrice to follow. "If you wish, of course."

"Yes, please," Lizzie insisted, starting after the other two men.

Mr. Gibson made no objection to the women coming along, though he did raise an eyebrow. The marquis quickly made room, and Lizzie noted, briefly, that his legs were wooden. That would account for his manner of walking, but it did not seem to hinder him a jot.

It was six blocks to the German political ministry, and it was fully dark when they arrived. Still, the men exited the car—Lizzie and Beatrice following—and took turns pounding on the door and ringing the bell. There was no hint of life from the inside, no lights flickering on, no shuffling of feet nearing the door.

Hopeless, Lizzie thought to herself with a heavy groan. *Utterly hopeless.*

Just as she was ready to suggest they return to the car, the great oak door heaved open, and a disgruntled concierge answered.

"No one home," he grunted, preparing to close the door in their faces.

Mr. Gibson pressed a hand to the door, holding it open. "Where is von der Lancken?" he demanded.

The concierge seemed aware that arguing with this man would not get him very far at all. "The theater," he begrudgingly relented. "*Le Bois Sacre* in Rue d'Arenberg."

"Excellent," Gibson exclaimed in approval, pushing the door wider and striding in. "Send for him. Take our car. We shall wait."

Lizzie clamped down on a startled laugh and followed the marquis and Maître de Leval into the ministry, despite the startled and irritable expression of the poor concierge.

"Remind me to keep on Mr. Gibson's good side," Beatrice whispered to her, a hint of laughter in her tone.

Maître de Leval ushered them into chairs while Mr. Gibson and the marquis ordered the concierge to do as directed. Eventually, he left, and she could hear the car driving away.

Rush and then wait, rush and then wait. That seemed to be the process of the night, and it was a maddening management of time. She distracted herself by taking in this grand ministry of the Germans, their offices of politics from which they marched on towns and burned them to the ground.

Politics, indeed.

The ceilings of the parlor were higher than she expected, and the furniture was white enamel with yellow satin upholstery. The room exuded tradition, refinement, even gentility, which was a mighty paradox with the actions of the Germans. What had this place been before they had taken over? Who had worked here, lived here? Would she have felt the paradox so completely then?

It was after 10:30 when the ministry doors were thrown open, thundering against the walls of the entry. Three finely dressed men entered the parlor, and the center one, in the process of stripping off his gloves, seemed genuinely surprised to see those within.

"Still here?" he grumbled in English.

Mr. Gibson, Maître de Leval, and the marquis rose upon their entry.

"Baron von der Lancken, we have come to appeal on behalf of the British nurse, Edith Cavell," Mr. Gibson said.

The baron groaned and threw up his hands. *"Ach, nein!"*

"Oh, yes, sir," Mr. Gibson insisted, undeterred. "We have it on most excellent authority that she is to be shot in the morning."

Baron von der Lancken scoffed with a loud rudeness Lizzie found incredibly disrespectful. He switched to French, either for the ease of it or to prevent Lizzie and Beatrice from understanding, though they were both fluent in the language. "Impossible. Who is the source of your information?"

Mr. Gibson shook his head firmly from side to side. "An excellent and credible one, sir."

"It cannot be official, then," the baron said with a shrug.

Maître de Leval stepped forward. "Without doubt, I consider my information trustworthy, but I must refuse to tell you from whom I received it. Besides, what difference does it make? If the information is true, our presence at this hour is justified. If it is not true, I am ready to take the consequences of my mistake."

The baron looked at him in disgust. "Orders are never issued with such precipitation! And especially when a woman is concerned. *Gott im Himmel,* how, at this hour, can I obtain any information? The governor general must certainly be sleeping!"

"Telephone the prison, then," Gibson suggested easily. "That will tell you of the validity of our claim."

Baron von der Lancken looked mildly less irritated at that suggestion. "I had not thought of that. One moment." He strode from the room with the same grandeur with which he had entered.

His lackeys, whoever they were, remained in the parlor but said nothing.

It was a scant few minutes before the baron returned, his bluster all but gone, color in his cheeks. "You are right," he announced in French. "Miss Cavell will be shot in the morning."

Maître de Leval handed him the letter from Mr. Whitlock.

The baron sat to read it, a sarcastic little smile appearing on his face as he did so. He finally shook his head and handed the letter back to de Leval. "Is there also a formal plea for mercy?"

De Leval handed that over.

Again, the baron read quickly, then made another scoffing sound. "What do you expect me to do about that spy?"

"It is not a question of spying," Mr. Gibson protested hotly. "It is a question of the life of a woman—a life that has been devoted to charity, to the service of others. She has nursed wounded soldiers— has even nursed German wounded since the beginning of the war— and now she is accused of but one thing: of having helped British soldiers make their way toward Holland."

"Is that not enough?" the baron asked with an almost sneer.

Mr. Gibson shook his head. "She may have been imprudent, she may have acted against the laws of the occupying power, but she was not a spy. She was not accused of being a spy, she has not been convicted of spying, and she does not merit the death of a spy."

Baron von der Lancken had no direct reply and resorted to rubbing his hands over his face.

"I find it a great pity," one of the lackeys chimed in, "that we have not three or four English women to shoot."

Lizzie gasped and stared at the man in horror, and she sensed that most of the other men in the room did so as well.

Baron von der Lancken, though, nodded.

The lackey was unabashed in his statements. "The life of one German soldier seems much more important than that of all the old English nurses."

Mr. Gibson glowered. "Given the service our capable English nurses have done for your precious German soldiers, I wonder that you value them so little. We have two such nurses with us now. Will you slander them again?" He gestured toward Lizzie and Beatrice.

The man looked over at them, then shrugged.

Baron von der Lancken looked toward the antique French clock on the far side of the room, yawning. "It is a shame that the minister himself could not come. Not important enough for him, perhaps?"

Mr. Gibson stiffened in response, while Maître de Leval's hands formed fists at his side.

The baron offered a patronizing smile. "Why don't you go home reasonably?" he suggested. "Sleep quietly and come back in the morning, and we'll talk about it. *Nicht wahr?*"

"Are you entirely serious?" Maître de Leval burst out, his control snapping. "A woman's life hangs in the balance! Wait until morning? By your own admission, she will have been shot by then, and it will be too late!"

Mr. Gibson nodded his agreement. "It would seem we have come on a fool's errand, presenting ourselves here. The entire German political party has clearly been engaging in falsification and subterfuge, including the failure to inform the Legation of the sentence, even after we had been given the word of honor of one of yours to do so."

The baron's head swung around to him, a coldness in his eyes that told Lizzie that specific accusation stung.

"The offense charged against Miss Cavell," Gibson continued, "has long been accomplished. As she has already been in prison for many weeks, a slight delay in carrying out the sentence could not possibly endanger the German cause. Have you considered, Baron, the effects that a deed such as the summary execution of a death sentence against a woman would have upon public opinion? Not only in Belgium, but in America. In Britain. In Spain." He gestured to the marquis standing by his side. "In many, many places. And after Louvain was burned down and the *Lusitania* sunk? It will be more than enough, this act. There is a great possibility of reprisals against it."

"It does not matter," Baron von der Lancken broke in. "Governor von Lüttwitz is the supreme authority in such matters, and I have no authority to intervene. Under the provisions of German martial law, it lays within the discretion of the military governor whether he would accept or refuse an appeal for clemency."

"Oh, come now!" the Spanish marquis interrupted loudly, his accent giving his French a firmer note. "We are speaking of a woman; you cannot shoot a woman like that!" He marched toward the baron. "Call the Great Headquarters at Charleville and learn if the Kaiser himself is there tonight. Surely, he will grant a stay."

The three Germans reared back in almost comical unison. "In Germany, diplomats are not on such informal terms with our rulers," the baron remonstrated. He shuddered, seeming to shake off the very suggestion. "Come, gentlemen. It is past eleven o'clock. What can be done? *Nichts!*"

Maître de Leval folded his arms, standing firm in his place. "Until you call Governor von Lüttwitz, we will not be removing ourselves. The sooner you do so, the sooner you might be rid of us."

The baron glared at him, at Gibson, at the marquis, even at Lizzie and Beatrice, before heaving himself out of his chair and grumbling in German as he started out of the room again.

Lizzie sank onto a sofa after he departed and began to silently pray.

The men conversed with the two lackeys whose names she had never caught, reiterating their arguments, but she could not bring herself to listen closely.

It was too much, this back and forth, this rationalization of a wrong, this fighting for a course of sense that should have been a simple answer. But of course, if Edith's fate was in the hands of Governor von Lüttwitz alone, hope was already gone.

Lizzie glanced over at the lackeys. The one who had said such beastly things earlier was paring his nails with a pocketknife and yawning. The other was still in conversation with the men, and he at least looked sympathetic, which was something, she supposed. Outside, the rain continued to fall, pelting against the window in a regular and steady pattern.

No one would be out in the rain at this hour. The streets would be entirely empty, rather like the prospects of this meeting.

Was there any hope at all to be found in this night?

It was ages before the dreadful baron returned, looking a trifle pale, which gave an odd little jolt to Lizzie's sorrowing heart before it dropped in despair.

"I am exceedingly sorry," he began, sounding more shaken than repentant. "The governor was slightly intoxicated at home following an evening at the Théâtre de la Monnaie. He was . . . brusque. He tells me that the execution was decided upon and he will not change his decision. Making use of his prerogative, he even refuses to receive the plea for mercy. Therefore, no one, not even the Kaiser, can do anything for you."

The room fell entirely silent. Lizzie looked around at her allies, those who were fighting so hard for Edith, waiting for one of them to have a retort or suggest a plan.

No one said anything.

Then the grizzled Spanish marquis hobbled over to Baron von der Lancken and took him by the coat. "Come," he barked. "I must speak with you." He pulled on the taller German until he led him into an anteroom, no doubt to give them privacy.

But his voice sounded clearly to the lot of them.

"It is an idiotic thing you are going to do!" he raged. "You will have another Louvain! It is not only a crime, but a crass stupidity—thousands of British soldiers will rise up to avenge her!"

It was the sort of noble speech that made Lizzie want to cheer, but she settled for clenching her hands in her lap.

Then the marquis's voice lowered, and his words were not intelligible to any of them.

Maître de Leval sighed heavily. "It seems incredible that not even a single day can be granted to stay the execution. It is without any legal precedent whatever!"

The Germans had no response to this, so de Leval stepped closer to Mr. Gibson. "Desperate measures? We could call the Kaiser by telephone and explain. Or send him a telegram. Or visit in person. Charleville is but a few hours' fast drive; we could make it."

Mr. Gibson opened his mouth to respond when von der Lancken and de Villalobar returned to the room. Von der Lancken was red in the face, looking as though he had been soundly beaten without actually bearing a mark, and the Spaniard was positively fuming.

But one look at their faces told everyone in the room that the decision had been made and their visit was not going to produce the result they'd hoped for.

Maître de Leval scoffed loudly, shaking his head. He strode from the room toward the door, and Lizzie and Beatrice followed at a quick signal from Mr. Gibson. The marquis brought up the rear, not one of them speaking another word to the Germans. They took their coats and hats and ventured out into the rainy night with more despair than that with which they'd arrived.

They drove back to the ministry in silence and, upon their entrance, spotted a few more nurses waiting for them, along with Mrs. Whitlock and Reverend and Mrs. Gahan.

Maître de Leval was pale, and Mr. Gibson rubbed his forehead. As they gave a report to those waiting, Lizzie sank onto a nearby chair and let her tears rush down her cheeks at the utter futility of it all.

One of her fellow nurses rubbed her back, and a glass of sherry was placed in her hand. She sipped it absently through her tears, barely noticing it.

She barely noticed anything now.

"Come, Lizzie," Beatrice murmured, nudging her after a while. "We should go home."

Home? How could she go home when Edith would not be there? Would never be there?

Yet she stood, her legs shaky.

Mr. Gibson came over and took her hand in farewell. "I will ring doorbells all night and all morning long, if I have to. Call whoever I must. Every last link."

Lizzie swallowed hard and nodded. "Thank you, Mr. Gibson. For everything." She looked beyond him to Maître de Leval. "And you, sir. And the marquis. Thank you all for your efforts."

They nodded wordlessly, and Lizzie, along with her fellow nurses, left the ministry in the company of the equally silent Gahans.

"I don't want to go home," Lizzie murmured. "Not yet."

"Where should we go, then?" Beatrice asked.

She sniffled and wiped at her cheeks. "I want to go to the prison.

Perhaps we might catch a glimpse of her before . . ." She could not bear to say it, and looked away, leaving the dreaded words unspoken.

They all turned, though, and started in that direction. Their steps slow, but firm.

All the while, the rain fell about their heads.

CHAPTER 28

Edith lay on the bed in her cell, fully awake, staring up into the bright light upon the ceiling. They had not been permitted to lower the lights in their cells, not since one of her fellow accused had hanged himself. The Germans did not want any of the rest of them to escape their rightful fates by taking matters into their own hands.

She was not tempted to do so, at any rate.

She had been able to rest for a few hours after Reverend Gahan had left, finding a new serenity and comfort in his words. She was not about to shake her fist at heaven for the injustice of it all. Bemoan her forthcoming end for being too soon. Weep endlessly for what might have been, had she been spared.

There was something of beauty in suffering and uncertainty. Some magnificent gap of time and self where one had to let go of the known and move into the unknown with only faith as their guide. What brilliance such a refining fire had produced in ancient times, and with more recent saints, and with those individuals who felt themselves far too insignificant for such notice, but whose travails had brought them into a higher, holier plane.

This was, and had been, Edith's refining fire, she was certain. How brilliant its result would be, she could not say. She might never know, in this mortal experience. The effect could be some light to shine for others, rather than for herself.

She hoped that would be the case. She would much rather be a beacon to others than a lone figure on some unnecessary pedestal.

Edith blinked and looked at the small watch set upon the chair near her bed.

Five minutes to five.

She swallowed a brief flare of apprehension and rose from her bed. She padded to the small jug and basin in the corner of the room and washed her face, the cold water igniting an icy chill that rippled down her spine.

She was going to die shortly.

And yet she felt no panic at that statement. No clawing, gaping chasm of fear. She did not wish to die, of course, but she could honestly say she was not afraid of it. She was sorry for the pain it would cause her mother, her sisters, and her brother. Her cousin Eddy. Her friends. Lizzie. Her dear nurses.

But such pain was also an expression of love and affection, and she was so very blessed to have had such bonds that would render those pains at her death.

How many could say they were so fortunate?

She folded the linens of her bed, the actions reminding her of the chores of the clinic, the tasks she had done as a junior nurse, and even as a governess. Such simple things, and so habitual. She looked about the small space, finding her scant belongings already rather neat in their places. No need to fuss about there.

She had decided the night before that she would wear the same clothes from her trial on this day. Removing her nightgown, she pulled on her blue skirt, followed by her white blouse. Doing up the buttons seemed to take longer than normal, yet her fingers never fumbled even once. She slid her arms into the sleeves of the matching blue coat and fastened those buttons. Then came the gold stud on her collar, the gray fur stole, the hat with a tortoiseshell pin.

There was no looking glass in the cell, but she knew how she would look, and she exhaled with the satisfaction one might sensibly feel upon viewing a reflection.

Then she knelt beside her bed, clasping her hands together and bowing her head.

What she said, how she said it, how much she confessed—all were lost to her. There was less conversation in this prayer and more a reaching of her deepest emotions. A craving for a connection to heaven that would see her through the next few hours. A desire to glimpse the glories she might find after the shots were fired.

A need to touch the hem of the Lord's garment and be made whole.

The reaching of a fragile plant toward a glorious source of light.

As the door to her cell opened, she exhaled deeply and swallowed hard.

"Mademoiselle Cavell," came the soft voice of Pastor Le Seur.

Edith nodded and slowly rose, turning toward the door and offering the kind man a smile. "Pastor. Thank you for coming."

His smile was full of compassion, if not sadness. "Are you ready?"

She glanced behind her, nodding again. "I have packed everything into the carpetbag there. It is not much, but it is my property." She turned back, looking at the guard beside the pastor. "Is that all right?"

The guard nodded, his eyes less cold than she had seen before.

"Come," Pastor Le Seur said, holding out a hand to her.

She went to him, head held high, and together they walked slowly down the long corridor of the prison toward the entrance. Several guards in their spiked helmets lined the way, and many of them lowered their heads as she passed.

She nodded thanks to each of them, hoping that, in their mutual silence of the moment, there might be found a hint of benevolence on both sides.

They turned through the entrance to the prison, the pre-dawn light of Brussels adding its own special silence to each breath and footstep. Cars waited for them, and Pastor Le Seur led her toward one. From behind her, she heard voices and glanced to see Philippe Baucq and his Catholic priest following.

Philippe met her eyes, emotion and resignation laced into his features. He gave her a faint smile and nodded.

Edith took the chance to glance around at this beloved city, this home she had made for herself away from the home of her childhood, this place that had adopted her so well.

A small group of women stood nearby, and she knew them at once.

Her nurses.

Lizzie stood in the center, her pale cheeks stained with tears, her eyes fixed on Edith with the rawness of finality.

Edith tried to smile but found the effort too great to bear. She turned her attention to the car before her, taking the pastor's hand as he helped her in.

"Matron!"

"Madame! Madame!"

Their cries reached her ears with a warm familiarity that took her back to the clinic, to her training sessions, to her chats with the nurses in the evenings, and, even in their sounds of distress, she found comfort in knowing of their care for her.

She silently prayed they would know how deeply she cared for them too.

The cars pulled away from the prison, and the cries of her nurses faded into silence. Silence filled the car, and Edith did not bother looking out the window or even through the windshield. She was only aware of every breath entering and exiting her body, and the calm, steady way she moved with each.

Soon the Tir National loomed before them, the massive edifice miraculously free from moss and ivy, unlike so many other stately buildings of a similar age and condition. The two narrow fronting minarets added to its majesty and grandeur. It had been used as a rifle range by the Belgians before the war. Now it was used for the same purpose by the Germans occupying the land.

Shot by Germans on a Belgian firing range.

There was something darkly ironic in that.

The cars pulled to a stop, and Edith glanced out the window, startled to see what had to be a full company of soldiers lined up and waiting for them, practically leading the way to the scene of her death.

A show of strength toward those who would soon no longer be here.

Edith cleared her throat as she exited the car, glancing down at her skirt with a slight frown. She turned to the nearest guard. "Could I have several large pins, please?"

He seemed surprised by the request, but moments later she was handed some.

"Thank you." She stooped, gathering the fabric of her skirt and pinning the folds together. She took another pin and secured the length of her skirts around her ankles, smoothing the lines so she would still look presentable. There was no telling what her body would do once it was shot, and she needed to ensure her skirt would not flare up before the soldiers.

It was, perhaps, a small thing, an errant thought to have at such a time, but she was willing to follow through if it would help her feel more prepared as she walked down that hill to her fate.

Nodding at the new security of her skirts, Edith rose and handed the remaining pins back to the guard.

He looked at her handiwork, then back at her. "Good thought," he grunted.

She nodded at his strange compliment and started toward the front with Pastor Le Seur, Philippe and the priest following behind. The soldiers shifted their rifles in brisk, coordinated motions to present the weapons as they passed. It was a strange, solemn sight to walk down the line of armed and uniformed soldiers, none of whom knew her or Philippe, none of whom knew the specifics of their supposed crimes, none of whom would have any sort of personal stake in what was about to take place.

And what of the ones who would fire upon them? Would they feel the weight of their responsibility? Of snuffing out a life on the orders of others who outranked and overpowered their own wishes? Did they consider such things in their moments of private reflection?

Or was it simply part of a soldier's duty and nothing more?

Compassion filled Edith as she looked at the men she passed, forgiving each and every one for the things they were required to do that might never have been thought of in times of peace. War could make monsters out of anyone, and she would not be their judge.

They reached the bottom of the hill, a separate line of eight soldiers bearing rifles standing away off. Several paces across from them were two vertical white planks.

There. There would be her final breath of mortality.

She stared at the planks with the sort of detachment one might have observing a car passing in the street.

Someone cleared their throat, and she turned to see Mr. Stoeber from the trial standing by the soldiers, papers in his hand.

Before he could speak, Philippe stepped forward. "Brothers," he announced in clear French, "in the presence of death, we are all comrades!"

The guard nearest him pulled him back a few steps, silencing him at once.

Mr. Stoeber gave him a dark look, then turned back to his paper. "Philippe Baucq, you are hereby brought to the Tir National for the fulfilling of your lawfully determined sentence, which is death by firing squad. Edith Cavell, you are also hereby brought to the Tir National for the fulfilling of your lawfully determined sentence, which is death by firing squad. Please escort the prisoners to their positions."

Paster Le Seur took Edith gently by the elbow and turned her in the direction of the plank, walking with her.

Her steps seemed heavier than ever in her life, but her legs still moved, the crunch of the grass beneath her feet rough and unfamiliar. She caught sight of a simple yellow coffin set beyond each white plank, lids leaning against the wood. They would be buried immediately after they were shot, then. Quick and simple, all done in the dark of the morning.

Edith swallowed, her throat suddenly dry, her stomach clenching as they neared the planks.

Pastor Le Suer took her hand as they walked, pressing it firmly. "The Grace of our Lord Jesus Christ and the love of God and the Communion of the Holy Ghost be with you forever. Amen."

Edith returned the pressure. "Amen."

"Remember the words of our Lord: 'I will not leave you

comfortless: I will come to you. Yet a little while, and the world seeth me no more; but ye see me: because I live, ye shall live also.'" He squeezed her hand again. "The fate of the truly faithful, mademoiselle."

"Yes," she whispered, gripping his hand more tightly. "Thank you for being here, Pastor. I hold no enmity toward you. May God bless you for your faith and service."

He nodded and led her the rest of the way to the plank. Edith turned and set her back against the smooth wood, her heart racing as she stared at his compassionate face. "Ask Mr. Gahan to tell my loved ones later on that my soul, as I believe, is safe, and that I am glad to die for my country."

Pastor Le Seur smiled in encouragement, though the pain never left his eyes. "God bless you, mademoiselle. All will be well."

It was an odd thing to say, she thought at first, considering a guard had moved behind the plank to fasten her wrists together. But as the ropes tightened around her, the pastor's words took on a new light, easing the tension in her chest.

All *would* be well. Not shortly, not in the next few minutes, or perhaps even longer, depending on . . .

Well, on how accurate the shots were.

But all would be well soon enough. She would be free of this world and its chains, free of the pain and suffering she had witnessed, free of all worldly cares.

That was well, indeed.

Nodding at the kind pastor, Edith leaned her head back against the surface of the plank and turned her attention to the soldiers preparing their rifles.

The guard finished the knots at her wrists, then came around the front, linen bandage in hand.

A shaky breath escaped Edith, and she glanced at Philippe, still in conversation with his priest. He paused, looking back at her. His shoulders moved on a heavy exhale, and his sad smile filled her with a measure of peace.

She was not alone. Would not be alone. Philippe was here, would endure the same, and she had been assured that God was with her.

She nodded at Philippe and returned her attention to the guard before her, who watched her carefully.

She blinked as she gave him a firm nod, surprised to feel tears fall from her eyes. Her lips and jaw trembled, echoed further down by her knees, and her eyes filled with more tears.

The guard stepped forward and placed the bandage around her eyes, tying it securely behind her head.

All was darkness now, and she could hear steps fading away from her. Low murmuring still came from her right side—Philippe and his priest exchanging words of consolation and hope.

Her breath sounded much louder now, air scraping against her lungs and her throat, rippling across her lips with a sensitivity that made her cold. Her fingers ached as though they had been submerged in ice. A faint breeze crossed in front of her, rippling her pinned skirts slightly, the snapping of fabric against her legs thunderous in the surrounding silence.

Tears fell from her bound eyes, trickling down into the fabric of the bandage and becoming lost within it.

How long would they make her wait? Time stretched on and on, seconds turning into years, minutes into eons. She had been nowhere else in her life but this plank, had never seen beyond this linen, had never walked freely.

"Bereit!" called out a deep, authoritative voice.

Edith gasped, the unfamiliar word sending ice into her stomach. *"Ziel!"*

The world fell silent. She held her breath, stiffening.

"Long live Belgium!" Philippe bellowed from her left.

"Feuer!"

A deafening crack rent the air.

Then there was darkness. And light.

CHAPTER 29

How any of them managed to walk the dreary route home from the prison, Lizzie would never know. She could not feel her feet, could not feel the ground beneath her, could not feel anything but the tears on her face and the burning agony in her chest.

They had watched their beloved Edith being driven off to her death, staring after the gray car as though expecting it to turn about and return to them at any moment.

But it had not.

And would not.

No divine intervention had been granted, no miracle from Mr. Gibson or the rest. It had all been for nothing.

Lizzie had insisted they wait at the prison until they were certain nothing more would happen, and when the cars returned with the guards and priests, but without Edith or Mr. Baucq . . .

The skies had never seemed so dark. The rain was its iciest, the wind its most brutal, and every ache in her body more acute.

Yet nothing had changed, as far as she could see and tell.

It only felt its absolute worst.

Not one of their small group spoke a word as they walked back to the clinic in Uccle. A place Edith had dreamed of, planned on, worked for, and had never seen completed. A place that would never have been possible without her influence, her passion, her work.

An entire profession whose progression might not have occurred without her. Certainly not in Belgium.

And now she was gone.

What did a world without Edith Cavell look like? What did it feel like? How did one live in it?

Lizzie did not want to know, did not want to feel.

After the cars had returned, she had gone to the prison office to inquire about fetching Edith's belongings, and they had informed her that she would need to return in three days to do so. Lizzie had been made the executor of Edith's will, so her possessions would be released to her eventually, and more information would follow at that time.

More information. What more did she need to know? Edith was dead. That was all that mattered.

They arrived at the clinic, and Lizzie stared at it without emotion. "I want to go to Rue de la Culture," she announced, her voice hoarse.

The other nurses turned to her, only half of them looking surprised.

Sister Taylor, who had come out to greet them, nodded and came to her side, taking her arm. "I'll go with you."

"So will I," Beatrice added tearfully.

"And I," three others chimed in.

Lizzie nodded and started walking again, the effort to simply breathe in and out proving to be almost too much.

Dawn was fast approaching, which seemed impossible after the events of the night and what had just transpired. How could there be another dawn ever again?

"I do not know that I can go into her rooms there," one of the nurses murmured. "It must look as though she has only gone for a walk and will return soon to sit with Jack by the fire."

"Poor Jack," someone else said. "He has been pining for her all these weeks, and now . . ."

Sister Taylor sniffled. "We will shower him with all the love the matron would have given him."

"I suppose . . . I suppose we must pack away her things now."

That brought them all to silence. Every book, every photograph, every piece of needlework, and every diary would need to be packed away and sent home to England. Or taken back the next time one of them departed. There would be no need for any of the items now.

"Do you think they will announce her death?" Jacqueline inquired. "Post statements?"

"I have no doubt they will," Sister Taylor replied. "With the fervor they arrested, tried, and murdered her? There will be announcements, mark my words."

"I hope there will be an outcry in Britain for what they have done."

Lizzie wanted to nod at that but could not. Edith would not want vengeance or reprisals, would not think of wielding a sword against the very people who had abused her. But not everyone was Edith, and the indignities she suffered ought to have consequences. If Lizzie had learned anything from the night before, it was that there would be hell to pay from several sides for these acts.

Time alone would tell just what that might entail.

"What do we tell people?" one of the young nurses asked. "What do we say?"

Lizzie stopped walking, nearly causing a few of them to crash into her. She blinked, took in a breath, and turned with a smile that she hoped would convey the spirit of Edith within it.

"We tell people that we had the honor and privilege to know and work with Edith Cavell," she told them softly. "We tell them of her devotion, her fortitude, her humanity, and her sacrifice. Her integrity and her loyalty, her faith and her intellect. We tell them she feared nothing and no one but God in heaven, and she lived her life as she believed. A Christian woman of unconquerable spirit and everlasting faith. We tell them that we loved her, and she loved us. We tell them—" She swallowed, her emotions rising with a new rawness. "We tell them that countless numbers owe her their very lives and that on this day, one of the greatest people who has ever walked this earth was taken from us. But that she lives on through us, through our work, and through every noble and selfless act until the end of time."

There was not a dry eye among them, and Lizzie was no exception. Tears rolled freely down her face unchecked, a tide of them rushing upon her in waves.

"Well said," Beatrice managed as she wiped at her eyes, the other nurses bobbing their heads in agreement.

Lizzie turned back to their path, clinging to Jacqueline's hand on the left and leaning into Sister Taylor on the right as they started to walk again.

Dawn broke upon the horizon, a gap in the endless clouds allowing the sun's first morning beams to shine upon them.

It stole Lizzie's breath to see such a moment, and, eventually, she smiled into the brightness, a tenuous but deepening peace taking root in her heart like a timid plant determined to stand fast.

She sighed at the faint warmth, closing her eyes as though the sun shone high above and enveloped them all in its glowing rays. "Hello, Edith. God bless you."

The sun seemed to blink behind a sliver of cloud and then shone upon them once more, accompanying them to the last place their beloved matron had been truly among them, and where so much of her too-short life had been so fully lived.

EPILOGUE

May 19, 1919

London, for all its natural and grand majesty, had never looked like this.

Not to Elizabeth Wilkins, at any rate.

But that was as it should be. Today, three and a half years after her death, Edith Cavell could be laid to rest.

No efforts from any politicians or parliamentary offices had induced the Germans to exhume her body from where she had been hastily buried immediately following her execution while the Germans had still occupied Belgium and while the war had continued to rage across Europe.

Now that the war was over, the treaties signed, and peace finally secured, it was time.

Lizzie would have given a great deal to be in Belgium last week when Edith's coffin had been carried through the crowd-lined streets of Brussels to the Gard du Nord. When Reverend Gahan, in the presence of Edith's sisters, had given what must have been a stirring service of memorial. Edith's mother and brother had passed since the matron's death, but her dear Jack was still well and living in the chateau Bellignies with the de Croÿ household.

So much of those precious Belgian memories had faded in Lizzie's mind with the years. She had returned to England in November 1915; Belgium was never quite the same without Edith. She had continued her work as a nurse and had been given the post of matron at the Cottage Hospital of Chard in Somerset a year after her return. It became part of her daily routine to ask herself what Edith Cavell would do, and she could ask for no greater inspiration in her work than that.

She rarely spoke of Brussels and Edith, finding it easier to keep that chapter of her life in the rear of her memories. But today it would all be brought to the forefront.

London had come out in grand splendor, the streets lined with crowds standing five or six deep from Victoria to Westminster. In Lizzie's short walk to her place with the other ranks of nurses marching in the procession, she had seen soldiers and civilians alike standing in respectful anticipation.

After Edith's death, she had become a symbol of resistance against the Germans and their allies. Her story had been dramatized for effect, posters and postcards had been plastered with drawings of her prone figure on the ground with a German soldier pointing a pistol at her head, and the uproar across the world had happened just as Mr. Gibson and Maître de Leval had predicted.

Edith would have hated the fuss, especially those details that had been exaggerated, but knowing that her death had caused enough of an outcry to bring more than ten thousand new volunteers into the ranks of the British Army would have made her proud.

As would the influence her sacrifice had had on the nursing profession.

Nurses in London had flocked to St. Paul's Cathedral in late October of 1915 for a memorial service on Edith's behalf. Lizzie had still been in Belgium at the time, but she had heard about it from some of her own nurses in Somerset. What a hallowed experience that must have been! And how Lizzie could have used it at such a time.

Today, however, all of London would honor Edith.

Ahead of the eleven thousand nurses were rows upon rows of Coldstreamers, followed by the Welsh and Scots guard bands, who had been warming up their instruments as each prepared for the procession. There were soldiers on horses and soldiers to march, and, if she understood correctly, yet more soldiers to follow behind the gun carriage upon which the coffin was placed.

She glanced behind her now; the sight of the flag-draped coffin strewn with red and white carnations would be enough to bring a lump to any throat. But knowing it was Edith who lay within, her friend and mentor, her matron and her guide . . .

An exquisite blend of agony and pride filled Lizzie's chest.

And with it, a blessed sense of relief.

They had been forced to leave her body in Belgian soil, placed there by the monsters who had executed her, without even a marker for her grave. Now she was free from that plot and would be honored in the way she ought to have been nearly four years ago.

Swallowing the wash of emotion, Lizzie turned her face forward, inhaling the fresh fragrance of spring in London, noting every flag flying at half-staff, and the cloudless sky above them. What a day for honoring the greatest woman Lizzie had ever known. All of the posters that had showered England after Edith's death had returned to the buildings for the day. Banners bearing her name and her cause hung from windows and storefronts. Likenesses of Edith had been erected on fabric and paper and scattered throughout the city, raising the honor and praise of her nearly to that of sainthood.

Victory was the fragrance of the day. Victory over the Germans, over von Lüttwitz, over Quien, Bergan, Mayer. Victory over anyone who had stood in Edith's way or attempted to bring her down. Victory over her murder, which was now that of martyrdom, whether she would have wished it or not.

Victory. That was what Edith Cavell had accomplished today.

A quiet, solemn, firm, and absolute victory.

At last.

A faint bellowing of an officer could be heard up ahead, and the dull murmuring of those waiting in the procession faded at its sound. Then the soldiers began to move, the bands striking up, and, when the time came, the nurses began their walk.

It was a strange, majestic thing to be walking in this procession, surrounded by fellow nurses and soldiers, the music of the bands filling the air. To see tears streaming down the faces of adults and children alike in the crowd. To see former soldiers bowing their heads in advance of the coffin. To see London as a whole grow so still and silent for this woman and the honors due to her.

"There's a card from Queen Alexandra on the carnations, you know," a fellow nurse nearby said to the woman next to her. "The dowager queen selected the flowers herself, and there are arum lilies in there."

"What does the card say?" her companion asked in awe.

"I caught sight of it earlier. It read, 'In memory of our brave, heroic, never-to-be-forgotten Nurse Cavell. Life's race well run, Life's work well done, Life's crown well won, Now comes rest. From Alexandra.' Such an elegant woman, and such a fitting tribute."

Lizzie smiled to herself as she continued to walk. These nurses had likely never met Edith, had known only of her reputation and, most likely, her death. But even they knew an apt tribute when they heard it.

They would simply never understand just how perfectly apt it really was.

Westminster Abbey loomed before them now, its magnificence gleaming in the brilliant sunlight and pristine skies as though heaven itself had placed it there. The bands began to play Chopin's "Funeral March" as they reached the Abbey itself, the soldiers and sailors peeling off from the procession to form an honor guard for the coffin. Most of the nurses followed suit, but Lizzie, as one of the few individuals in attendance who had truly known Edith, had a seat reserved near the front for the service.

She nodded at the guards at the door and walked quickly down the long nave, noting with pride that the entire Abbey was filled with guests for the service. All were listening to the funeral march from the band outside, the Grenadier Guards standing at attention rather than playing themselves. Moving into the Quire, she noted with some surprise that the dowager queen and Princess Victoria were in attendance, as was the Earl of Athone, brother of the present queen.

Royalty in attendance and represented for Edith Cavell. She would never have imagined that.

Lizzie found her seat just in time for the entire gathering to rise as the coffin was brought into the Abbey. Borne on the shoulders of eight servicemen, the Grenadier Guards played solemn and sobering tones that matched the slow and careful cadence of the paces. There was no other sound in the entire Abbey, only the music and the clipped notes of boots on stone.

It seemed an age before the procession reached those in the Quire section of the Abbey, and nothing could have prepared Lizzie for the poignancy of seeing the coffin being carried by somber servicemen, so reminiscent of the men Edith had hidden away at the clinic all those years ago in Brussels. She had rescued them from danger, healed them, and given them a step toward hope and freedom, raising them from a previously hopeless state.

Now it was she who was physically raised upon their shoulders, her soul already embraced in the light of hope, her body soon finding its lasting rest.

The coffin was carefully and methodically placed on the dais, the flag straightened in places, and then the servicemen stepped back and marched away in neat lines.

The choir began to sing, their pure voices echoing angelically in the towering halls of Westminster. The words had been printed in the program they had all received, and Lizzie read along as the music continued.

> *I am the resurrection and the life, saith the Lord: he that believeth in me, though he were dead, yet shall he live: and whosoever liveth and believeth in me shall never die.*
>
> *I know that my Redeemer liveth, and that he shall stand at the latter day upon the earth. And though after my skin worms destroy this body, yet in my flesh shall I see God: whom I shall see for myself, and mine eyes shall behold, and not another.*
>
> *We brought nothing into this world, and it is certain we can carry nothing out. The Lord gave, and the Lord hath taken away; blessed be the name of the Lord.*

The Lord is my shepherd: therefore can I lack nothing.

He shall feed me in a green pasture: and lead me forth beside the waters of comfort.

He shall convert my soul: and bring me forth in the paths of righteousness, for His Name's sake.

Yea, though I walk through the valley of the shadow of death, I will fear no evil: for Thou art with me; Thy rod and Thy staff comfort me.

Thou shalt prepare a table before me against them that trouble me: Thou hast anointed my head with oil, and my cup shall be full.

But Thy loving-kindness and mercy shall follow me all the days of my life: and I will dwell in the house of the Lord for ever.

Glory be to the Father, and to the Son: and to the Holy Ghost;

As it was in the beginning, is now, and ever shall be: world without end. Amen.

As the music concluded, Lizzie blinked back tears, recalling the number of times Edith had been heard to recite the words of Psalm Twenty-Three. It had likely been the most oft-quoted scripture she had ever recited, and she always meant the words as though she had written them herself.

Even now, Lizzie could not think of the psalm without growing emotional.

The Dean of Westminster stepped forward, his smile slight, his countenance serene. "The Lesson shall be taken out of the Twenty-first Chapter of the Revelation of Saint John the Divine.

"And I saw a new heaven and a new earth: for the first heaven and the first earth are passed away; and the sea is no more. And I saw the

Holy City, new Jerusalem, coming down out of heaven from God, made ready as a bride adorned for her husband.

"And I heard a great voice out of the throne saying, Behold, the tabernacle of God is with men, and he shall dwell with them, and they shall be his peoples, and God himself shall be with them, and be their God: And he shall wipe away every tear from their eyes; and death shall be no more; neither shall there be mourning, nor crying, nor pain, any more: the first things are passed away.

"And he that sitteth on the throne saith, Behold, I make all things new. And he saith, Write: for these words are faithful and true. And he said unto me, They are come to pass. I am the Alpha and the Omega, the beginning and the end. I will give unto him that is athirst of the fountain of the water of life freely. He that overcometh shall inherit these things; and I will be his God, and he shall be my son."

The Precentor stepped to the center, the book open before him. "Lord, have mercy upon us," he recited.

Lizzie and the rest of the congregation replied, "Christ, have mercy upon us."

Again, the Precentor said, "Lord, have mercy upon us."

All in the Abbey bowed their heads, and in unison, recited together:

> *Our Father which art in Heaven, Hallowed be Thy Name. Thy kingdom come. Thy will be done, in earth as it is in heaven. Give us this day our daily bread. And forgive us our trespasses, As we forgive them that trespass against us. And lead us not into temptation; But deliver us from evil. Amen.*

The Dean stepped forward again, offering another invocation on Edith's behalf. The words rolled over Lizzie without truly reaching her mind, her thoughts turning only to Edith. Was she with them in this cathedral? Had she found the rest she so richly deserved? Or had she been given the task of angelic ministry, perhaps even now tending to the hearts of her beloved nurses?

The Dean cleared his throat, and then ended his prayers with, "The grace of our Lord Jesus Christ and the love of God and the fellowship of the Holy Ghost be with us all evermore. Amen."

Lizzie opened the program to see what would follow as she murmured her amen, and her chest tightened.

Edith's hymn.

The Grenadier Guards began their introduction, and soon the entire Abbey was singing the words that Edith had so loved, the words that Reverend Gahan had said he and Edith had recited the evening before her death.

> *Abide with me; fast falls the eventide;*
> *The darkness deepens; Lord, with me abide;*
> *When other helpers fail, and comforts flee,*
> *Help of the helpless, O abide with me.*

Lizzie closed her eyes on streaming tears, the image of Edith rising in her mind's eye. She cleared her throat on the clog of welling emotion and raised her voice higher for the final verse.

As the music faded, the sound of sniffling could be heard throughout the congregation, handkerchiefs dabbing at most of the eyes present as the Dean stepped forward once more.

"The peace of God, which passeth all understanding, keep your hearts and minds in the knowledge and love of God, and of his Son Jesus Christ our Lord: and the blessing of God Almighty, the Father, the Son, and the Holy Ghost, be amongst you and remain with you always. Amen."

Lizzie sniffed back tears. "Amen."

The haunting, piercing strains of "The Dead March" from

Handel's *Saul* began to soar among the rafters of the Abbey, the Grenadier Guards again showering their talents on the congregation. It was a stirring piece, and under such influence, more and more memories of Edith sprang to Lizzie's mind.

Their entire professional career together passed before her, and the friendship and sisterhood that had developed along the way. Each and every aspect of Lizzie's life that Edith had touched had helped her own faith and confidence bloom.

She would not have become the person or the nurse that she now was without Edith Cavell. And yet, through it all, Edith had only ever claimed to be a plain, ordinary Christian.

If she had been plain and ordinary, what could be said for the rest of them?

The song ended, its last notes seeming to take an age to completely fade. No sooner had it done so than a choir of bugles sounded.

Lizzie caught her breath, the power and stirring spirit of "The Last Post" not lost on any of them. She closed her eyes, letting the notes sink deep into her soul. Though not a member of the British armed forces, Edith had certainly done enough to honor those ranks to warrant the playing of the song now.

The notes from the bugles echoed and ricocheted throughout the building, seeming to be calls from heaven of soldiers and sailors, all wishing to pay tribute to this humble woman. Then they, too, fell silent.

Drums filled the Abbey almost at once, leading majestically into "The Reveillé," which accompanied Lizzie's slowly rolling tears with a tenderness and poignancy she had not expected. This was how Edith ought to be remembered, what ought to have played in her honor as she was buried in that cold grave in Belgium. This ought to have sounded from every rooftop in England when the news of her death had been received.

But at least it was playing now that she was returned to her home country.

Servicemen appeared as the song was concluding, hoisting the coffin onto their shoulders once more. Chopin's "Funeral March" was struck up again as they carried her back down the Quire and into the Nave, headed for the gun carriage that had brought her here. Lizzie and the others due to join the return procession followed them, matching their slow, measured steps in time with the song.

The day was just as glorious as it had been when they had arrived, and the march toward Liverpool Street Station was still lined with crowds. Flowers were tossed into the street ahead of the gun carriage, heads were bowed, hearts were covered, tears were shed.

It was a somber yet triumphant experience, this hallowed walk to the station. A special train had been arranged for the occasion, bound for Norwich so that Edith could be laid to rest in her home cathedral and near her parents. Exactly how she would have wanted it.

It would be a small, simple service, and Lizzie was one of the fortunate few who had been invited.

There were flowers and wreaths from far and wide that would travel with them, including one from Elizabeth, Queen of the Belgians. A softer rendition of Edith's favorite hymns would be played, no doubt, and her sisters would likely find the occasion more to Edith's taste.

That would be the service Edith would have planned for herself.

This one had been for England. To honor what they had lost. To welcome a lost daughter home. To mark, once and for all, just how valuable she had been to the world.

Lizzie smiled softly to herself as they reached the station and the servicemen began the process of transferring the coffin from gun carriage to train car.

One more journey, and then Edith would be home for good. Home to stay.

Though, if Edith were here beside her, watching the same sight, she would have reminded Lizzie that she *was* home. And had been from the day she had left this earth.

Lizzie swallowed and shook herself, moving toward the train platform and pulling her ticket from her pocket. She had never been to Norwich, but she knew in her heart she would feel the same love, warmth, charity, and goodness there that she had always known from its most famous daughter.

She felt a new smile cross her lips as she boarded the train and sighed at the peace that now resided in her heart. The peace that Edith had known and lived by.

Her true legacy to the world.

ACKNOWLEDGMENTS

Many thanks to Chris Schoebinger, Lisa Mangum, Heidi Gordon, and the entire team at Shadow Mountain for their help, guidance, and hard work on this project, as well as their belief in me to carry it off.

Thanks to Heather Moore and Jen Johnson for their advice and assistance throughout the project, to Lorie Humpherys for helping me clean it up, and to Shaela Odd for beta reading for content critiques.

Thanks to the Rev. Dom Guido, Fr Dana Lockhart, and Fr John Chorlton for their insight and help with religious details. Additional thanks to Fr John Chorlton for sending me photos and mementos from his own trip to Norwich Cathedral after helping me with this book.

Special thanks to Nick Miller, the unofficial expert on Edith Cavell, for taking time of out of his busy schedule to advise me and point me in the right direction.

Thanks also to the Florence Nightingale Museum for the references and notes they were so good as to send me.

And thanks to my mom, Lisa Connolly, for indulging in my Edith Cavell nerdiness on our UK trip in 2022. You're the best!

EDITH CAVELL

December 4, 1865 – October 12, 1915

AUTHOR'S NOTE

Devotion. Fortitude. Sacrifice. Humanity.

Those are the words that adorn the monument to Edith Cavell in London, and which seem to define all that she was. The daughter of a devoted clergyman, she was no stranger to good works, service, and charity, but where many people would simply claim these as good habits, for Edith Cavell, they became a part of her. She devoted her entire life to serving others, to tending the sick and injured, but also to the raising of spirits. She revolutionized the profession of nursing in Belgium when it was an unpopular option for a young woman, creating not only professional women in medical sciences, but world-class ones.

Edith was in London visiting her mother when the Germans invaded Belgium, and despite the danger, she chose to return to her nurses and her clinic. She chose to serve. She was in Brussels when the Germans marched into that city, and in many ways, her fate was sealed from the moment she first clashed swords with Governor von Lüttwitz.

When next I travel to England, I plan to lay a wreath for her to pay my respects. This remarkable woman has been relatively lost to history due to time and the tragedies that would later befall the world, and it has been a privilege to learn of her, to write of her, and to feel that I know her, in some small way.

There will always be stories of hope and goodness in the midst of darkness. It is important to tell those stories and to honor those who have acted with courage, faith, and determination against all obstacles.

There were other governors general throughout the time Edith was engaged in her activities during the war, but for the sake of simplicity in this book, they were all condensed into the person of Governor General von Lüttwitz.

Likewise, there were many nurses and probationers who interacted and worked with Edith Cavell in Belgium. For the sake of convenience, experiences of some were combined with those of others to keep the numbers of nurses less confusing for readers. Sister Taylor is based on Sister Whitelock, who took the place of Sister White after her return to England.

The nurse whose father relayed the information about Edith's sentence was Germaine van Aershodt. As she had not played a significant role in the book, I gave that role to Helen Wegels.

There is no proof that Elizabeth Wilkins ever went by Lizzie, but I made the choice in order to provide a greater difference between the names of Edith and Elizabeth.

None of the other prisoners condemned to death in the same trial as Edith and Philippe had their sentences carried out. The worldwide outcry at the German injustice was so intense that even the Kaiser himself was displeased with the outcome.

Louise Thuliez and Marie de Croÿ went on to help soldiers escape in much the same way during the Second World War.

Gaston Quien was arrested after the war and put on trial for his betrayal of Edith Cavell. He was sentenced to death. Elizabeth Wilkins went to the trial and testified against him. She wore her full nursing uniform.

Elizabeth went on to serve as a nurse for the rest of her life. She became matron of the Cottage Hospital in Chard and was awarded an OBE in 1920. She died on February 23, 1965, one day before her eighty-first birthday.

Edith Cavell was buried in the cemetery of her home cathedral in Norwich, England. She lies there to this day.

Edith Cavell (seated center) with a group of her multinational student nurses, whom she trained in Brussels. They are sitting in a garden, presumably outside the training hospital.

Edith Cavell sitting in a garden with her two dogs.
The dog on the right, Jack, was by Edith's side much
of her life and was rescued after her execution.

Elizabeth Wilkins with Edith Cavell's dog, Jack

DISCUSSION QUESTIONS

1. Despite vowing to rise above nationalities in the war, Edith agrees to shelter and hide soldiers from the German authorities. Why do you think she made that decision?

2. Edith's faith was a central part of her life and personality. How do you think this helped or hindered her in her work with the Belgian resistance?

3. Elizabeth Wilkins starts off as an unwitting participant in the first action of Edith's resistance against the Germans. How would you have felt in such a position?

4. When we think about World War I today, the name Edith Cavell almost never comes up. Why do you think she has been forgotten by history?

5. Elizabeth is questioned at least twice by the German authorities for her participation. How would such an experience shape her life moving forward?

6. The arrest, imprisonment, and trial of Edith and her compatriots

has been a topic of speculation and criticism from modern historians. What impressions do you have about how those events played out?

7. There were many things Edith taught her nurses throughout her career. What do you believe was her most lasting lesson for them?

8. If you were placed in Edith's situation, knowing how it played out, what would you have chosen to do? What might you have done differently? Was her sacrifice worth it?

BIBLIOGRAPHY

Archives, The National. n.d. "The National Archives - Homepage." The National Archives. Accessed January 15, 2022. https://www.national archives.gov.uk/education/resources/significant-people-collection/edith -cavell/.

Arthur, Terri. 2014. *Fatal Decision: Edith Cavell, World War I Nurse.* Milwaukee, WI: Henschelhaus Publishing, Inc.

A'kempis, Thomas. 2019. *Of the Imitation of Christ.* S.L.: Hansebooks.

"Battrum, Millicent Louise (Oral History)." 1965. Imperial War Museums. https://www.iwm.org.uk/collections/item/object/80006661.

BBC News. 2015. "Nurse Edith Cavell and the British World War One Propaganda Campaign," October 11, 2015, sec. Norfolk. https://www .bbc.com/news/uk-england-norfolk-34401643.

Beck, James M. 2011. *The Case of Edith Cavell: A Study of the Rights of Non-Combatants.* Minneapolis, MN: Filiquarian Publishing.

Cammaerts, Emile. 2018. *Through the Iron Bars: Two Years of German Occupation in Belgium.* Read Books Ltd.

Chorlton, John. Email communication with author. January 17, January 18, and May 28, 2022.

Cockburn, DJ. 2015. "Inspirations: The Legend of Edith Cavell." Cockburn's

Eclectics. October 21, 2015. https://cockburndj.wordpress.com/2015/10/21/inspirations-the-legend-of-edith-cavell/.

Croy, Marie. 1932. *War Memories*. London: Macmillan.

"Edith Cavell: An Unexpected Heroine | Findmypast." 2021. YouTube.com. https://www.youtube.com/watch?v=G2pzbuMnj-Y.

"Edith Cavell Letter Gifted to Cathedral." n.d. www.cathedral.org.uk. Accessed January 14, 2022. https://cathedral.org.uk/news/edith-cavell-letter-gifted-to-cathedral/.

"Edith Cavell Memorial Service—1915—St Paul's Cathedral." 2013. Stpauls.co.uk. 2013. https://www.stpauls.co.uk/history-collections/history/history-highlights/edith-cavell-memorial-service-1915.

"Edith Cavell Story—BECCG Brussels Belgium." 2015. www.edith-Cavell-Belgium.eu. http://www.edith-cavell-belgium.eu/edith-cavell-story.html.

Evans, Jonathan. 2008. *Edith Cavell*. London: Royal London Hospital Museum.

Gibson, Hugh. 1917. *A Journal from Our Legation in Belgium, by Hugh Gibson*. New York: Grosset And Dunlop.

Got, Ambroise. 1921. *L'affaire Miss Cavell, d'Après Les Documents Inédits de La Justice Allemande*. Paris (8, Rue Garancière): Impr.-Libr.-Éditeurs Plon-Nourrit Et Cie, (1Er Juin).

Grey, Elizabeth. 1968. *Friend within the Gates*. Dell.

Hallett, Christine E, Natasha Mcenroe, Tig Thomas, and Florence Nightingale Museum. 2014. *The Hospital in the Oatfield : The Art of Nursing in the First World War ; [... Accompanies the Exhibition "the Hospital in the Oatfield" Displayed in the Florence Nightingale Museum in 2014 as Art of the First World War Centenary]*. London: Florence Nightingale Museum.

Hoehling, A A. 1958. *Edith Cavell*. Cassell.

https://www.westminster-abbey.org/media/9403/edith-cavell-funeral-service.pdf. Accessed January 8, 2022.

Judson, Helen. 1941. *Edith Cavell*. New York: The Macmillan Company.

March, Francis A, and Richard J Beamish. 1919. *History of the World War: An Authentic Narrative of the World's Greatest War*. Vol. 4. Philadelphia;

Chicago: Published for the United Publishers of the United States and Canada.

Memorial Service for the Late Miss Edith Cavell. 1915. RE Thomas and Co.

Miller, Nick. 2014. *Edith Cavell: A Forgotten Heroine.* Cambridge, Eng. Grove Books Limited.

Nightingale, Florence, and Maureen Shawn Kennedy. 2020. *Notes on Nursing: What It Is and What It Is Not.* Philadelphia: Wolters Kluwer.

Noel, Boston. 1965. *The Dutiful Edith Cavell.* Norwich, Eng.: Norwich Cathedral.

Pacific Coast Journal of Nursing. 1919. *Google Books.* Vol. 15. Pacific Coast Journal of Nursing. https://books.google.com/books?id=1pMXAQAAIA AJ&lpg=PA607&ots=4vB8xqmJO6&dq=rev%20gahan%20service%20 brussels%20train%20station&pg=PA607#v=onepage&q=rev%20 gahan%20service%20brussels%20train%20station&f=false.

Paisey, David. (1986) 2013. *Gottfried Benn: Selected Poems and Prose.* Carcanet Press Limited.

"Pastor Le Seur's Testimony." 2015. Edith Cavell 1865–1915. July 15, 2015. https://edithcavell.org.uk/edith-cavells-life/pastor-le-seurs-testimony/.

pixeltocode.uk, PixelToCode. n.d. "Edith Cavell." Westminster Abbey. Accessed January 8, 2022. https://www.westminster-abbey.org/abbey -commemorations/commemorations/edith-cavell.

Powell, Anne. 2013. *Women in the War Zone: Hospital Service in the First World War.* Stroud: The History Press.

Protheroe, Ernest, and Edith Cavell. 1916. *A Noble Woman: The Life-Story of Edith Cavell.* London: Kelly.

Ryder, Rowland. 1975. *Edith Cavell.* London: Parnell Book Services.

Scovil, Elisabeth Robinson. 1915. "An Heroic Nurse." *The American Journal of Nursing* 16 (2): 118. https://doi.org/10.2307/3406248.

"Secrets and Spies: The Untold Story of Edith Cavell—BBC Sounds." 2015. www.bbc.co.uk. September 15, 2015. https://www.bbc.co.uk/sounds /play/b069wth6.

Souhami, Diana. 2010. *Edith Cavell.* London: Quercus.

"St. John's Daily Star, 1915-11-03." 2021. Collections.mun.ca. 2021. https://collections.mun.ca/digital/collection/daily_star/id/2664.

"Uncle Sam's Diplomats in War Zone Do Him Honor Famous War Correspondent Tells of Crises Met Sturdily and Wisely by Representatives of This Nation in the Writhing Lands of Europe." 1914. *The Archive of American Journalism*. New York Times. https://nebula.wsimg.com/925ca 56977e7a168bba8911016cc0e50?AccessKeyId=94861742399A59C7B18A &disposition=0&alloworigin=1.

Van Til, Jacqueline. 2015. *With Edith Cavell in Belgium*.

"Viscount Burnham and Maitre de Level on Nurse Cavell. Her Last Words Recorded." 1919. The Hospital. https://pdfs.semanticscholar.org/d1e5 /d057b802ca0c15cab778e53dd86bb1d3569f.pdf.

Whitlock, Brand, and Allan Nevins. 1936. *The Letters and Journal of Brand Whitlock*. New York, London, D. Appleton-Century Co.

———. 2020. "Edith Cavell: The Other Nightingale." Ojin.nursingworld. org. May 2020. https://ojin.nursingworld.org/MainMenuCategories /ANAMarketplace/ANAPeriodicals/OJIN/TableofContents/Vol-25 -2020/No2-May-2020/Edith-Cavell-The-Other-Nightingale.html

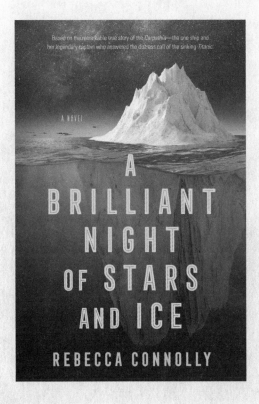